Graded Examinations

Woodwind

Flute
Jazz Flute (new)
Clarinet
Jazz Clarinet
Saxophone (formerly Classical Saxophone)
Jazz Saxophone

Other woodwind syllabuses are available as follows:

- Double Reed Instruments: Oboe and Bassoon
- Recorder

Valid from
2002

This syllabus is valid from 2002 until one year after the issue of a replacement syllabus.
Please contact Guildhall Examinations for current information.

ISBN 0-900423-80-3

GUILDHALL
School of Music & Drama

QCA Accredited Examinations

The Guildhall School's examinations from Grade 1 through to Grade 8 in this syllabus are accredited by the regulatory body the Qualifications and Curriculum Authority (QCA) and the corresponding regulatory authorities in Wales (ACCAC) and Northern Ireland (CCEA). The QCA has set out rigorous 'accreditation criteria' which stipulate rules about the content and assessment of qualifications. Only those qualifications that meet these stringent criteria are admitted to the framework, ensuring that they are assessed thoroughly and fairly.

National Qualifications Framework (NQF)

The framework shows how national qualifications relate to each other and serves to guarantee the quality of accredited qualifications. Qualifications in the NQF are arranged in six levels, from Entry Level awards to professional qualifications at Level 5. The higher the level of a qualification, the greater the depth and breadth of knowledge, skills and understanding that candidates have to show to pass it.

Guildhall School Graded Examinations map into the National Qualifications Framework as indicated in the table of equivalence below:

Graded Exam	NQF Level	General Qualifications
6 – 8	3	A and AS Level
4 – 5	2	GCSE A* – C
1 – 3	1	GCSE D – G

Structure and Content of Qualifications

The structure of this syllabus provides:
- a common pattern of progressively graded and differentiated content;
- a common pattern of assessment;
- a common structure of examining performance;
- a common assessment system.

The syllabus structure ensures:
- equivalent levels of demand and progression across each endorsed instrumental discipline;
- differentiation and progression between grades;
- comparability between endorsed instrumental disciplines.

Contents

A syllabus for
the post-grade 8
Certificate in
Performance
CertGSMD(P) is
available from
Guildhall Exams.

The Aims of this Syllabus

The Guildhall School believes in the intrinsic value of engaging in artistic forms of experience. Most importantly, music and the arts offer a fundamental way of enabling us to connect to the world, to each other, to other cultures, to other forms of human experience, to ourselves.

This syllabus aims to:

- develop, extend and sustain the skills, knowledge and understanding necessary to perform and enjoy music;
- support personal, social, cultural, and spiritual development through the experience of making and sharing music;
- apply the ability to critically and constructively listen, think and engage with making music;
- encourage lifelong learning by fostering imagination, creativity and achievement in and through performance;
- promote a perceptive, sensitive and imaginative response to the diverse and dynamic heritage of music.

It is important for teachers and students to have confidence in examinations and results. That is why the Guildhall selects, as examiners, people who specialise in the disciplines they are assessing. Each of them is then carefully and systematically trained to use the **Clear** system before becoming part of the examining team.

Affirming Achievement
A leaflet explaining how Guildhall School Examiners assess performance is available from the Help Desk 020 7382 7167

You can email questions about **Clear** to clear@gsmd.ac.uk

Larger print?

This syllabus is available to download from our website **www.gsmd.ac.uk** in a larger size.

Foreword

Eric Hollis
Director of Initial Studies
Guildhall School of
Music & Drama, London

Welcome

This Guildhall woodwind syllabus builds on the success of the School's approach to teaching and learning. It is the product of years of research and experience in curriculum development and working with teachers in our professional development programmes.

We have worked closely with Boosey & Hawkes on the development of their *Boosey Woodwind Method* series, which provides core repertoire books for our Flute, Jazz Flute, Clarinet, Jazz Clarinet, Saxophone and Jazz Saxophone syllabuses in the early grades. This material is, of course, supplemented by an enormous range of attractive repertoire drawn from other sources, too.

We recognise that repertoire is a central medium in liberating the power of music and choosing suitable repertoire requires great skill. Not only must we be concerned with appropriate technical progression and consolidation but also with motivation and the developing expressive awareness of our students. Our selections are chosen by experienced specialist teachers and have been matched against the Guildhall School's curriculum outlines and the criteria that our examiners use when assessing performances. This ensures a progressive framework for anyone using the syllabus.

Suggested optional warm-up exercises for all grades are included in the syllabus to help musicians perform at their best in the exam. Facility exercises have been added at every grade to reflect the importance of flexibility, intonation, articulation, tone and control skills. *The Scales Wizard*, a new publication from Camden Music written by Guildhall staff, makes scale learning fun and relevant. To help establish confidence, the student can choose the first scale or arpeggio to be played at each grade and the scale and arpeggio requirements now include elements of rhythm, tempo, character, articulation and dynamic. These changes will have a beneficial impact on the way pupils practise their scales generally and not only when preparing for examinations.

We have made changes to the way sight-reading is handled up to Grade 5 with the student having two attempts.

The quality assurance that is provided by the Guildhall's **Clear**® Performance Assessment System completes the picture. You can have confidence that the structure, progression and assessment provided by our curricular approach is underwritten by the experience of one of the world's leading training institutions.

This woodwind syllabus embodies the Guildhall School's commitment to good teaching and curriculum planning. I hope that you will enjoy teaching with our programme and that your students will enjoy meeting our examiners.

Please visit our website **www.gsmd.ac.uk** for up-to-date information on the Guildhall's woodwind provision.

Recommended Warm-up Exercises

The warm-up exercises given in this syllabus do not form part of the examination. However, a short but well structured warm-up routine should always form part of every musician's preparation to play. The examination context is no exception to this, so we recommend that candidates prepare for their exam by warming up immediately before entering the examination room. The candidate's usual warm-up routine could be used. As an alternative, or in addition, the following exercises may be helpful. If you feel dizzy when doing breathing exercises, stop and have a rest.

FLUTE / JAZZ FLUTE

More comprehensive notes on posture can be found in *The Boosey Woodwind Method, flute book 1* (B&H M060112898).

Grade 1

Posture
Adopt a comfortable playing posture, standing alert and flexible. Your feet should be a hip-width apart, your knees unlocked, and your arms, shoulders and face relaxed. Aim for the head to be evenly balanced, without undue tension in the neck, and looking gently to the left. The flute should be held lightly, allowing the chest to remain open, and your elbows hanging loose.

Controlled breathing and support
Exhale and inhale to counts of 2, 4 and 8 (at $\quarternote$ = 60), using the abdominal (tummy) muscles to support the outbreath as if playing the instrument.

Grade 2

Posture
Adopt a comfortable playing posture, standing alert and flexible. Your feet should be a hip-width apart and pointing to the right of music stand, your knees unlocked, and your arms, shoulders and face relaxed. Aim for the head to be evenly balanced, without undue tension in the neck, and looking gently to the left. The flute should be held lightly, allowing the chest to remain open, with a triangle of space between right shoulder, right hand and mouth, and your elbows hanging loose. Wrists and hands should be well aligned to the instrument with the fingers close to keys. Check your embouchure too.

Controlled breathing and support
Exhale and inhale to counts of 2 – 10 (at $\quarternote$ = 60), using the abdominal (tummy) muscles to support the outbreath as if playing the instrument.

Grade 3

Posture
As grade 2

Controlled breathing and support
Exhale and inhale to counts of 2 – 10 (at $\quarternote$ = 60), using the abdominal muscles to support the outbreath as if playing the instrument.

Grade 4

Posture: standing
As grade 2

Posture: sitting
Sit comfortably on an upright chair, aiming to distribute your weight evenly on both sitting bones, with any rotation in the spine kept to a minimum, and the spine tall and flexible. Legs should be without tension and feet flat on the floor in front of the chair.

Controlled breathing and support
Exhale and inhale to counts of 2 – 12 (at $\quarternote$ = 60), using the abdominal muscles to support the outbreath as if playing the instrument.

Grade 5

Posture: standing
As grade 2

Posture: sitting
As grade 4

Controlled breathing and support
Exhale and inhale to counts of 2 – 12 (at $\quarternote$ = 60), using the abdominal muscles to support the outbreath as if playing the instrument.

Grade 6

Posture: standing
As grade 2

Posture: sitting
As grade 4

Controlled breathing and support
Exhale and inhale to counts of 2 – 12 (at ♩ = 60), using the abdominal muscles to support the outbreath as if playing the instrument.

Grade 7

Posture: standing
As grade 2

Posture: sitting
As grade 4

Controlled breathing and support
Exhale and inhale to counts of 2 – 16 (at ♩ = 60), using the abdominal muscles to support the outbreath as if playing the instrument.

Grade 8

Posture: standing
As grade 2

Posture: sitting
As grade 4

Controlled breathing and support
Exhale and inhale to counts of 2 – 16 (at ♩ = 60), using the abdominal muscles to support the outbreath as if playing the instrument.

CLARINET / JAZZ CLARINET

More comprehensive notes on posture can be found in *The Boosey Woodwind Method, clarinet book 1* (B&H M060112904).

Grade 1

Posture
Adopt a comfortable playing posture, standing alert and flexible. Your feet should be a hip-width apart, your knees unlocked, and your arms, shoulders and face relaxed. Aim for the head to be evenly balanced without undue tension in the neck, and hold your instrument lightly, with as little disruption to your normal stance as possible.

Controlled breathing and support
Exhale and inhale to counts of 2, 4 and 8 (at ♩ = 60), using the abdominal (tummy) muscles to support the outbreath as if playing the instrument.

Grade 2

Posture
Adopt a comfortable playing posture, standing alert and flexible. Your feet should be a hip-width apart, your knees unlocked, and your arms, shoulders and face relaxed. Aim for the head to be evenly balanced without undue tension in the neck, and hold your instrument lightly, with as little disruption to your normal stance as possible. Wrists and hands should be well aligned to the instrument with the fingers close to keys. Check your embouchure too.

Controlled breathing and support
Exhale and inhale to counts of 2 – 10 (at ♩ = 60), using the abdominal muscles to support the outbreath as if playing the instrument.

Grade 3

Posture
As grade 2

Controlled breathing and support
Exhale and inhale to counts of 2 – 10 (at ♩ = 60), using the abdominal muscles to support the outbreath as if playing the instrument.

Grade 4

Posture: standing
As grade 2

Posture: sitting
Sit comfortably on an upright chair, aiming to distribute your weight evenly on both sitting bones, with the spine tall and flexible. Legs should be without tension and feet flat on the floor in front of the chair.

Controlled breathing and support
Exhale and inhale to counts of 2 – 12 (at ♩ = 60), using the abdominal muscles to support the outbreath as if playing the instrument.

Grade 5

Posture: standing
As grade 2

Posture: sitting
As grade 4

Controlled breathing and support

Exhale and inhale to counts of 2 – 12 (at ♩ = 60), using the abdominal muscles to support the outbreath as if playing the instrument.

Grade 6

Posture: standing

As grade 2

Posture: sitting

As grade 4

Controlled breathing and support

Exhale and inhale to counts of 2 – 12 (at ♩ = 60), using the abdominal muscles to support the outbreath as if playing the instrument.

Grade 7

Posture: standing

As grade 2

Posture: sitting

As grade 4

Controlled breathing and support

Exhale and inhale to counts of 2 – 16 (at ♩ = 60), using the abdominal muscles to support the outbreath as if playing the instrument.

Grade 8

Posture: standing

As grade 2

Posture: sitting

As grade 4

Controlled breathing and support

Exhale and inhale to counts of 2 – 16 (at ♩ = 60), using the abdominal muscles to support the outbreath as if playing the instrument.

SAXOPHONE / JAZZ SAXOPHONE

More comprehensive notes on posture can be found in *The Boosey Woodwind Method,
saxophone book 1* (B&H M060112911).

Grade 1

Posture

Adopt a comfortable playing posture, standing alert and flexible. Your feet should be
a hip-width apart, your knees unlocked, and your arms, shoulders and face relaxed.
Aim for the head to be evenly balanced without undue tension in the neck, and hold
your instrument lightly, with as little disruption to your normal stance as possible,
and the instrument assembly (including sling adjustment) adjusted to produce an
effective playing posture.

Controlled breathing and support

Exhale and inhale to counts of 2, 4 and 8 (at ♩ = 60), using the abdominal (tummy)
muscles to support the outbreath as if playing the instrument.

Grade 2

Posture

Adopt a comfortable playing posture, standing alert and flexible. Your feet should be
a hip-width apart, your knees unlocked, and your arms, shoulders and face relaxed.
Aim for the head to be evenly balanced without undue tension in the neck, and hold
your instrument lightly, with as little disruption to your normal stance as possible,
and the instrument assembly (including sling adjustment) adjusted to produce an
effective playing posture. Wrists and hands should be well aligned to the instrument
with the fingers close to keys. Check your embouchure too.

Controlled breathing and support

Exhale and inhale to counts of 2 – 10 (at ♩ = 60), using the abdominal muscles to
support the outbreath as if playing the instrument.

Grade 3

Posture

As grade 2

Controlled breathing and support

Exhale and inhale to counts of 2 – 10 (at ♩ = 60), using the abdominal muscles to
support the outbreath as if playing the instrument.

Grade 4

Posture: standing

As grade 2

Posture: sitting

Sit comfortably on an upright chair, aiming to distribute your weight evenly on both sitting bones, with the spine tall and flexible. Legs should be without tension and feet flat on the floor in front of the chair.

Controlled breathing and support

Exhale and inhale to counts of 2 – 12 (at ♩ = 60), using the abdominal muscles to support the outbreath as if playing the instrument.

Grade 5

Posture: standing

As grade 2

Posture: sitting

As grade 4

Controlled breathing and support

Exhale and inhale to counts of 2 – 12 (at ♩ = 60), using the abdominal muscles to support the outbreath as if playing the instrument.

Grade 6

Posture: standing

As grade 2

Posture: sitting

As grade 4

Controlled breathing and support

Exhale and inhale to counts of 2 – 12 (at ♩ = 60), using the abdominal muscles to support the outbreath as if playing the instrument.

Grade 7

Posture: standing

As grade 2

Posture: sitting
As grade 4

Controlled breathing and support
Exhale and inhale to counts of 2 – 16 (at $\textpmbf{\downarrow}$ = 60), using the abdominal muscles to support the outbreath as if playing the instrument.

Grade 8

Posture: standing
As grade 2

Posture: sitting
As grade 4

Controlled breathing and support
Exhale and inhale to counts of 2 – 16 (at ♩ = 60), using the abdominal muscles to support the outbreath as if playing the instrument.

FLUTE

Grade 1

Warm-ups

Warm-ups do not form part of the examination, but it is highly recommended that candidates prepare by using warm-up exercises immediately before entering the examination room. See page 6.

The Examination

Facility Exercise

Play a long note with full tone for a prescribed number of beats (6 – 8 at ♩ = 60). The examiner will specify the note and the number of beats and will set the pulse.

Scales and Arpeggios

(See Notes on Scales and Arpeggios page 198)

To be played from memory. All scales and arpeggios should be prepared with the specifications listed in the grey box below. The examiner will request *one only* (e.g. one rhythm *or* one articulation *or* one character) when requesting each scale/arpeggio.

Range

Scales
G major (one octave)
C major (one octave)
A natural minor (one octave)

Arpeggios
G major (one octave)
C major (one octave)
A minor (one octave)

Rhythms	i) ♪ s grouped in 3s or 4s as appropriate; ii) as given in Ex.1 (see p.204) (scales only)
Dynamics	With a confident and consistent full tone
Tempi	♩ = 56 – 62
Articulations	Scales (i) tongued; (ii) slurred Arpeggios tongued only
Character	i) Spiky and angry (when tongued) ii) Smooth and calm (when slurred)

Pieces

Play TWO pieces, one to be chosen from each list.

List A

(See General Notes p.210)

From the *Boosey Woodwind Method, flute book 1*　　(B&H M060112898)

Trad.....................Dona, dona, p.22

Barratt.................Centre Stage, p.25

Trad.....................Land of the Silver Birch, p.31

*Wine &
Bayer Sager* ....A Groovy Kind of Love, p.32 [with CD track 46 *or* 47]

Anon., arr. Wye .....Sad Waltz, p.30 [top line] (Flute Class)　　(Novello NOV120738)

*Boehm, arr. Harris
& Adams* ....Du Du (Music Through Time Bk.1)　　(OUP N7181)

*Gluck, arr.
Wastall* ....Chorus from *Paris and Helen*, p.22
　　　　　　　　　(Learn As You Play Flute)　　(B&H M060029295)

*Rosseter, arr. Pearce
& Gunning* ....Elizabethan Dance (The Really Easy Flute Book)　　(Faber 0571508812)

*Brahms, ed.
Mumford*..............Lullaby (What Else Can I Play? Flute Grade 1)　　(IMP 3303A)

*Haydn, arr.
Barratt*.................Minuet (Bravo! Flute)　　(B&H M060106736)

*Czerny, ed./arr.
Hare*.....................Sunrise (The Magic Flute)　　(B&H M060094538)

*Gershwin, arr.
Harris* ....Funny Face (Easy Gershwin for Flute)　　(OUP N6676)

*Granados, arr. Harris
& Adams* ....My Son Eduardo (Music Through Time Bk.1)　　(OUP N7181)

Lewin ....Just Drifting (Up Front Album for Flute)　　(Brass Wind 0304)

Ridout, arr. Wye....Dawn from *Dawn Until Night*
　　　　　　　　　(A Very Easy 20th Century Album)　　(Novello NOV120682)

Barratt.................Safe Haven (Bravo! Flute)　　(B&H M060106736)

Norton ....Softly Does It, No.7
　　　　　　　　　(The Microjazz Flute Collection 1)　　(B&H M060109089)

Norton ....A Stroll, No.9 (The Microjazz Flute Collection 1)   (B&H M060109089)

List B

> (See General Notes p.210)
>
> From the *Boosey Woodwind Method, flute book 1*   (B&H M060112898)
>
> *Trad.* ....Kalinka, p.28
>
> *Trad.* ....Hine ma tov, p.36
>
> *Marks* ....The Flute Rap, p.36
>
> *Trad.* ....When the Saints go Marching in, p.26

Harris ....Scapino, No.1 (Clowns)   (Novello NOV120644)

Ridout, arr. Wye....Rustic Dance, No.13
(A Beginner's Book for the Flute Part 1)   (Novello NOV120584)

*Trad., arr. Pearce
& Gunning* ....Slovakian Hoop Dance
(The Really Easy Flute Book)   (Faber 0571508812)

Barratt.................Wimbledon Waltz (Bravo! Flute)   (B&H M060106736)

*Olechowski, ed.
Durán* ....Flute Song, No.8
(The Duran Collection Volume 1 Flute Song)   (Schott ED12654)

*Lutoslawski, arr.
Denley*..................Zalotny (Time Pieces for Flute Vol.1)   (ABRSM 186096 042 1)

*Hook, arr.
Wastall* ....Minuetto from *Sonata No.3, Op.99*, p.22
(Learn As You Play Flute)   (B&H M060029295)

*Mozart, arr. Harris
& Adams*..............Slave Dance (Music Through Time Bk.1)   (OUP N7181)

*Praetorius, arr
Harris & Adams*...Gavotte (Music Through Time Bk.1)   (OUP N7181)

Trad., arr. Wye......Maypole Dance, No.37
(A Beginner's Book for the Flute Part 1)   (Novello NOV120584)
(N.B. Also in Flute Class, p.28 [top line])   (Novello NOV120738)

*Mozart, arr. Pearce
& Gunning* ....Air from *Figaro*, No.13 (The Really Easy Flute Book)   (Faber 0571508812)

*Purcell, ed.
Mumford*..............Rigadoon (What Else Can I Play? Flute Grade 1)   (IMP 3303A)

List C: Study

Play ONE study, to be chosen from the list below.

> (See General Notes p.210)
>
> From the *Boosey Woodwind Method, flute book 1*   (B&H M060112898)
>
> *Marks* ....Wave Machine, p.35

Bullard ....Restful Flute, No.3 (Fifty Pieces for Flute Bk.1)   (ABRSM 185472 866 0)

Harris, ed. Harris
& Adams ....No.4 (76 Graded Studies for Flute Bk.1)   (Faber 0571514308)

Harris, ed. Harris
& Adams ....No.5 (76 Graded Studies for Flute Bk.1)   (Faber 0571514308)

Adams, ed. Harris
& Adams ....No.8 (76 Graded Studies for Flute Bk.1)   (Faber 0571514308)

Popp, arr.Vester .....No.16 (125 Easy Classical Studies for Flute)   (Universal UE16042)

Bullard ....Sad Flute, No.2 (Fifty Pieces for Flute Bk.1)   (ABRSM 185472 866 0)

Ben-Tovim ....No.4 (The Young Orchestral Flautist Bk.1)   (Pan PEM110)

Ben-Tovim ....No.7 (The Young Orchestral Flautist Bk.1)   (Pan PEM110)

Ben-Tovim ....No.18 (The Young Orchestral Flautist Bk.1)   (Pan PEM110)

Popp, arr.Vester .....No.10 (125 Easy Classical Studies for Flute)   (Universal UE16042)

Gariboldi, arr.
Vester....................No.2 (125 Easy Classical Studies for Flute)   (Universal UE16042)

Gariboldi, arr.
Vester....................No.14 (125 Easy Classical Studies for Flute)   (Universal UE16042)
(N.B. also to be found in 76 Graded Studies for Flute Bk.1, No.11)   (Faber 0571514308)

Wastall ....Unit 11, Ex.3, p.28 *and* Unit 12, Ex.3, p.30
              (Learn As You Play Flute)   (B&H M060029295)

Sight-reading (see p.209)

Aural Tests *or* Initiative Tests (see p.207)

Musicianship Questions (see p.208)

Grade 2

Warm-ups

Warm-ups do not form part of the examination, but it is highly recommended that candidates prepare by using warm-up exercises immediately before entering the examination room. See page 6.

The Examination

Facility Exercises

- Play a long note with full tone for a prescribed number of beats (6 – 8 at ♩ = 60). The examiner will specify the note and the number of beats and will set the pulse.
- Exercise

Scales and Arpeggios

(See Notes on Scales and Arpeggios page 198)

To be played from memory. All scales and arpeggios should be prepared with the specifications listed in the grey box below. The examiner will request *one only* (e.g. one rhythm *or* one articulation *or* one character) when requesting each scale/arpeggio.

Range

Note Centres

Candidates should prepare the following note centre:

G (a twelfth).

N.B. Candidates should use the B♭ fingering (not the B♭ thumb key).

The following should be prepared:

- the major scale
- the major arpeggio

Rhythms	i) ♪ s grouped in 3s or 4s as appropriate ii) As given in Ex.2 (see p.204) (scales only)
Dynamics	With a confident and consistent full tone
Tempi	♩ = 56 – 62
Articulations	Scales (i) tongued (ii) slurred Arpeggios tongued only
Character	i) Happy and bright ii) Sad and dragging

- the natural minor scale
- the minor arpeggio
- the dorian scale

Candidates may pause between individual scales and arpeggios.

Pieces

Play TWO pieces, one to be chosen from each list.

List A

(See General Notes p.210)

From the *Boosey Woodwind Method, flute book 1*   (B&H M060112898)

Trad.....................I Love my Love, p.62 [flute 1 part]

Cacavas................I'll Set my Love to Music, p.46 [flute 1 part]

Jenkins ....Cantilena, p.54

Trad.....................Scarborough Fair, p.39

Marks ....Rambling Man, p.39 [with CD track 61 *or* 62]

From the *Boosey Woodwind Method, flute book 2*   (B&H M060112928)

Trad.....................On the Waves of Lake Balaton, p.8

Norton ....Off the Rails, p.11 [flute 1 part, with CD track 8 *or* 9]

Handel ....March (Music Through Time Bk.2)   (OUP N7182)

Mozart, arr.
Wastall ....Minuet from *Divertimento* No.2, K229, p.40
                       (Learn As You Play Flute)   (B&H M060029295)

Petzold, arr.
Denley..................Menuet in G (Time Pieces for Flute Vol.1)   (ABRSM 186096 042 1)

Rameau, arr.
Barratt ....Sarabande (Bravo! Flute)   (B&H M060106736)

Finnish Folk Melody
arr. Denley ....A Rose there bloomed
                       (Time Pieces for Flute Vol.1)   (ABRSM 186096 042 1)

Cooke, ed. Wye.......Piece No.1, Moderato from *Two Pieces*, No.37
                       (A Very Easy Flute Treasury)   (Novello NOV120852)

Gershwin, arr.
Harris ....Love Walked In (Easy Gershwin for Flute)   (OUP N6676)

Harris	Pierrot, No.2 *or* Columbine, No.4 (Clowns)	(Novello NOV120644)
Hart	Day Dreamin' (All Jazzed Up for Flute)	(Brass Wind 1301)
Lewin	Canton Garden (Up Front Album for Flute)	(Brass Wind 0304)
Lyons	Andante Semplice (Useful Flute Solos Bk.1)	(Useful Music U6)
Ridout, arr. Wye	Morning (A Very Easy 20th Century Album)	(Novello NOV120682)
	Morning (A Very Easy Flute Treasury)	(Novello NOV120852)

List B

> (See General Notes p.210)
>
> From the *Boosey Woodwind Method, flute book 1*   (B&H M060112898)
>
> *Attrib. Henry VIII,*
> *arr. Barratt* ....Hélas madame, p.53 [top part, with *either* flute duet
> accompaniment *or* CD track 81]
>
> *Trad.* ....Athol Highlanders' Jig, p.55
>
> *Trad.* ....Dodi li, p.60 [with CD track 90]
>
> From the *Boosey Woodwind Method, flute book 2*   (B&H M060112928)
>
> *Norton* ....Regretfully Yours, p.9
>
> *Marks* ....Long Shadows, p.10

Gershwin, arr. *Harris*	Swanee (Easy Gershwin for Flute)	(OUP N6676)
Gorb	Belly Dance (Up Front Album for Flute)	(Brass Wind 0304)
Janáček, arr. *Harrison*	Psanicko (Amazing Solos for Flute)	(B&H M060084683)
Mueller, arr. *Harrison*	The Wang Wang Blues (Amazing Solos for Flute)	(B&H M060084683)
Norton	Duet, No.2 (The Microjazz Flute Collection 2)	(B&H M060110603)
Prokofiev, arr. *Harrison*	Troika (Amazing Solos for Flute)	(B&H M060084683)
Trad., arr. *Harrison*	Peruvian Dance Tune (Amazing Solos for Flute)	(B&H M060084683)
Boyle	Panache, No.5 (Pieces of Pan)	(B&H M060081644)
Wiggins	Graceful Dance, No.2 (The Flautist's Debut)	(Studio Music 045359)
Mower	March Wind (Landscapes)	

(Itchy Fingers Publications/B&H M708010340)

Boismortier, ed.
Wye .... Bourée, No.9 (A Very Easy Flute Treasury) (Novello NOV120852)

Humperdinck, arr.
Denley .... Brother, come and dance with me
(Time Pieces for Flute Vol.1) (ABRSM 186096 042 1)

Praetorius, arr.
Harrison .... Tanz des Bürgermeisters (Amazing Solos for Flute) (B&H M060084683)

Wye .... Tambourin, p.42 (Flute Class) (Novello NOV120738)

Vivaldi .... Autumn (Music Through Time Bk.2) (OUP N7182)

Schubert, ed./arr.
Hare .... Ecossaises (The Magic Flute) (B&H M060094538)

List C: Study

Play ONE study, one to be chosen from the list below.

(See General Notes p.210)

From the *Boosey Woodwind Method, flute book 1* (B&H M060112898)

Morgan .... Imaginary Dancer, p.42

Marks .... Upstairs, Downstairs, p.38

Marks .... Step by Step, p.49

From the *Boosey Woodwind Method, flute book 2* (B&H M060112928)

Trad. .... The Irish Washerwoman, p.16

Trad. .... Ghana Alleluia, p.18 [Call 1, followed by the top part of
the Response]

Ben – Tovim .... No.1 (The Young Orchestral Flautist Bk.1) (Pan PEM110)

Ben – Tovim .... No.2 (The Young Orchestral Flautist Bk.1) (Pan PEM110)

Ben – Tovim .... No.15 (The Young Orchestral Flautist Bk.1) (Pan PEM110)

Kohler, arr.
Vester .... No.22 (125 Easy Classical Studies for Flute) (Universal UE16042)

Kohler, arr.
Vester .... No.23 (125 Easy Classical Studies for Flute) (Universal UE16042)

Popp, arr.
Vester .... No.17 (125 Easy Classical Studies for Flute) (Universal UE16042)

Popp, arr.
Vester .... No.32 (125 Easy Classical Studies for Flute) (Universal UE16042)

Baermann, ed.
Harris & Adams ...No.14 (76 Graded Studies for Flute Bk.1)   (Faber 0571514308)

Gariboldi, ed.
Harris & Adams ...No.15 (76 Graded Studies for Flute Bk.1)   (Faber 0571514308)

Anon., arr.
Harrison ....Medieval Dance Tune, No.12
                    (Amazing Studies for Flute)   (B&H M060103858)

Bullard ....Dancing Flute, No.10 (Fifty Pieces for Flute Bk.1)   (ABRSM 185472 866 0)

Bullard ....Gracious Flute, No.13 (Fifty Pieces for Flute Bk.1)   (ABRSM 185472 866 0)

Sight-reading (see p.209)

Aural Tests *or* Initiative Tests (see p.207)

Musicianship Questions (see p.208)

Grade 3

Warm-ups

Warm-ups do not form part of the examination, but it is highly recommended that candidates prepare by using warm-up exercises immediately before entering the examination room. See page 6.

The Examination

Facility Exercises

- Play a long note with full tone for a prescribed number of beats (6 – 12 at $\downarrow$ = 60). The examiner will specify the note and the number of beats and will set the pulse.
- Exercise

N.B. Do not use the B♭ thumb key. Remember to raise the left hand first finger for E♭.

Scales and Arpeggios

(See Notes on Scales and Arpeggios page 198)

To be played from memory. All scales and arpeggios should be prepared with the specifications listed in the grey box below. The examiner will request *one only* (e.g. one rhythm *or* one articulation *or* one character) when requesting each scale/arpeggio.

Range

Note Centres

Candidates should prepare the following note centres: D *and* G.

When the examiner names a note centre the candidate will play:

- the major scale (two octaves)
- the major arpeggio (two octaves)
- the natural minor scale (two octaves)
- the minor arpeggio (two octaves)
- the pentatonic major scale (one octave)
- the chromatic scale (one octave)

Rhythms	i) ♪ s grouped in 3s or 4s as appropriate ii) as given in Ex.3 (see p.204); (two octave scales only) Candidates may if they wish devise their own rhythms for pentatonic and chromatic scales.
Dynamics	With a confident and consistent full tone
Tempi	♩ = 56 – 62
Articulations	i) Tongued; ii) slurred
Character	i) Vivace; ii) Pesante; iii) Dolce; iv) Maestoso sostenuto

Candidates may pause between individual scales and arpeggios.

Pieces

Play TWO pieces, one to be chosen from each list.

List A

(See General Notes p.210)

From the *Boosey Woodwind Method, flute book 1* (B&H M060112898)

Marks & York.......Image, p.56

From the *Boosey Woodwind Method, flute book 2* (B&H M060112928)

Marks ....Tiger Leap, p.26

Weiss &
Shearing...............Lullaby of Birdland, p.27 [with CD track 28]

Trad.....................Jewish Wedding Song, p.48

Bach, J.S., arr.
Harrison ....Minuet for *Anna Magdalena*
(Amazing Solos for Flute)   (B&H M060084683)

Boyce ....Menuetto (Music Through Time Bk.3)   (OUP N7183)

Mozart, arr.
Lyons ....Papageno's Song (Useful Flute Solos Bk.1)   (Useful Music U6)

Schubert ....Menuetto and Trio (Music Through Time Bk.3)   (OUP N183)

Purcell, arr.
Reisen ....Air, No.1 (Two Pieces)   (B&H M060021572)

Trad., ed.
Mumford..............The Lark in the Clear Air
(What Else Can I Play? Flute Grade 3)   (IMP 3305A)

Brahms, ed./arr.
Hare.....................Love Song (The Magic Flute)   (B&H M060094538)

Sullivan, arr.
Wye......................Oh Foolish Fay from *Iolanthe*
(A Gilbert & Sullivan Album)   (Emerson 256)

Sullivan, ed.
Wye......................Twilight, No.28 (A Very Easy Flute Treasury)   (Novello NOV120852)

Satie·····················No.2 (Three Gymnopèdies)   (De Haske F110 or Kevin Mayhew 3611552)

Mower ....Still Waters (Landscapes)   (Itchy Fingers Publications/B&H M708010340)

McDowall............Waltz (Six Pastiches)   (Pan PEM40)

Norton ....Young at Heart, No.9
(The Microjazz Flute Collection 2)   (B&H M060110603)

Popp, arr.
Wastall ....Andantino, No.15 (First Repertoire Pieces for Flute)   (B&H M060040733)

List B

(See General Notes p.210)

From the *Boosey Woodwind Method, flute book 1*   (B&H M060112898)

Barratt.................Quirk, p.59 [either part, with *either* the flute duet
part *or* CD accompaniment]

Norton ....Club Soda, p.61 [flute 1 part]

Vivaldi.................Spring, p.60

From the *Boosey Woodwind Method, flute book 2*   (B&H M060112928)

Barratt.................Italian Connection, p.25

Trad. ....Hero's Farewell, p.28

Norton ....A Sad Tale, p.46

Bernstein, arr.
Harrison ....America (Amazing Solos for Flute)   (B&H M060084683)

Bizet, arr.
Harrison ....Seguidilla (Amazing Solos for Flute)   (B&H M060084683)

Desmond, arr.
Hart.....................Take Five (All Jazzed Up for Flute)   (Brass Wind 1301)

Dvořák ....Humoresque (Pop Go The Classics Encore!)   (Cramer 90055)

Gershwin, arr.
Harris ....Sweet & Low Down *or* Fascinating Rhythm
                              (Easy Gershwin for Flute)   (OUP N6676)

Harris ....Harlequin, No.5 (Clowns)   (Novello NOV120644)

Hart.....................No Dice (All Jazzed Up for Flute)   (Brass Wind 1301)

Horovitz, arr.
Wye ....Rumba (A Very Easy 20th Century Album)   (Novello NOV120682)

McDowall............Hornpipe (Six Pastiches)   (Pan PEM40)

Norton ....Easy does it, No.4 *or* Scottisch, No.8
                              (The Microjazz Flute Collection 2)   (B&H M060110603)

Pogson..................Rock in Time (The Way to Rock)   (B&H M060087264)

Sousa....................The Liberty Bell (Pop Go the Classics Encore!)   (Cramer 90055)

Gordon ....Waltz and Trio (Ländler) (A Little Suite)   (Janus Music 008835)

Martin, ed.
Mumford..............Puppet on a String (What Else Can I Play? Flute Grade 3)   (IMP 3305A)

Sculthorpe.............Left Bank Waltz (Two Easy Pieces)   (Faber 057151751X)

Mower ....The Great Outside (Landscapes)   (Itchy Fingers Publications/B&H M708010340)

Attaingnant, arr.
Denley..................Que je chatoulle ta fossette
                              (Time Pieces for Flute Vol.2)   (ABRSM 186096 043 X)

Schubert, arr.
Denley..................Marche Militaire (Time Pieces for Flute Vol.2)   (ABRSM 186096 043 X)

Trad., ed.
Mumford..............The Wraggle Taggle Gypsies
                              (What Else Can I Play? Flute Grade 3)   (IMP 3305A)

List C: Study

Play ONE study, to be chosen from the list below.

(See General Notes p.210)

From the *Boosey Woodwind Method, flute book 2*   (B&H M060112928)

Marks ....Chromatic Cheesecake, p.26

Trad. ....The Parson's Farewell, p.38

Marks ....Clean Air, p.39

Ben – Tovim ....No.11 (The Young Orchestral Flautist Bk.1)   (Pan PEM110)

Ben – Tovim ....No.14 (The Young Orchestral Flautist Bk.1)   (Pan PEM110)

Dick, arr. Wye ....Dorset Street (A Very Easy 20th Century Album)   (Novello NOV120682)

Gariboldi, arr.
Vester ....No.5 (100 Classical Studies for Flute)   (Universal UE12992)

(N.B. also to be found in 76 Graded Studies for Flute Bk.1, No.27)   (Faber 0571514308)

Gariboldi, arr.
Vester ....No.7 (100 Classical Studies for Flute)   (Universal UE12992)

Soussman, arr.
Vester ....No.36 (125 Easy Classical Studies for Flute)   (Universal UE16042)

Soussman, arr.
Vester ....No.38 (125 Easy Classical Studies for Flute)   (Universal UE16042)

Gariboldi, ed. Harris
& Adams ....No.22 (76 Graded Studies for Flute Bk.1)   (Faber 0571514308)

Anon., ed. Harris
& Adams ....The Sun from the East, No.20
                        (76 Graded Studies for Flute Bk.1)   (Faber 0571514308)

Bullard ....Cheerful Flute, No.18 (Fifty Pieces for Flute Bk.1)   (ABRSM 185472 866 0)

Bullard ....Romantic Flute, No.16 (Fifty Pieces for Flute Bk.1)   (ABRSM 185472 866 0)

Sight-reading (see p.209)

Aural Tests *or* Initiative Tests (see p.207)

Musicianship Questions (see p.208)

Grade 4

Warm-ups

Warm-ups do not form part of the examination, but it is highly recommended that
candidates prepare by using warm-up exercises immediately before entering the
examination room. See page 6.

The Examination

Facility Exercises

* Play a long note *mf* for a prescribed number of beats (8 – 12 at ♩ = 60).
  The examiner will specify the note and the number of beats and will set the pulse.
* Embouchure flexibility

All notes are to be played with equal strength.

Scales and Arpeggios

(See Notes on Scales and Arpeggios page 198)

To be played from memory. All scales and arpeggios should be prepared with the
specifications listed in the grey box on the following page. The examiner will request
one only (e.g. one rhythm *or* one articulation *or* one character) when requesting each
scale/arpeggio.

Range

Note Centres

Candidates should prepare the following note centres: C (two octaves, except where specified) *and* A (two octaves, except where specified).

When the examiner names a note centre the candidate will play:

- the major scale
- the major arpeggio
- the natural minor scale
- the melodic minor scale
- the minor arpeggio
- the pentatonic major scale
- the whole tone scale (one octave)
- the chromatic scale

Candidates may pause between individual scales and arpeggios.

Rhythms	i) ♪s grouped in 3s or 4s as appropriate ii) as given in Ex.3 (see p.204) (major and minor scales only) Candidates may if they wish devise their own rhythms for pentatonic, whole tone and chromatic scales.
Dynamics	Within the range *mp – f,* i) sustaining a level throughout; ii) cresc.; iii) decresc.
Tempi	Scales ♩= 72 – 84 Arpeggios ♩= 60 – 66
Articulations	i) Tongued; ii) slurred
Character	i) Staccato and light; ii) Heavy and accented; iii) Douce et très passioné

Pieces

Play TWO pieces, one to be chosen from each list.

List A

Milford, arr. Harris & Adams ....Air (Music Through Time Bk.3)   (OUP N7183)

Mozart, arr. Harris & Adams ....Theme & Variation (Music Through Time Bk.3)   (OUP N7183)

Bach, J.S., arr. Vester....................Minuet I and II in C Major and A Minor (15 Easy Baroque Pieces)   (Universal UE17669)

MacDowell, arr. Fish ....To a Wild Rose (Festival for Flute Book 1)   (Kevin Mayhew 3611085)

Bach, J.S., arr. Fish ....Gavotte (Festival for Flute Book 1)   (Kevin Mayhew 3611085)

Moyse...................Rippling Water, No.2 (Six Easy Pieces)   (Presser/Universal PR1880)

Moyse...................Hopscotch, No.3 (Six Easy Pieces)   (Presser/Universal PR1880)

McDowall...........Romantic Song (Six Pastiches)   (Pan PEM40)

Le Thiere, arr.
Wastall ....Romance (First Repertoire Pieces for Flute)   (B&H M060040733)

Trad., arr.
Harrison ....Stars, No Moon (Amazing Solos for Flute)   (B&H M060084683)

List B

Gershwin, arr.
Harris ....I Got Plenty of Nothin' (Easy Gershwin for Flute)   (OUP N6676)

Joplin, arr.
Harrison ....Original Rags (Amazing Solos for Flute)   (B&H M060084683)

Lyons ....Set Free (Useful Flute Solos Bk.1)   (Useful Music U6)

McDowall...........Comic Song (Six Pastiches)   (Pan PEM40)

Norton ....Folk Shuffle, No.13 *or* Song, No.12 *or* Springboard, No.14
   (The Microjazz Flute Collection 2)   (B&H M060110603)

Parker ....Buggy (Jazzed Up Too for Flute)   (Brass Wind 1310)

Pogson..................Ska-Face *or* Little David (The Way to Rock)   (B&H M060087264)

Warlock, arr.
Harrison ....Basse Dance (Amazing Solos for Flute)   (B&H M060084683)

Sullivan,
arr.Wye ....I am a Courtier Grave and Serious
   (A Gilbert & Sullivan Album)   (Emerson 256)

Dodgson ....Polka (Up Front Album for Flute)   (Brass Wind 0304)

Porter, ed. Steel......It's Alright With Me (What Else Can I Play? Flute Grade 4)   (IMP 7047A)

Purcell, arr.
Revell ....Hornpipe, No.2 (Two Pieces)   (B&H M060021572)

Tchaikowsky, arr.
Cathrine...............March from *The Nutcracker* (Favourite Classics)   (Presser/Universal PR2626)

Handel, arr.
Wastall ....Giga from *Sonata in F*, No.10
   (First Repertoire Pieces for Flute)   (B&H M060040733)

Telemann, arr.
Wastall ....Minuet, No.8 (First Repertoire Pieces for Flute)   (B&H M060040733)

(N.B. also to be found in Suite in A Minor No.4b)   (Hinrichsen/Peters H882A)

Vivaldi, arr.
Wastall ....Allegro, No.14 (First Repertoire Pieces for Flute)   (B&H M060040733)

List C: Study

Play ONE study, to be chosen from the list below.

Ben – Tovim ....No.32 *and* No.48 (The Young Orchestral Flautist Bk.2)   (Pan PEM111)

Ben – Tovim ....No.48 *and* No.50 (The Young Orchestral Flautist Bk.2)   (Pan PEM111)

Ben – Tovim ....No.40 (The Young Orchestral Flautist Bk.2)   (Pan PEM111)

Gariboldi, arr.
Vester ....No.21 (100 Classical Studies for Flute)   (Universal UE12992)

Kohler, arr.
Vester ....No.27 (100 Classical Studies for Flute)   (Universal UE12992)

(N.B. also to be found in Progress in Flute Playing, Op.33, Bk.1, No.1)   (Chester/Music Sales CH55791)

Popp, arr. Vester ....No.82 (125 Easy Classical Studies for Flute)   (Universal UE16042)

(N.B. also to be found in 76 Graded Studies for Flute Bk.1, No.40)   (Faber 0571514308)

Tulou, arr.
Vester ....No.15 (100 Classical Studies for Flute)   (Universal UE12992)

Bullard ....Baroque Flute, No.30 (Fifty Pieces for Flute Bk.1)   (ABRSM 185472 866 0)

Toulou, ed. Harris
& Adams ....No.29 (76 Graded Studies for Flute Bk.1)   (Faber 0571514308)

(N.B. also to be found in 100 Classical Studies for Flute, No.14)   (Universal UE12992)

Popp, arr. Vester ....No.94 (125 Easy Classical Studies for Flute)   (Universal UE16042)

Popp, arr.Vester .....No.95 (125 Easy Classical Studies for Flute)   (Universal UE16042)

(N.B. Also to be found in 76 Graded Studies for Flute Bk.1, No.34)   (Faber 0571514308)

Gariboldi, arr.
Harrison ....No.10 (Amazing Studies for Flute)   (B&H M060103858)

(N.B. Also found in 100 Classical Studies for Flute, No.40)   (Universal UE12992)

Gariboldi, arr.
Harrison ....No.11 (Amazing Studies for Flute)   (B&H M060103858)

Sight-reading (see p.209)

(see p.209)

Aural Tests *or* Initiative Tests (see p.207)

(see p.207)

Musicianship Questions (see p.208)

(see p.208)

Grade 5

Warm-ups

Warm-ups do not form part of the examination, but it is highly recommended that candidates prepare by using warm-up exercises immediately before entering the examination room. See page 6.

The Examination

Facility Exercises

- Play a long note *mf* for a prescribed number of beats (8 – 12 at ♩ = 60).
  The examiner will specify the note and the number of beats and will set the pulse.
- Flexibility

Breathe where necessary.

Scales and Arpeggios

(See Notes on Scales and Arpeggios page 198)

To be played from memory. All scales and arpeggios should be prepared with the specifications listed in the grey box below. The examiner will request *one only* (e.g. one rhythm *or* one articulation *or* one character) when requesting each scale/arpeggio.

Range

Note Centres

Candidates should prepare the following note centres: E (two octaves) *and* F (two octaves).

When the examiner names a note centre the candidate will play:

- the major scale
- the major arpeggio
- the melodic minor scale
- the minor arpeggio
- the pentatonic major scale

Rhythms	i) ♪s grouped in 3s or 4s as appropriate ii) as given in Ex.4 (see p.204) (major and minor scales only) Candidates may if they wish devise their own rhythms for pentatonic, whole tone, chromatic and blues scales.
Dynamics	Within the range *mp – f,* i) sustaining a level throughout; ii) cresc.; iii) decresc.
Tempi	Scales ♩ = 72 – 84 Arpeggios ♩ = 60 – 66
Articulations	i) Tongued; ii) slurred
Character	i) Sehr ruhig; ii) Rasch und feuerig; ii) Trotzig; iii) Lebhaft und mit wut

- the whole tone scale
- the chromatic scale
- the blues scale

Candidates may pause between individual scales and arpeggios.

Pieces

Play TWO pieces, one to be chosen from each list.

List A

Gluck, arr.
Malcolm ....Dance of the Blessed Spirits from *Orfeo*
  (3 Masterpieces for Flute)   (Pan PEM36)

(Also available in an arrangement by Hunt)   (Schott ED10719)

Bach, J.S. ....Sonata No.4 in C Major, 3rd Movt: Adagio
  (Bach Sonatas Vol.2)   (Peters 4461B)

Pepusch &
Coeillet, ed.
Moyse ....Sonata in G Major, 1st Movt: Adagio *and* 2nd
  Movt: Gigue (Flute Music of the Baroque)   (Schirmer/Music Sales GS33033)

Arrieu ....Sonatine, 1st Movt: Allegro moderato   (Amphion/UMP 24054)

Laken ....Misty (Flute Magic 1)   (IMP 03852)

Gaubert ....Orientale, No.2 (Two Esquisses)   (Heugel/UMP HE26583)

Hart ....City Life, No.2 (City Life)   (Brass Wind 2301)

Mancini, arr.
Laken ....Moon River (Flute Magic 1)   (IMP 03852)

Fauré, arr. Biglio...Sicilienne, Op.78   (Chester/Music Sales CH55156)

Debussy ....En Bateau   (Durand/UMP 071150)

Rutter ....Chanson, No.5 (Suite Antique)   (OUP N8691)

Olechowski, ed.
Durán ....Lullaby for an Indian Baby, No.2 (The Duran
  Collection Volume 3 Romance and Fantasie)   (Schott ED12656)

List B

Delibes ....No.1 (Three Original Pieces)   (OUP Y5595)

Garner, arr.
McCabe ....March of the Fool (Portraits)   (Novello NOV120529)

McDowall ....Music Hall (Six Pastiches)   (Pan PEM40)

Norton ....Carthorse Rag, No.28 or Swing Out Sister, No.19 *or*
　　　　　　　　Riff Laden, No.21 (The Microjazz Flute Collection 2)　(B&H M060110603)

Pogson ....The Paper Boy *or* Rockette (The Way to Rock)　(B&H M060087264)

Vaughan
Williams...............Humoresque, No.2 (Suite de Ballet)　(OUP N9282)

Milford ....Sonatina in F, 3rd Movt: Vivo non troppo　(OUP N7807)

Handel ....Sonata in F Major, HWV 369, 2nd Movt: Allegro
　　　　　　　　(Eleven Sonatas)　(Bärenreiter/Faber BA4225)

Telemann ....Sonata in C Major, TWV 41:C2, 2nd Movt: Allegro
　　　　　　　　(Four Sonatas from *Der getreue Musikmeister*)　(Bärenreiter/Faber HM6)

Quantz, ed. Ruf....Sonata in E Minor, 4th Movt: Vivace　(Schott FTR61)

Pepusch &
Coeillet ed. Moyse..Sonata in F Major, 2nd Movt: Allegro
　　　　　　　　(Flute Music of the Baroque)　(Schirmer/Music Sales GS33033)

List C: Study

Play ONE study, to be chosen from the list below.

Anderson, arr.
Vester....................No.18 (100 Classical Studies for Flute)　(Universal UE12992)

Castérède..............No.8 (Douze Etudes)　(Leduc/UMP AL23139)

Drouet ....No.1 (25 Studies for the Flute)　(Broekmans and Van Poppel BRP1510)

(N.B. Also to be found in 100 Classical Studies, No.69)　(Universal UE12992)

Gariboldi, arr.
Vester....................No.42 (100 Classical Studies for Flute)　(Universal UE12992)

(N.B. Also to be found in 76 Graded Studies for Flute Bk.1, No.45)　(Faber 0571514316)

Kohler, arr. Vester..No.29 (100 Classical Studies for Flute)　(Universal UE12992)

(N.B. Also to be found in Progress in Flute Playing, Op.33, Bk.1, No.3)　(Chester/Music Sales CH55791)

Kohler, arr. Vester..No.31 (100 Classical Studies for Flute)　(Universal UE12992)

(N.B. Also to be found in Progress in Flute Playing, Op.33, Bk.1, No.7)　(Chester/Music Sales CH55791)

Soussmann, arr.
Blakeman ....No.4 (Flute Player's Companion Vol.2)　(Chester/Music Sales CH55841)

Demersseman, ed.
Harris & Adams...No.58 (76 Graded Studies for Flute Bk.2)　(Faber 0571514316)

(N.B. Also to be found in 100 Classical Studies for Flute, No.36)　(Universal UE12992)

Drouet, ed. Harris
& Adams ....No.61 (76 Graded Studies for Flute Bk.2)   (Faber 0571514316)

(N.B. Also to be found in 25 Etudes Célèbres, No.6)   (Leduc/UMP AL17113)

Kohler, ed. Harris
& Adams ....No.64 (76 Graded Studies for Flute Bk.2)   (Faber 0571514316)

(N.B. Also to be found in Kohler Op.33 Bk.1, No.12)   (Chester/Music Sales CH55791)

Ferling, ed. Harris
& Adams ....No.50 (76 Graded Studies for Flute Bk.1)   (Faber 0571514318)

Sight-reading (see p.209)

Aural Tests *or* Initiative Tests (see p.207)

Musicianship Questions (see p.208)

Grade 6

Warm-ups

Warm-ups do not form part of the examination, but it is highly recommended that candidates prepare by using warm-up exercises immediately before entering the examination room. See page 6.

The Examination

Facility Exercises

- Play a long note *mf* for a prescribed number of beats (4 – 10 at ♩ = 60).
  The examiner will specify the note and the number of beats and will set the pulse.
- Play a long note *f* for a prescribed number of beats (4 – 6 at ♩ = 60).
  The examiner will specify the note and the number of beats and will set the pulse.
- Intonation exercise

To be played in the key requested by the examiner. The examiner will state the starting note.

Scales and Arpeggios

(See Notes on Scales and Arpeggios page 198)

To be played from memory. All scales and arpeggios should be prepared with the specifications listed in the grey box below. The examiner will request *two only* (e.g. one rhythm *and* one dynamic or one articulation *and* one character) when requesting each scale/exercise.

Range

Note Centres

Candidates should prepare the following note centres: B♭ (two octaves) *and* F♯ (two octaves).

When the examiner names a note centre the candidate will play:

- the scale/arpeggio exercise on p.203
- the pentatonic major scale
- the whole tone scale
- the blues scale

Candidates may pause between individual scales and arpeggios.

Rhythms	Scale/arpeggio exercise as written; other scales ♪ s grouped in 3s or 4s as appropriate. Candidates may if they wish devise their own rhythms for pentatonic, whole tone and blues scales.
Dynamics	Within the range *pp – ff* i) sustaining a level throughout; ii) cresc. throughout each scale/arpeggio; iii) decresc. throughout each scale/arpeggio
Tempi	♩ = 94+
Articulations	i) Tongued; ii) slurred. Candidates may if they wish offer additional articulation patterns of their own.
Character	Candidates to offer a selection of at least four of their own contrasting choices which may include familiar Italian/German terms of expression or terms from any other language provided an explanation can be given.

Pieces

Play TWO pieces, one to be chosen from each list. Candidates may offer one piece on the piccolo as their List A choice.

List A

Abel ....Sonata in E Minor, Op.6/3, 1st Movt: Adagio *and* 2nd
Movt:Allegro (Zwei Sonaten Op.6/2 & 3)   (Schott FTR123)

Bach, C.P.E. ....Sonata in G Major, 1st Movt: Andante *and* 2nd Movt:
Allegro (Sonatas Bk.1)   (Bärenreiter/Faber HM71)

Bach, J.S. ....Suite in B Minor, Sarabande *and* Badinerie   (B&H M060010859)

Blavet ....Sonata No.6 in A Minor, *La Bouget*, 1st Movt: Adagio
         and 2nd Movt: Allemande (Sonatas Vol.2)   (B&H M060091810)

Handel ....Sonata in G Major, HWV 363b, 1st Movt: Adagio
         and 2nd Movt: Allegro (Eleven Sonatas)   (Bärenreiter/Faber BA4225)

Mozart ....Concerto in D, KV314 2nd Movt:
         Adagio ma non troppo   (Any reliable edition)

Piccolo

*Mozart, arr. Wye
& Morris* ....Turkish March, p.22 (A Piccolo Practice Book)   (Novello NOV120658)

or

Vivaldi ....Concerto in C, F VI, 4, 2nd Movt: Largo   (Any reliable edition)

List B

Tomasi ....Complainte – Danse de Mowgli   (Billaudot/UMP GB6417)

Seiber ....Dance Suite, 1st Movt: Novelty Foxtrot
         and 4th Movt: Mazurka   (Schott ED12426)

Heath ....Gentle Dreams *and* Shiraz   (Camden Music CM113)

Bizet ....Entr'acte *or* Minuet (Entr'acte and Minuet)   (Universal UE17627)

*Taffanel, ed.
Blakeman* ....Allegro Grazioso *or* Allegretto Scherzando
         (Allegro Grazioso and Allegretto Scherzando)   (Pan PEM50)

*Roussel, ed.
Roorda* ....Joueurs de Flûte, 2nd Movt:
         Tityre *and* 3rd Movt: Krishna   (Broekmans and Van Poppel BRP1573)

Hart ....City Life, No.3 (City Life)   (Brass Wind 2301)

Poulenc ....Sonata, 2nd Movt: Cantilena   (Chester/Music Sales CH01605)

*Rachmaninov, ed.
Peck* ....Vocalise (Solos for Flute: 36 Repertoire Pieces)   (Fischer/B&H M060001048)

List C: Study

Play a study, an orchestral alternative, or a study on the piccolo, to be chosen from the list below. N.B. A piccolo study may only be chosen if the candidate offers a flute piece as their List A choice.

*Blavet, arr.
Vester* ....No.8 (50 Classical Studies for Flute)   (IMC/Universal 2037)

*Drouet, arr.
Blakeman* ....No.15 (The Flute Player's Companion Vol.2)   (Chester/Music Sales CH55841)

Kohler, ed.
Blakeman ....No.8 *or* No.9 *or* No.11
               (Progress in Flute Playing Op.33, Bk.1)   (Chester/Music Sales CH55791)

Quantz, ed.
Preston ....No.2 (16 Pieces for Solo Flute)   (Pan PEM32)

Reade ....Aspects of a Landscape, 2nd Movt:
               Birdsong *and* 3rd Movt: Bird Movements   (Hunt Edition HE31)

Hindemith ....Acht Stücke, 3rd Movt: Sehr langsam,
               frei im zeitmass *and* 5th Movt: Sehr lebhaft   (Schott 4760)

Mower ....Go With the Flow, No.8
               (20 Commandments)   (Itchy Fingers Publications/B&H M708010333)

Piazzola ....No.4 (Tango Etudes)   (Lemoine/UMP HL 24897)

Orchestral Alternatives

Mozart, ed.
Smith ....Symphony No.41, Andante, p.16 *and* Allegro, p.17
               (Orchestral Studies for the Flute Bk.1)   (UMP)

or

Ben – Tovim ....No.14 *and* No.15 *and* No.24
               (The Young Orchestral Flautist Vol.3)   (Pan PEM112)

Piccolo

Bach, J.S. arr.
Eden ....Sarabande, p.34 (Piccolo! Piccolo! Bk.1)   (Just Flutes EDE010)

or

Hoffmeister, arr.
Eden ....Etude, p.24 (Piccolo! Piccolo! Bk.2)   (Just Flutes EDE020)

Sight-reading (see p.209)

Aural Tests *or* Initiative Tests (see p.207)

Musicianship Questions (see p.208)

Grade 7

Warm-ups

Warm-ups do not form part of the examination, but it is highly recommended that candidates prepare by using warm-up exercises immediately before entering the examination room. See page 6.

The Examination

Facility Exercises

- Play a long note *p/mf* for a prescribed number of beats (4 – 12 at ♩ = 60).
  The examiner will specify the note and the dynamic, choose the number of beats and set the pulse.
- Play a long note *f* for a prescribed number of beats (4 – 8 at ♩ = 60).
  The examiner will specify the note and the number of beats and will set the pulse.
- Control, positioning and intonation

Play this exercise on D, E♭, E or F, as requested by the examiner.

Scales and Arpeggios

(See Notes on Scales and Arpeggios page 198)

To be played from memory. All scales and arpeggios should be prepared with the specifications listed in the grey box opposite. The examiner will request *two only* (e.g. one rhythm *and* one dynamic *or* one articulation *and* one character) when requesting each scale/exercise.

Range

Note Centres

Candidates should prepare the following note centres: C♯, F, G *and* E♭ (all two octaves).

When the examiner names a note centre the candidate will play:

- the scale/arpeggio exercise on p.203
- the whole tone scale
- the diminished scales (both forms)
- the blues scale

Candidates may pause between individual scales and arpeggios.

Rhythms	Scale/arpeggio exercise as written; other scales ♪s grouped in 3s or 4s as appropriate. Candidates may if they wish devise their own rhythms for whole tone, diminished and blues scales.
Dynamics	Within the range *pp – ff*, i) sustaining a level throughout; ii) cresc. throughout each scale/arpeggio; iii) decresc. throughout each scale/arpeggio.
Tempi	♩ = 94+
Articulations	i) tongued; ii) slurred; Candidates may if they wish offer additional articulation patterns of their own.
Character	Candidates to offer a selection of at least four of their own contrasting choices which may include familiar Italian/German terms of expression or terms from any other language provided an explanation can be given.

Pieces

Play TWO pieces, one to be chosen from each list. Candidates may offer one piece on the piccolo as their List B choice.

List A

Bach, C.P.E. ....Sonata in E Minor, 1st Movt: Adagio
and 2nd Movt: Allegro (Sonatas Bk.1)   (Bärenreiter/Faber HM71)

Bach, J.S. ....Solo Sonata in A Minor, 3rd Movt: Sarabande
and 4th Movt: Bourrée anglaise   (Peters P3332)

Gluck ....Concerto in G, 1st Movt: Allegro non molto
and 2nd Movt: Adagio   (Kalmus/Maecenas KO9250)

Telemann ....Fantasie No.8 in E Minor, TWV 40:9,
1st Movt: Largo *and* 2nd Movt: Spirituoso
(Twelve Fantasias for Flute)   (Bärenreiter BA2971/Musica Rara MR2167)

Vivaldi ....Concerto in A Minor, F vi, 1st Movt:
Allegro non molto *and* 2nd Movt: Larghetto   (IMC/Universal 2219)

Mozart.................Concerto in G Major, KV313, 2nd Movt:
Adagio ma non troppo   (Any reliable edition)

List B

Mouquet................La Flûte de Pan, 2nd Movt: Pan et Les Oiseaux   (Lemoine/UMP 19743)

Roussel, ed.
Roorda.................Joueurs de Flûte, 4th Movt:
M. de la Péjaudie   (Broekmans and Van Poppel BRP1573)

Bozza...................Aria   (Leduc/UMP AL20208)

Bennett...............Summer Music, 2nd Movt:
Siesta and 3rd Movt: Games   (Novello NOV120560)

Donjon, ed.
Roorda.................Offertoire   (Broekmans/Universal 1624)

Donjon, ed. Wye....Offertoire (Flute Solos Vol.3)   (Chester/Music Sales CH55122)

Saint-Saëns..........Romance Op.37   (UMP)

Vaughan
Williams...............Suite de Ballet, Gavotte and Passepied   (OUP N9282)

Taffanel, ed.
Blakeman.............Andantino and Andante   (Pan PEM52)

Heath...................Out of the Cool   (Chester/Music Sales CH55693)

Piccolo

Shostakovitch,
arr. Maganini.......Polka (The Golden Age Op.22 for Piccolo and Piano)   (MusT M829)

Janáček, ed.
Burmeister............March for Piccolo and Piano   (Peters P9868)

List C: Study

Play a study, both orchestral alternatives, or a study on the piccolo, to be chosen from the list below. N.B. A piccolo study may only be chosen if the candidate offers a flute piece as their List B choice.

Boehm..................No.3 (24 Capriccios, Op 26)   (Chester/Music Sales CH55209)

Castérède..............No.11 (Douze Etudes)   (Leduc/UMP AL23139)

Gariboldi, arr.
Blakeman.............No.7 (The Flute Player's Companion Vol.2)   (Chester/Music Sales CH55841)

Kohler, ed.
Blakeman.............No.7 (Progress in Flute Playing, Op 33, Bk.2)   (Chester/Music Sales CH55792)

Prill, arr.
Blakeman.............No.8 (The Flute Player's Companion Vol.2)   (Chester/Music Sales CH55841)

Quantz, ed.
Preston ....No.9 (16 Pieces for Solo Flute)   (Pan PEM32)

Reade ....Aspects of a Landscape, 6th Movt: Lament
      and 7th Movt: Celebration   (Hunt Edition HE31)

Hindemith ....Acht Stücke, 7th Movt: Recitativ *and* 8th Movt: Finale   (Schott 4760)

Piazzolla ....No.5 (Tango Etudes)   (Lemoine/UMP HL24897)

Mower ....Boiling Point, No.10
      (20 Commandments)   (Itchy Fingers Publications/B&H M708010333)

Orchestral Alternatives

Bizet, ed. Durichen/
Kratsch ....Carmen – Vorspiel (Orchester Probespiel)   (Peters P8659)

And (i.e. candidate should play both)

Dvořák, ed.
Durichen/Katsch ...Symphony No.9 (Orchester Probespiel)   (Peters P8659)

Piccolo

Damare, arr.
Eden ....Etude, p.51 (Piccolo! Piccolo! Bk.2)   (Just Flutes EDE020)

Hindemith, arr.
Wye ....March & Pastorale from *Nobilissima Visione*,
      p.28 (A Piccolo Practice Book)   (Novello NOV120658)

Delius, arr.
Wye ....La Calinda, p.76 (A Piccolo Practice Book)   (Novello NOV120658)

Sight-reading (see p.209)

Aural Tests *or* Initiative Tests (see p.207)

Musicianship Questions (see p.208)

Grade 8

Warm-ups

Warm-ups do not form part of the examination, but it is highly recommended that candidates prepare by using warm-up exercises immediately before entering the examination room. See page 6.

The Examination

Facility Exercises

- Play a long note *pp/p/mf* for a prescribed number of beats (4 – 16 at ♩ = 60). The examiner will specify the note and the dynamic, choose the number of beats and set the pulse.
- Play a long note *f* for a prescribed number of beats (4 – 10 at ♩ = 60).
  The examiner will specify the note and the number of beats and will set the pulse.
- Embouchure facility

- Dynamic control

To be played on any two notes an octave apart. The examiner will state the starting note and starting dynamic.

Scales and Arpeggios

(See Notes on Scales and Arpeggios page 198)

To be played from memory. All scales and arpeggios should be prepared with the specifications listed in the grey box opposite. The examiner will request *two only* (e.g. one rhythm *and* one dynamic *or* one articulation *and* one character) when requesting each scale/exercise.

Range

Note Centres

Candidates should prepare the following note centres: G♯, B, E *and* B♭ (all two octaves, except where specified).

When the examiner names a note centre the candidate will play:

- the scale/arpeggio exercise on p.203
- the whole tone scale
- the diminished scales (both forms)
- the blues scale
- the crabwise major scale (one octave, starting either on the note centre or on C – candidate's choice)

Candidates may pause between individual scales and arpeggios. Where there is more than one possible starting pitch within the range (e.g. crabwise scale starting on C), the starting pitch is at candidate's choice.

Rhythms	Scale/arpeggio exercise as written; crabwise as written (see page 199); other scales ♪ s grouped in 3s or 4s as appropriate. Candidates may if they wish devise their own rhythms for whole tone, diminished and blues scales.
Dynamics	Within the range *pp – ff*, i) sustaining a level throughout; ii) cresc. throughout each scale/arpeggio; iii) decresc. throughout each scale/arpeggio.
Tempi	♩ = 94+
Articulations	i) tongued; ii) slurred. Candidates may if they wish offer additional articulation patterns of their own.
Character	Candidates to offer a selection of at least four of their own contrasting choices which may include familiar Italian/German terms of expression or terms from any other language provided an explanation can be given.

Pieces, studies and orchestral alternatives for Grade 8

Options are given for flute, piccolo and alto flute in the lists below. Candidates may offer one piece/study/orchestral alternative on the piccolo *or* alto flute, but must offer at least TWO choices on the flute.

Pieces

Play TWO pieces, one to be chosen from each list.

List A

Options are given for flute and for piccolo.

Bach, C.P.E. ....Sonata in G, 'Hamburger Sonata' [complete]　　(Schott FTR1)

Bach, J.S. ....Sonata in E♭ Major, BWV1031 [complete]　　(Any reliable edition)

Mozart................Concerto in G Major, KV313, 1st Movt:
Allegro maestoso *or* Concerto in D Major,
KV314, 1st Movt: Allegro aperto   (Any reliable edition)

Mozart, ed. Proehle
& Gabor................Rondo in D, KV373   (EMB/B&H M080085219)

Quantz ....Concerto in G, 1st Movt: Allegro Assai   (De Haske F359)

Telemann ....Fantasia No.3 in B minor,
TVW 40:4 *or* Fantasia No.7 in D major,
TVW 40:8 [complete]   (Bärenreiter BA2971/Musica Rara MR2167)

Vivaldi................Concerto in F, *La Tempesta di Mare*   (EMB/B&H M080071885)

Piccolo

Gounod, arr. Wye
& Morris..............Ballet Music from *Faust*, p.56 (A Piccolo Practice Book)   (Novello 120658)

Verdi, arr. Wye
& Morris..............Finale from *Aida*, p.80 (A Piccolo Practice Book)   (Novello 120658)

Sibelius, arr. Wye
& Morris..............Alla Marcia from *Karelia Suite*,
(A Piccolo Practice Book)   (Novello 120658)

List B

Options are given for flute and for alto flute.

Clarke ....The Great Train Race   (Just Flutes CLA035)

Fukushima ....Requiem   (Zerboni/Elkin 5325)

Mower ....Sonata Latino, 1st Movt:
Salsa Montunate   (Itchy Fingers Publications/B&H M708010326)

Roussel, ed.
Roorda ....Joueurs de Flûte, 1st Movt: Pan   (Broekmans/Universal BRP1573)

Copland ....Duo for Flute and Piano, 2nd Movt:
Poetic, somewhat mournful
and 3rd Movt: Lively, with bounce   (B&H M051590193)

Muczynski............Sonata, Op.14, 1st Movt: Allegro Deciso   (Schirmer/Music Sales GS33612)

Hindemith............Sonata, 1st Movt: Heiter bewegt
or 2nd Movt: Sehr langsam   (Schott ED2522)

Poulenc.................Sonata, 3rd Movt: Allegro Giocoso   (Chester/Music Sales CH01605)

Prokofiev..............Sonata No.2, Op.94, 1st Movt: Moderato   (B&H M060021176)

Reinecke ....Ballade, Op.288   (Zimmerman/Elkin ZM1991)

Reinecke ....Sonata Undine, 1st Movt: Allegro   (IMC/Universal 1757)

Alto Flute

Mower ....No.2 (Sonnets – Two Pieces
for Alto Flute and Piano)   (Itchy Fingers Publications / B&H M708010395)

List C: Study

Play a study or orchestral alternative(s), to be chosen from the list below. Options are given for flute, piccolo and alto flute.

Boehm ....No.9 *or* No.24 (24 Caprices, Op.26)   (Any reliable edition)

Castérède ....No.4 (Douze Etudes)   (Leduc/UMP AL23139)

Holcombe ....Etude in B♭, p.8 (24 Jazz Etudes for Flute)   (Studio Music JE001)

Kohler ....No.10 *or* No.11 *or* No.12
(Progress in Flute Playing, Op.33, Bk.2)   (Chester/Music Sales CH55792)

Andersen ....No.5 *or* No.18 (24 Studies Op.15)   (IMC/Universal 1664)

Martinů ....Scherzo   (Panton PAN000404)

Taffanel, ed.
Blakeman ....Sicilienne Etude for Flute and Piano (1885)   (Pan PEM53)

Mower ....Final Demand, No.20
(20 Commandments)   (Itchy Fingers Publications/B&H M708010333)

Piazzolla ....No.3 (Tango Etudes)   (Lemoine/UMP HL24897)

Orchestral Alternatives

Dvořák, ed.
Durichen/
Kratsch ....Symphony No.8 (Orchester Probespiel)   (Peters P8659)

And (i.e. candidates should play both)

Bach, ed. Durichen/
Kratsch ....St Matthew Passion (Orchester Probespiel)   (Peters P8659)

Alto Flute

Maxwell Davies ...Nocturne   (B&H M060064463)

Orchestral Alternative for Alto Flute

Stravinsky, arr. Wye
& Morris ....Le Sacre du Printemps, Deuxième partie
(The Alto Flute Practice Book)   (Novello NOV120781)

Orchestral Alternatives for Piccolo

Ravel, ed. Durichen/
Kratsch.................Ma Mere L'Oye [Mother Goose] (Orchester Probespiel)   (Peters P8659)

Or

Rossini, ed.
Durichen/Kratsh ..Die Seidene Leiter [The Silken Ladder]
               (Orchester Probespiel)   (Peters P8659)

Sight-reading (see p.209)

Aural Tests *or* Initiative Tests (see p.207)

Musicianship Questions (see p.208)

JAZZ FLUTE

Grade 1

Warm-ups

Warm-ups do not form part of the examination, but it is highly recommended that candidates prepare by using warm-up exercises immediately before entering the examination room. See page 6.

The Examination

Facility Exercise

Play a long note with full tone for a prescribed number of beats (6 – 8 at $\downarrow$ = 60). The examiner will specify the note and the number of beats and will set the pulse.

Scales and Arpeggios (Chord Shapes)

(See Notes on Scales and Arpeggios page 198)

To be played from memory. All scales and arpeggios should be prepared with the specifications listed in the grey box below. The examiner will request *one only* (e.g. one rhythm *or* one articulation *or* one character) when requesting each scale/arpeggio.

Range

Creative Exercise

Choose one of the scales or arpeggios from the list for this Grade and perform a creative version using elements chosen from the menu on page 205 and/or from the grey box for this Grade.

Candidates may notate their creative exercise and read from

Rhythms	$\eighthnote$ s grouped in 3s or 4s as appropriate; i) straight; ii) medium swing
Dynamics	With a confident and consistent full tone
Tempi	$\downarrow$ = 72+
Articulations	Scales i) tongued; ii) legato; Arpeggios tongued only Swing $\sheetmusic$
Character	i) Spiky and angry (when tongued) ii) Relaxed and laid back (when legato)

this or simply improvise a version. In either case the same exercise should be performed twice so as to clarify the musical intentions. Candidates will be rewarded for adventure and invention.

Note Centres

Candidates should prepare the following note centre: G (one octave).

The following should be prepared:

- the major scale followed by the major seventh arpeggio
- the dorian scale followed by the minor seventh arpeggio

Candidates may pause between pairs of scales and arpeggios.

Improvisation

Module 1, either A, B, or C (candidate's choice), from the GSMD publication *Jazz Improvisation*. See p.210 for details and for further useful publications.

Pieces

Play TWO pieces, one to be chosen from each list.

List A

(see General Notes p.210)

From the *Boosey Woodwind Method, flute book 1*   (B&H M060112898)

Wine/Bayer Sager.A Groovy Kind of Love, p.32 [with CD track 46]

Young...................Sweet Sue – Just You (Classic Jazz for Flute)   (Wise/Music Sales AM937057)

Furber..................Limehouse Blues (Blues for Flute)   (Wise/Music Sales AM952017)

Bennett ....Road Hog (Jazz Club Flute Grades 1-2)   (IMP 7530A)

Wilson..................Gospel Joe (Creative Variations Vol.1)   (Camden Music CM173)

Ellington..............In a Mellow Tone [omit D.S. and go straight
                   to Coda] (Blues for Flute)   (Wise/Music Sales AM952017)

List B

(see General Notes p.210)

From the *Boosey Woodwind Method, flute book 1*   (B&H M060112898)

Marks ....The Flute Rap, p. 36

Trad....................When the Saints go Marching in, p. 26

Miles...................Setting Off (Jazz Routes)   (Camden Music CM175)

Miles...................Arriving Home (Creative Variations Vol.1)   (Camden Music CM173)

Norton ....Mango Juice, No.12 *or* Fine Views, No.13
               (The Microjazz Flute Collection 1)   (B&H M060109089)

Rae ....North Circular [omit repeat] (Easy Jazz Flute)   (Universal UE16581)

List C: Study

Play ONE study, to be chosen from the list below.

Taylor ....I Wish I knew how it would Feel to be Free [omit repeat]
               (Classic Jazz for Flute)   (Wise/Music Sales AM937057)

Stokes ....No.1 *or* No.3 (Easy Jazz Singles)   (Hunt Edition HE36)

Rae ....No.44 *and* No.45 (Progressive Jazz
               Studies for Flute Easy Level)   (Faber 0571513603)

Sight-reading (see p.209)

Aural Tests *or* Initiative Tests (see p.207)

Musicianship Questions (see p.208)

Grade 2

Warm-ups

Warm-ups do not form part of the examination, but it is highly recommended that candidates prepare by using warm-up exercises immediately before entering the examination room. See page 6.

The Examination

Facility Exercise

Play a long note with full tone for a prescribed number of beats (6 – 8 at ♩ = 60). The examiner will specify the note and the number of beats and will set the pulse.

Scales and Arpeggios (Chord Shapes)

(See Notes on Scales and Arpeggios page 198)

To be played from memory. All scales and arpeggios should be prepared with the specifications listed in the grey box on the following page. The examiner will request *one only* (e.g. one rhythm *or* one articulation *or* one character) when requesting each scale/arpeggio.

Range

Creative Exercise

Choose one of the scales or arpeggios from the list for this Grade and perform a creative version using elements chosen from the menu on page 205 and/or from the grey box for this Grade.

Rhythms	♪ s grouped in 3s or 4s as appropriate; i) straight; ii) medium swing
Dynamics	With a confident and consistent full tone
Tempi	♩ = 72+
Articulations	i) tongued; ii) legato; Swing ♫♫♩
Character	i) Medium 'up' and dance-like; ii) Bluesy and dragging

Candidates may notate their creative exercise and read from this or simply improvise a version. In either case the same exercise should be performed twice so as to clarify the musical intentions. Candidates will be rewarded for adventure and invention.

Note Centres

Candidates should prepare the following note centre: D (two octaves).

The following should be prepared:

- the major scale followed by the major seventh arpeggio
- the dorian scale followed by the minor seventh arpeggio
- the mixolydian scale followed by the dominant seventh arpeggio (starting and finishing on the note centre)

Candidates may pause between pairs of scales and arpeggios.

Improvisation

Module 2, either A, B, or C (candidate's choice), from the GSMD publication *Jazz Improvisation*. See p.210 for details and for further useful publications.

Pieces

Play TWO pieces, one to be chosen from each list.

List A

(see General Notes p.210)

From the *Boosey Woodwind Method, flute book 1* (B&H M060112898)

Cacavas...............I'll Set my Love to Music, p.46 [flute 1 part]

Marks ....Rambling Man, p. 39 [with CD track 61 *or* 62]

From the *Boosey Woodwind Method, flute book 2* (B&H M060112928)

Norton ....Off the Rails, p. 11 [flute 1 part, with CD track 8 *or* 9]

Kern ....Yesterdays (Blues for Flute) (Wise/Music Sales AM952017)

Bennett ....Southern Fried *or* Orbiting Venus
(Jazz Club Flute Grades 1-2) (IMP 7530A)

Wilson..................J's Dream (Creative Variations Vol.1) (Camden Music CM173)

Hudson, De Lange
& Mills ....Moonglow (Classic Jazz for Flute) (Wise/Music Sales AM937057)

List B

(see General Notes p.210)

From the *Boosey Woodwind Method, flute book 1* (B&H M060112898)

Trad.....................Swing Low, Sweet Chariot, p. 50

Marks ....Blue 4 U, p. 47 [with CD track 71 *or* 72]

From the *Boosey Woodwind Method, flute book 2* (B&H M060112928)

Norton ....Calypso Facto, p. 55

Hart.....................Day Dreamin' (All Jazzed Up for Flute) (Brass Wind 1301)

O'Neill ....A Bossa for Betty, p.53 (The Jazz Method for Flute) (Schott ED 12450)

Miles....................Vintage Steam (Jazz Routes) (Camden Music CM175)

Miles....................Abigail's Song (Creative Variations Vol.1) (Camden Music CM173)

Hamer..................Easy Going (Play It Cool) (Spartan Press SP560)

List C: Study

Play ONE study, to be chosen from the list below.

Howard................Fly Me to the Moon (Classic Jazz for Flute) (Wise/Music Sales AM937057)

Stokes ....No.6 (Easy Jazz Singles) (Hunt Edition HE36)

Rae ....No.54 (Progressive Jazz Studies for Flute Easy Level) (Faber 0571513603)

Sight-reading (see p.209)

Aural Tests *or* **Initiative Tests** (see p.207)

Musicianship Questions (see p.208)

Grade 3

Warm-ups

Warm-ups do not form part of the examination, but it is highly recommended that candidates prepare by using warm-up exercises immediately before entering the examination room. See page 6.

The Examination

Facility Exercise

Play a long note with full tone for a prescribed number of beats (6 – 12 at ♩ = 60). The examiner will specify the note and the number of beats and will set the pulse.

Scales and Arpeggios (Chord Shapes)

(See Notes on Scales and Arpeggios page 198)

To be played from memory. All scales and arpeggios should be prepared with the specifications listed in the grey box below. The examiner will request *one only* (e.g. one rhythm *or* one articulation *or* one character) when requesting each scale/arpeggio.

Range

Creative Exercise

Choose one of the scales or arpeggios from the list for this Grade and perform a creative version using elements chosen from the menu on page 205 and/or from the grey box for this Grade.

Rhythms	♪ s grouped in 3s or 4s as appropriate; i) straight; ii) medium swing
Dynamics	With a confident and consistent full tone
Tempi	♩ = 72+
Articulations	i) tongued; ii) legato; Swing ♫♫♩
Character	i) Latin 'feel'; ii) Rock groove; iii) Like a ballad i.e. melodic and sensitive

Candidates may notate their creative exercise and read from this or simply improvise a version. In either case the same exercise should be performed twice so as to clarify the musical intentions. Candidates will be rewarded for adventure and invention.

Note Centres

Candidates should prepare the following note centre: A (a twelfth, except where specified).

The following should be prepared:

- the major scale followed by the major seventh arpeggio
- the dorian scale followed by the minor seventh arpeggio
- the mixolydian scale followed by the dominant seventh arpeggio (starting and finishing on the note centre)
- the pentatonic major scale (one octave)

Candidates may pause between pairs of scales and arpeggios.

Improvisation

Module 3, either A, B, or C (candidate's choice), from the GSMD publication *Jazz Improvisation*. See p.210 for details and for further useful publications.

Pieces

Play TWO pieces, one to be chosen from each list.

List A

(see General Notes p.210)
From the *Boosey Woodwind Method, flute book 1*   (B&H M060112898)
York & Marks.......Image, p. 56
From the *Boosey Woodwind Method, flute book 2*   (B&H M060112928)
Trad.....................Yellow Bird, p. 17
Weiss &   *Shearing*...............Lullaby of Birdland, p.27 [with CD track 28]

Waller &
Brooks ....Ain't Misbehavin' (Classic Jazz for Flute)   (Wise/Music Sales AM937057)

Cuzner.................Billy's Waltz [omit repeats]
(3 Jazz Jingles for Flute and Piano)   (Hunt Edition HE28)

Jobim. ....How Insensitive [play twice – on repeat play an
octave higher and embellish] (Jazz Gems)   (Hal Leonard/Music Sales HLE0084)

Wilson ....Joe's New Words (Creative Variations Vol.1) (Camden Music CM173)

Isacoff...................The Gospel Truth (Jazz Time for Flute and Keyboard) (B&H M060087356)

Miles...................Waltz for Richard (Jazz Routes) (Camden Music CM175)

Hamer..................Casa Mia (Play It Cool) (Spartan Press SP560)

List B

(see General Notes p.210)

From the *Boosey Woodwind Method, flute book 1* (B&H M060112898)

Norton ....Club Soda, p. 61 [flute 1 part]

From the *Boosey Woodwind Method, flute book 2* (B&H M060112928)

Norton ....Crayfish, p. 34 [flute 1 part]

Norton ....Feeling Sunny, p. 42 [flute 1 part]

Norton ....Don't Wannabe, p. 37

Norton ....Golden Sand, p. 39

Hart.....................Checkout (All Jazzed Up for Flute) (Brass Wind 1301)

Gumbley...............Fast Food Funk (Cops, Caps and Cadillacs) (Saxtet Publications 206)

Bennett ....Mango Number 5 [omit repeat unless using
CD backing track] (Jazz Club Flute Grades 1-2) (IMP 7530A)

Bennett ....Bad Hair Day (Jazz Club Flute Grades 1-2) (IMP 7530A)

Norton ....Easy Does It (The Microjazz Flute Collection 2) (B&H M060110603)

Norton ....Seashore, No.19 (The Microjazz Flute Collection 1) (B&H M060109089)

Miles...................Who's Got the Answer? (Creative Variations Vol.1) (Camden Music CM173)

List C: Study

Play ONE study, to be chosen from the list below.

Stokes ....No.16 (Easy Jazz Singles) (Hunt Edition HE36)

Rae ....No.62 (Progressive Jazz Studies for Flute Easy Level) (Faber 0571513603)

Zawinul...............Mercy, Mercy, Mercy [omit repeat]
(Classic Jazz for Flute) (Wise/Music Sales AM937057)

Sight-reading (see p.209)

Aural Tests *or* Initiative Tests (see p.207)

Musicianship Questions (see p.208)

Grade 4

Warm-ups

Warm-ups do not form part of the examination, but it is highly recommended that candidates prepare by using warm-up exercises immediately before entering the examination room. See page 6.

The Examination

Facility Exercise

Play a long note *mf* for a prescribed number of beats (8 – 12 at ♩ = 60).
The examiner will specify the note and the number of beats and will set the pulse.

Scales and Arpeggios (Chord Shapes)

(See Notes on Scales and Arpeggios page 198)

To be played from memory. All scales and arpeggios should be prepared with the specifications listed in the grey box below. The examiner will request *one only* (e.g. one rhythm *or* one articulation *or* one character) when requesting each scale/arpeggio.

Range

Creative Exercise

Choose one of the scales or arpeggios from the list for this Grade and perform a creative version using elements chosen from the menu on page 205 and/or from the grey box for this Grade.

Rhythms	♪ s grouped in 3s or 4s as appropriate; i) straight; ii) medium up swing
Dynamics	Within the range *mp – f*, i) sustaining a level throughout; ii) cresc.; iii) decresc.
Tempi	♩ = 96+
Articulations	i) tongued; ii) legato; Swing ♫♫♪
Character	i) Staccato and light; ii) Heavy and accented

Candidates may notate their creative exercise and read from this or simply improvise a version. In either case the same exercise should be performed twice so as to clarify the musical intentions. Candidates will be rewarded for adventure and invention.

Note Centres

Candidates should prepare the following note centre: C (two octaves, with major scale two and a half octaves).

The following should be prepared:

- the major scale followed by the major seventh arpeggio
- the dorian scale followed by the minor seventh arpeggio
- the mixolydian scale followed by the dominant seventh arpeggio (starting and finishing on the note centre)
- the melodic *or* harmonic minor scale (candidate's choice) followed by the minor arpeggio with the major seventh
- the pentatonic major scale
- the chromatic scale

Candidates may pause between pairs of scales and arpeggios.

Improvisation

Module 4, either A, B, or C (candidate's choice), from the GSMD publication *Jazz Improvisation*. See p.210 for details and for further useful publications.

Pieces

Play TWO pieces, one to be chosen from each list.

List A

Schertzinger ....Tangerine [play twice; on repeat play an
octave higher and embellish] (Jazz Gems) (Hal Leonard/Music Sales HL00841132)

*McHugh &
Fields* ....Don't Blame Me (Blues for Flute)
(Wise/Music Sales AM952017)

*Desmond, arr.
Hart*......................Take Five (All Jazzed Up for Flute)
(Brass Wind 1301)

Jobim. ....Wave (Classic Jazz for Flute)
(Wise/Music Sales AM937057)

Wilson ....Bossa [play octave higher] (Jazz Album)
(Camden Music CM097)

Wilson ....Hey Joe...Let's Meet (Creative Variations Vol.1)
(Camden Music CM173)

Isacoff...................A Little Mo'Satch (Jazz Time for Flute & Keyboard)
(B&H M060087356)

*Silver, arr.
Dr. Hill, Jnr*..........The Preacher [play the tune, transposing up an
octave on repeat, followed by solo on p.17]
(Approaching the Standards Vol.1, C Edition)
(Warner Bros 7359A)

List B

Gumbley..............Cops, Caps and Cadillacs		
(Cops, Caps and Cadillacs)	(Saxtet Publications 206)	
O'Neill ....I'm In Love, p.69 [include short improvisation]		
(The Jazz Method for Flute)	(Schott ED12450)	
Norton ....Song *or* Springboard		
(The Microjazz Flute Collection 2)	(B&H M060110603)	
Miles....................Transformation (Jazz Routes)	(Camden Music CM175)	
Miles....................Three Views of Orford (Creative Variations Vol.1)	(Camden Music CM173)	

List C: Study

Play ONE study, to be chosen from the list below.

Stokes ....No.27 (Easy Jazz Singles)   (Hunt Edition HE36)

Stokes ....No.5 (Jazz Singles)   (Hunt Edition HE32)

Berg ....Example Improvisation, p.29
(Approaching the Standards Vol.1, C Edition)   (Warner Bros 7359A)

Jackson ....Example Improvisation, p.5
(Approaching the Standards Vol.1, C Edition)   (Warner Bros 7359A)

Sight-reading (see p.209)

(see p.209)

Aural Tests *or* Initiative Tests (see p.207)

(see p.207)

Musicianship Questions (see p.208)

(see p.208)

Grade 5

Warm-ups

Warm-ups do not form part of the examination, but it is highly recommended that candidates prepare by using warm-up exercises immediately before entering the examination room. See page 6.

The Examination

Facility Exercise

Play a long note *mf* for a prescribed number of beats (8 – 12 at ♩ = 60).
The examiner will specify the note and the number of beats and will set the pulse.

Scales and Arpeggios (Chord Shapes)

(See Notes on Scales and Arpeggios p.198)

To be played from memory. All scales and arpeggios should be prepared with the specifications listed in the grey box below. The examiner will request *one only* (e.g. one rhythm *or* one articulation *or* one character) when requesting each scale/arpeggio.

Range

Rhythms	$\flat$s grouped in 3s or 4s as appropriate; i) straight; ii) medium up swing
Dynamics	Within the range $mp - f$, i) sustaining a level throughout; ii) cresc.; iii) decresc.
Tempi	$\downarrow = 96+$
Articulations	i) tongued; ii) legato; Swing ♫♫♪
Character	i) Earthy and soulful; ii) Restrained and gentle

Creative Exercise

Choose one of the scales or arpeggios from the list for this Grade and perform a creative version using elements chosen from the menu on page 205 and/or from the grey box for this Grade.

Candidates may notate their creative exercise and read from this or simply improvise a version. In either case the same exercise should be performed twice so as to clarify the musical intentions. Candidates will be rewarded for adventure and invention.

Note Centres

Candidates should prepare ONE of the following note centres: E (two octaves) *or* F (two octaves).

For the chosen note centre, the following should be prepared:

- the major scale followed by the major seventh arpeggio
- the dorian scale followed by the minor seventh arpeggio
- the mixolydian scale followed by the dominant seventh (starting and finishing on the note centre)
- the melodic *or* harmonic minor scale (candidate's choice) followed by the minor arpeggio with the major seventh
- the pentatonic major scale
- the pentatonic minor scale
- the blues scale
- the chromatic scale

Candidates may pause between pairs of scales and arpeggios.

Improvisation

Module 5, either A, B, or C (candidate's choice), from the GSMD publication *Jazz Improvisation*. See p.210 for details and for further useful publications.

Pieces

Play TWO pieces, one to be chosen from each list.

List A

Strayhorn ....Chelsea Bridge [play last nine bars an octave higher]
(Classic Jazz for Flute)   (Wise/Music Sales AM937057)

Hagen ....Harlem Nocturne (Blues for Flute)   (Wise/Music Sales AM952017)

Wilson ....Jazz Waltz [play an octave higher] (Jazz Album)   (Camden Music CM097)

O'Neill ....It's All Yours, p.88 (The Jazz Method for Flute)   (Schott ED 12450)

Wilson ....Blues for Joseph (Creative Variations Vol.1)   (Camden Music CM173)

Silver, arr.
Dr. Hill, Jnr ....Satin Doll [play the tune and the solo on p.25,
sections of the tune may be played an octave
higher ad lib. Play the solo an octave higher throughout]
(Approaching the Standards Vol. 1, C Edition)   (Warner Bros 7359A)

List B

Norton ....Home Blues (The Microjazz Flute Collection 2)   (B&H M060110603)

Miles....................Blah-blah-blah! (Jazz Routes)   (Camden Music CM175)

Miles....................Bathwater Blues (Creative Variations Vol.1)   (Camden Music CM173)

Isacoff...................Like a Man Walking on Eggshells
(Jazz Time for Flute and Keyboard)   (B&H M06087356)

List C: Study

Play ONE study, to be chosen from the list below.

Stokes ....No.6 Jazz Singles   (Hunt Edition HE32)
Holcombe..............Etude in F Major [omit repeat]
(24 Jazz Etudes for Flute)   (Musicians Publications JE001)

Sight-reading (see p.209)

Aural Tests *or* Initiative Tests (see p.207)

Musicianship Questions (see p.208)

Grade 6

Warm-ups

Warm-ups do not form part of the examination, but it is highly recommended that candidates prepare by using warm-up exercises immediately before entering the examination room. See page 6.

The Examination

Facility Exercises

- Play a long note *mf* for a prescribed number of beats (4 – 10 at ♩ = 60).
  The examiner will specify the note and the number of beats and will set the pulse.
- Play a long note *f* for a prescribed number of beats (4 – 6 at ♩ = 60).
  The examiner will specify the note and the number of beats and will set the pulse.

Scales and Arpeggios (Chord Shapes)

(See Notes on Scales and Arpeggios p.198)

To be played from memory. All scales and arpeggios should be prepared with the specifications listed in the grey box below. The examiner will request *two only* (e.g. one rhythm *and* one dynamic *or* one articulation *and* one character) when requesting each scale/arpeggio.

Range

Creative Exercise

Choose one of the scales or arpeggios from the list for this Grade and perform a creative version using elements chosen from the menu on page 205 and/or from the grey box for this Grade.

Candidates may notate their creative exercise and read from

Rhythms	♪ s grouped in 3s or 4s as appropriate; i) straight; ii) fast swing
Dynamics	Within the range *pp – ff,* i) sustaining a level throughout; ii) cresc.; iii) decresc.
Tempi	♩ = 132+
Articulations	i) tongued; ii) legato; Swing ♫♫♩
Character	Candidates to offer a selection of at least four of their own contrasting choices which reflect the jazz idiom, provided an explanation can be given.

this or simply improvise a version. In either case the same exercise should be performed twice so as to clarify the musical intentions. Candidates will be rewarded for adventure and invention.

Note Centres

Candidates should prepare the following note centres: C#/Db (two octaves, with major scale two and a half octaves) *and* G (two octaves, with major scale extended down to lowest D).

When the examiner names a note centre the candidate will play:

- the major scale followed by the major seventh arpeggio
- the dorian scale followed by the minor seventh arpeggio
- the mixolydian scale followed by the dominant seventh arpeggio (starting and finishing on the note centre)
- the melodic minor scale
- the harmonic minor scale
- the minor arpeggio with the major seventh
- the blues scale
- the chromatic scale

Candidates may pause between pairs of scales and arpeggios.

Improvisation

Play once through then improvise two choruses of a modal tune, e.g., *Cantaloupe Island, Maiden Voyage, Impressions, Footprints, Little Sunflower, Milestones,* or a similar modal tune.

Or

Play once through then improvise two choruses of an original modally-based composition.

Candidates must provide a legible copy of the composition for the examiner's use.

Pieces

Play TWO pieces, one to be chosen from each list.

List A

Wilson	Bebop [play an octave higher] (Jazz Album)	(Camden Music CM097)
Lyons	Danish Blues (Useful Flute Solos Bk.2)	(Useful Music U25)
Lyons	Uncle Samba (Useful Flute Solos Bk.2)	(Useful Music U25)
Harbison	When? (20 Authentic Bebop Solos)	(Aebersold Jazz SU011T)
Wilson	After Charlie...Joe (Creative Variations Vol.2)	(Camden Music CM179)

List B

Genna ....First Flower (Contemporary Flute Solos in Pop/Jazz Styles)		(Musicians Publications FS001)
Miles ....A Bear In My Shed (Jazz Routes)		(Camden Music CM175)
Miles ....Candlelight (Creative Variations Vol.2)		(Camden Music CM179)
Holcombe ....Uptown (Contemporary Flute Solos in Pop/Jazz Styles)		(Musicians Publications FS001)

List C: Study

Play ONE study, to be chosen from the list below.

Mower ....Bluesangle (20 Commandments)   (Itchy Fingers Publications/B&H M708010333)

Ruwe ....Blues Etude in the Key of F
(Basic Blues Etudes In All Twelve Keys)   (Hal Leonard/Music Sales HL00030446)

Holcombe ....Etude in C Major *or* Etude in G Major
[omit repeat] (24 Jazz Etudes for Flute)   (Musicians Publications JE001)

Sight-reading (see p.209)

Aural Tests *or* Initiative Tests (see p.207)

Musicianship Questions (see p.208)

Grade 7

Warm-ups

Warm-ups do not form part of the examination, but it is highly recommended that candidates prepare by using warm-up exercises immediately before entering the examination room. See page 6.

The Examination

Facility Exercises

* Play a long note *p/mf* for a prescribed number of beats (4 – 12 at $\quarternote = 60$).
  The examiner will specify the note and the dynamic, choose the number of beats and set the pulse.
* Play a long note *f* for a prescribed number of beats (4 – 8 at $\quarternote = 60$).
  The examiner will specify the note and the number of beats and will set the pulse.

Scales and Arpeggios (Chord Shapes)

(See Notes on Scales and Arpeggios p.198)

To be played from memory. All scales and arpeggios should be prepared with the specifications listed in the grey box below. The examiner will request *two only* (e.g. one rhythm *and* one dynamic *or* one articulation and one character) when requesting each scale/arpeggio.

Range

Rhythms	♪ s grouped in 3s or 4s as appropriate; i) straight; ii) fast swing
Dynamics	Within the range *pp – ff*, i) sustaining a level throughout; ii) cresc.; iii) decresc.
Tempi	♩ = 132+
Articulations	i) tongued; ii) legato; Swing ♫♫♩
Character	Candidates to offer a selection of at least four of their own contrasting choices which reflect the jazz idiom, provided an explanation can be given.

Creative Exercise

Choose one of the scales or arpeggios from the list for this Grade and perform a creative version using elements chosen from the menu on page 205 and/or from the grey box for this Grade.

Candidates may notate their creative exercise and read from this or simply improvise a version. In either case the same exercise should be performed twice so as to clarify the musical intentions. Candidates will be rewarded for adventure and invention.

Note Centres

Candidates should prepare the following note centres: E♭ (two octaves, with major scale two and a half octaves) *and* A (two octaves, with major scale extended down to lowest E).

When the examiner names a note centre the candidate will play:

- the major scale followed by the major seventh arpeggio
- the dorian scale followed by the minor seventh arpeggio
- the mixolydian scale followed by the dominant seventh arpeggio (starting and finishing on the note centre)
- the harmonic minor *or* melodic minor *or* jazz melodic minor *or* Spanish Phrygian minor scale (candidate's choice) followed by the minor arpeggio with the major seventh
- the blues scale
- the chromatic scale

Candidates may pause between pairs of scales and arpeggios.

The following should also be prepared:

- the whole tone scale, two octaves, starting on lowest C
- the whole tone scale, two octaves, starting on C♯
- the augmented arpeggio, two octaves, starting on lowest C
- the augmented arpeggio, two octaves, starting on C♯

Improvisation

Play once through then improvise two choruses of a blues-based tune, e.g., *Now's the Time, Billie's Bounce, Tenor Madness, Blue Monk, Watermelon Man, West Coast Blues*, or a similar blues-based tune.

Or

Play once through then improvise two choruses of an original blues-based composition.

Candidates must provide a legible copy of the composition for the examiner's use.

Pieces

Play TWO pieces, one to be chosen from each list.

List A

Gordon, trans.
Niehaus ....Stanley the Steamer (Dexter
                Gordon Jazz Saxophone Solos)   (Hal Leonard/Music Sales HL00853780)

Miles....................tony7 (Jazz Routes)   (Camden Music CM175)

Wilson ....Just A Ballad For Joseph (Creative Variations Vol.2) (Camden Music CM179)

List B

Harbison ....Riding the Rails [play an octave higher
                from "4X" to the end, tempo: ♩ = 152+]
                (20 Authentic Bebop Solos)   (Aebersold Jazz SU011T)

Miles....................Sideways On (Creative Variations Vol.2)   (Camden Music CM179)

Mintzer ....Rhythm Check (14 Blues & Funk Etudes)   (Warner Bros 5330A)

Mintzer ....Slammin' (14 Blues & Funk Etudes)   (Warner Bros 5330A)

List C: Study

Play ONE study, to be chosen from the list below.

Ruwe .... Blues Etude in the Key of E
　　　　　　　(Basic Blues Etudes In All Twelve Keys)　(Hal Leonard/Music Sales HL00030446)

Mower .... Chilli Con Salsa
　　　　　　　(20 Commandments)　　　　(Itchy Fingers Publications/B&H M708010333)

Ruwe .... Blues Etude in the Key of A♭
　　　　　　　(Basic Blues Etudes In All Twelve Keys)　(Hal Leonard/Music Sales HL00030446)

Holcombe .... Etude in E Major [omit repeat]
　　　　　　　(24 Jazz Etudes for Flute)　　　　(Musicians Publications JE001)

Sight-reading (see p.209)

Aural Tests *or* Initiative Tests (see p.207)

Musicianship Questions (see p.208)

Grade 8

Warm-ups

Warm-ups do not form part of the examination, but it is highly recommended that candidates prepare by using warm-up exercises immediately before entering the examination room. See page 6.

The Examination

Facility Exercises

- Play a long note *pp/p/mf* for a prescribed number of beats (4 – 16 at ♩ = 60). The examiner will specify the note and the dynamic, choose the number of beats and set the pulse.
- Play a long note *f* for a prescribed number of beats (4 – 10 at ♩ = 60). The examiner will specify the note and the number of beats and will set the pulse.

Scales and Arpeggios (Chord Shapes)

(See Notes on Scales and Arpeggios p.198)

To be played from memory. All scales and arpeggios should be prepared with the specifications listed in the grey box on the following page. The examiner will request *two only* (e.g. one rhythm *and* one dynamic *or* one articulation *and* one character) when requesting each scale/arpeggio.

Range

Creative Exercise

Choose one of the scales or arpeggios from the list for this Grade and perform a creative version using elements chosen from the menu on page 205 and/or from the grey box for this Grade.

Candidates may notate their creative exercise and read from

Rhythms	♪ s grouped in 3s or 4s as appropriate; i) straight; ii) fast swing
Dynamics	Within the range *pp – ff*, i) sustaining a level throughout; ii) cresc.; iii) decresc.
Tempi	♩ = 132+
Articulations	i) tongued; ii) legato; Swing ♫♫♪
Character	Candidates to offer a selection of at least four of their own contrasting choices which reflect the jazz idiom, provided an explanation can be given.

this or simply improvise a version. In either case the same exercise should be performed twice so as to clarify the musical intentions. Candidates will be rewarded for adventure and invention.

Note Centres

Candidates should prepare the following note centres:

E (two octaves, except where specified, and with major scale two and a half octaves), A♭/G♯ (two octaves, except where specified) *and* C (three octaves, except where specified).

When the examiner names a note centre the candidate will play:

- the major scale followed by the major seventh arpeggio
- the dorian scale followed by the minor seventh arpeggio
- the mixolydian scale followed by the dominant seventh arpeggio (starting and finishing on the note centre)
- the harmonic minor *or* Spanish Phrygian minor scale (candidate's choice)
- the melodic minor *or* jazz melodic minor scale (candidate's choice)
- the minor arpeggio with the major seventh
- the blues scale
- the chromatic scale (starting on the lowest note of range and extended to cover the whole range for this Grade)

Candidates may pause between pairs of scales and arpeggios.

The following should also be prepared:

- the whole tone scale, two octaves, starting on lowest C
- the whole tone scale, two octaves, starting on C♯
- the augmented arpeggio, two octaves, starting on lowest C
- the augmented arpeggio, two octaves, starting on C♯

Improvisation

Play once through then improvise two choruses of a 32-bar song form, e.g., *Autumn Leaves, Whisper Not, Fly me to the Moon, Take the A Train, Stella by Starlight*, or a similar 32-bar song form.

Or

Play once through then improvise two choruses of a 'rhythm changes' tune, e.g. *I've got Rhythm, Oleo, Anthropology, Moose the Mooche, Lester Leaps in*, or a similar 'rhythm changes' tune.

Or

Play once through then improvise two choruses of an original 32-bar song form or 'rhythm changes' composition.

Candidates must provide a legible copy of the composition for the examiner's use.

Pieces

Play TWO pieces, one to be chosen from each list.

List A

Gordon, trans.
Niehaus................Cheesecake (Dexter Gordon
                              Jazz Saxophone Solos)   (Hal Leonard/Music Sales HL00853780)

Wilson..................Funky Joe (Creative Variations Vol.2)   (Camden Music CM179)

Mintzer...............See Forever (14 Blues & Funk Etudes)   (Warner Bros 5330A)

List B

Miles....................Pete's Picked a Pepperoni Pizza (Jazz Routes)   (Camden Music CM175)

Miles....................Struttin' in the Barbican
                              (Creative Variations Vol.2)   (Camden Music CM179)

Genna..................Weeping Willow (Contemporary
                              Flute Solos in Pop/Jazz Styles)   (Musicians Publications FS001)

List C: Study

Play ONE study, to be chosen from the list below.

Mower ....Dos Voces *or* Indianalee
     (20 Commandments)   (Itchy Fingers Publications/B&H M708010333)

Ruwe ....Blues Etude in the Key of D♭ *and*
     Basic Etude in the Key of D (Basic Blues
     Etudes In All Twelve Keys)   (Hal Leonard/Music Sales HL00030446)

Holcombe..............Etude in B♭ [omit repeat]
     (24 Jazz Etudes for Flute)   (Musicians Publications JE001)

Sight-reading (see p.209)

Aural Tests *or* Initiative Tests (see p.207)

Musicianship Questions (see p.208)

CLARINET

Grade 1

Warm-ups

Warm-ups do not form part of the examination, but it is highly recommended that candidates prepare by using warm-up exercises immediately before entering the examination room. See page 6.

The Examination

Facility Exercise

Play a long note with full tone for a prescribed number of beats (6 – 8 at ♩ = 60). The examiner will specify the note and the number of beats and will set the pulse.

Scales and Arpeggios

(See Notes on Scales and Arpeggios page 198)

To be played from memory. All scales and arpeggios should be prepared with the specifications listed in the grey box below. The examiner will request *one only* (e.g. one rhythm *or* one articulation *or* one character) when requesting each scale/arpeggio.

Range

Scales
G major (one octave)
G natural minor (one octave)

Arpeggios
G major (one octave)
G minor (one octave)

Rhythms	i) ♪s grouped in 3s or 4s as appropriate. ii) as given in Ex.1 (see p.204) (scales only)
Dynamics	With a confident and consistent full tone
Tempi	♩ = 56 – 62
Articulations	Scales i) tongued; ii) slurred; Arpeggios tongued only
Character	i) Spiky and angry (when tongued); ii) Smooth and calm (when slurred)

Pieces

Play TWO pieces, one to be chosen from each list.

List A

(see General Notes p.210)

From the *Boosey Woodwind Method, clarinet book 1*   (B&H M060112904)

Trad. ....Dona, dona, p.22

Barratt ....Centre Stage, p.23

Marks ....Rambling Man, p.26

Trad. ....Land of the Silver Birch, p.31

Wine &
Bayer Sager ....A Groovy Kind of Love, p.36 [with CD track 56 *or* 57]

Czerny, arr.
Hare ....Sunrise (The Magic Clarinet)   (B&H M060094545)

Haydn, arr.
De Smet ....Andante (Easy Pieces for Clarinet)   (Pan PEM87)

Trad. Russian, arr.
Griffiths ....Kalinka (10 Easy Tunes for Clarinet and Piano)   (De Haske F456)

Trad., arr.
Wilson ....The Skye Boat Song [top line] (Face to Face)   (Camden Music CM093)

Harris ....Haunted House p.19 (Clarinet Basics)   (Faber 0571518141)

Schumann, arr.
Wastall ....Humming Song, p.23 (Learn As You Play Clarinet)   (B&H M060029271)

Beethoven, arr.
De Smet ....Minuet (Easy Pieces for Clarinet)   (Pan PEM87)

Purcell, arr.
Griffiths ....Rigaudon (10 Easy Tunes for Clarinet and Piano)   (De Haske F456)

Bartók, arr.
Hare ....Dialogue from *Mikrokosmos* (The Magic Clarinet)   (B&H M060094545)

List B

(see General Notes p.210)

From the *Boosey Woodwind Method, clarinet book 1*   (B&H M060112904)

Trad.....................Kalinka, p.23

Naplan................Hine ma tov, p.37

Marks ....The Clarinet Rap, p.37

Trad.....................When the Saints go Marching in, p.26

Dring...................Jog Trot
                           (Jack Brymer Clarinet Series Elementary Bk.1)   (Weinberger/Elkin JW151)

Pilling.................Chalumeau (Seven Simple Pieces)   (Forsyth FPD08)

Trad. Czech, arr.
Davies & Harris...The Little Dove (The Really Easy Clarinet Book)   (Faber 0571510345)

Dowell ....Three Little Fishies, No.5 (What Else Can I Play? 1)   (IMP 3306A)

Henderson ....Don't Bring Lulu (What Else Can I Play? 1)   (IMP 3306A)

Harris..................Sonata in F, p.25 (Clarinet Basics)   (Faber 0571518141)

Lyons ....Storybook Waltz (New Clarinet Solos Bk.1 B♭/C)   (Useful Music U22/U53)

Dring...................Evening Song
                           (Jack Brymer Clarinet Series Elementary Bk.1)   (Weinberger/Elkin JW151)

Gershwin ....Funny Face (Easy Gershwin for Clarinet)   (OUP N6678)

Hare....................Variations on Goe From My Window
                           (The Magic Clarinet)   (B&H M060094545)

Reade ....Romance, No.5, p.5 (First Book of Clarinet Solos)   (Faber 0571504507)

List C: Study

Play ONE study, to be chosen from the list below.

(see General Notes p.210)

From the *Boosey Woodwind Method, clarinet book 1*   (B&H M060112904)

Marks ....Wave Machine, p.35

Purcell................Minuet, p.41

Demnitz, arr.
Davies & Harris...No. 5, p.2 (80 Graded Studies for Clarinet Bk.1)   (Faber 0571509517)

Demnitz, arr.
Davies & Harris...No.9, p.3 (80 Graded Studies for Clarinet Bk.1)   (Faber 0571509517)

Harris ....No.6, p.2 (80 Graded Studies for Clarinet Bk.1)   (Faber 0571509517)

Harris ....No.10, p.3 (80 Graded Studies for Clarinet Bk.1)   (Faber 0571509517)

Lazarus, arr.
Weston...................No.4, p.2 (50 Melodious Studies for Solo Clarinet)   (De Haske F500)

Rae ....In the Wings, No.6
                        (40 Modern Studies for Solo Clarinet)   (Universal UE19735)

Rae ....Sad Dance, No.3
                        (40 Modern Studies for Solo Clarinet)   (Universal UE19735)

Trad. English, arr.
Wastall ....Ellacombe, p.19 (Learn As You Play Clarinet)   (B&H M060029271)

Walters ....Country Dance (12 Pieces)   (Ricordi LD627)

Wastall ....Unit 8 exs.1 *and* 2, p.20 (Learn As You Play Clarinet)   (B&H M060029271)

Harris ....Hornpipe Study, p.28 (Clarinet Basics)   (Faber 0571518141)

Gumbley...............Frog Hop, p.1 (Cool School for Clarinet)   (Brass Wind 1318)

Lyons ....No.10 (Clarinet Studies)   (Useful Music U30)

Wilson ....Blue 'Nila' (Colour Studies)   (Camden Music CM180)

Sight-reading (see p.209)

Aural Tests *or* Initiative Tests (see p.207)

Musicianship Questions (see p.208)

Grade 2

Warm ups

Warm-ups do not form part of the examination, but it is highly recommended that candidates prepare by using warm-up exercises immediately before entering the examination room. See page 6.

The Examination

Facility Exercises

- Play a long note with full tone for a prescribed number of beats (6 – 8 at ♩ = 60). The examiner will specify the note and the number of beats and will set the pulse.
- Exercise

Scales and Arpeggios

(See Notes on Scales and Arpeggios page 198)

To be played from memory. All scales and arpeggios should be prepared with the specifications listed in the grey box below. The examiner will request *one only* (e.g. one rhythm *or* one articulation *or* one character) when requesting each scale/arpeggio.

Range

Note Centres

Candidates should prepare the following note centre: D (one octave).

The following should be prepared:

- the major scale
- the major arpeggio
- the natural minor scale
- the minor arpeggio
- the dorian scale

Rhythms	i) ♪s grouped in 3s or 4s as appropriate. ii) as given in Ex.1 (see p.204) (scales only)
Dynamics	With a confident and consistent full tone
Tempi	♩ = 56 – 62
Articulations	Scales i) tongued; ii) slurred; Arpeggios tongued only
Character	i) Happy and bright; ii) Sad and dragging

Candidates may pause between individual scales and arpeggios.

Pieces

Play TWO pieces, one to be chosen from each list.

List A

(see General Notes p.210)

From the *Boosey Woodwind Method, clarinet book 1* (B&H M060112904)

Barratt.................High Tide, p.44

Trad....................I Love my Love, p.62 [clarinet 1 part]

Oliviero...............I'll Set my Love to Music, p.46 [clarinet 1 part]

Jenkins ....Cantilena, p.41

Trad....................Scarborough Fair, p.29

From the *Boosey Woodwind Method, clarinet book 2* (B&H M060112935)

Trad....................On the Waves of Lake Balaton, p.8

Trad....................Dance of Displeasure, p.15

Lefevre, arr.
Harris ....Melody (Music Through Time Bk.2) (OUP N7185)

Macdowell, arr.
Davies &
Reade ....To a Wild Rose, No.20 (First Book of Clarinet Solos) (Faber 0571504507)

Schubert, arr.
Harrison ....Bliss, p.7 (Amazing Solos for Clarinet) (B&H M060084690)

Weill....................September Song (What Else Can I Play 2) (IMP 3307A)

Rose ....Valse (A Miscellany for Clarinet Bk.I) (ABRSM 185472 502 5)

Mozart, arr. Davies
& Reade..............Lullaby, No.18 (First Book of Clarinet Solos B♭/C) (Faber 0571504507)

Trad., arr.
Wilson.................Greensleeves [top line] (Face to Face) (Camden Music CM093)

Anon., arr. Davies
& Reade ....Shepherd's Hey, No.8 (First Book of Clarinet Solos) (Faber 0571504507)

Bartók, arr.
Harrison ....Scherzando (Amazing Solos for Clarinet) (B&H M060084690)

Diabelli, arr.
Davies &
Reade ....Scherzo, No.10 (First Book of Clarinet Solos) (Faber 0571504507)

Mozart, arr.
Griffiths ....Minuet from *Eine kleine Nachtmusik*
(10 Easy Tunes for Clarinet and Piano)   (De Haske F456)

Reinecke, arr.
Davies
& Reade ....Ländler, No.13 (First Book of Clarinet Solos)   (Faber 0571504507)

Sullivan, arr.
Hare ....The Policeman's Song (The Magic Clarinet)   (B&H M060094545)

Waldteufel ....The Skater's Waltz (What Else Can I Play 2)   (IMP 3307A)

List B

(see General Notes p.210)

From the *Boosey Woodwind Method, clarinet book 1*   (B&H M060112904)

Attrib. Henry VIII,
arr. Barratt ....Hélas madame, p.55 [top part, with *either* clarinet duet
accompaniment *or* CD track 83]

Trad. ....Athol Highlanders' Jig, p.56

Chen ....Dodi li, p.58 [with CD track 89]

Norton ....Tragic Consequences, p.63

From the *Boosey Woodwind Method, clarinet book 2*   (B&H M060112935)

Marks ....Long Shadows, p.10

Norton ....Regretfully Yours, p.10

Dring ....Rigadoon
(Jack Brymer Clarinet Series Elementary Bk.1)   (Weinberger/Elkin JW151)

Harris ....Merry-Go-Round, p.28
(Cambridge Clarinet Tutor)   (Cambridge University Press 0521283507)

Gunning ....A Nordic Tale, p.38 (Clarinet Basics)   (Faber 0571518141)

Flanders &
Swann ....The Hippopotamus (What Else Can I Play 2)   (IMP 3307A)

Lyons ....Bonjour (New Clarinet Solos Bk.2 B♭/C)   (Useful Music U23/U54)

Gershwin ....Summertime (Easy Gershwin for Clarinet)   (OUP N6678)

Pilling ....Snow Scene (Seven Simple Pieces)   (Forsyth FPD08)

Ridout ....Lullaby for Susan
(Jack Brymer Clarinet Series Elementary Bk.2)   (Weinberger/Elkin JW156)

Rodgers ....Blue Moon (What Jazz 'n' Blues Can I Play?)   (IMP 4771A)

List C: Study

Play ONE study, to be chosen from the list below.

(see General Notes p.210)

From the *Boosey Woodwind Method, clarinet book 1*   (B&H M060112904)

Morgan ....Imaginary Dancer, p.42

Marks ....Upstairs, Downstairs, p.39

Marks ....Step by Step, p.49

From the *Boosey Woodwind Method, clarinet book 2*   (B&H M060112935)

Trad. ....Ghana Alleluia, p.18 [play one of the Calls (candidate's choice) followed by the top part of the Response]

Demnitz, arr.
Weston ....No.1, p.5 (50 Classical Studies for Clarinet)   (De Haske F111)

Demnitz, arr.
Weston ....No.3, p.6 (50 Classical Studies for Clarinet)   (De Haske F111)

Demnitz, arr.
Davies &
Harris ....No.13, p.4 (80 Graded Studies for Clarinet Bk.1)   (Faber 0571509517)

Lazarus, arr.
Davies &
Harris ....No.15, p.5 (80 Graded Studies for Clarinet Bk.1)   (Faber 0571509517)

Lully, arr.
Wastall ....Ariette, p.29 (Learn As You Play Clarinet)   (B&H M060029271)

Rae ....Jumpin', No.4 (40 Modern Studies for Solo Clarinet) (Universal UE19735)

Rae ....Slow Motion, No.7
(40 Modern Studies for Solo Clarinet)   (Universal UE19735)

Trad., arr.
Wastall ....The Post, p.33 (Learn As You Play Clarinet)   (B&H M060029271)

Rose ....Folksong [unaccompanied]
(A Miscellany for Clarinet Bk.I)   (ABRSM 185472 502 5)

Rose ....Gavotte [unaccompanied]
(A Miscellany for Clarinet Bk.I)   (ABRSM 185472 502 5)

Arnold.................Twilight, p.51 (Clarinet Basics)   (Faber 0571518141)

Lyons ....No.12 (Clarinet Studies)   (Useful Music U30)

Wilson.................Grey Secrets (Colour Studies)   (Camden Music CM180)

Sight-reading (see p.209)

Aural Tests *or* Initiative Tests (see p.207)

Musicianship Questions (see p.208)

Grade 3

Warm-ups

Warm-ups do not form part of the examination, but it is highly recommended that candidates prepare by using warm-up exercises immediately before entering the examination room. See page 6.

The Examination

Facility Exercises

- Play a long note with full tone for a prescribed number of beats (6 – 12 at ♩ = 60). The examiner will specify the note and the number of beats and will set the pulse.
- Exercise

Scales and Arpeggios

(See Notes on Scales and Arpeggios page 198)

To be played from memory. All scales and arpeggios should be prepared with the specifications listed in the grey box on the following page. The examiner will request *one only* (e.g. one rhythm *or* one articulation *or* one character) when requesting each scale/arpeggio.

Range

Note Centres

Candidates should prepare the following note centre: A (two octaves, except where specified).

The following should be prepared:

- the major scale
- the major arpeggio
- the natural minor scale
- the minor arpeggio
- the pentatonic major scale
- the whole tone scale (one octave)
- the chromatic scale (one octave)

Candidates may pause between individual scales and arpeggios.

Rhythms	i) ♪s grouped in 3s or 4s as appropriate. ii) as given in Ex.3 (see p.204) (major and minor scales only) Candidates may if they wish devise their own rhythms for pentatonic, whole tone and chromatic scales.
Dynamics	With a confident and consistent full tone
Tempi	♩ = 56 – 62
Articulations	i) tongued; ii) slurred
Character	i) Vivace; ii) Pesante iii) Dolce; iv) Maestoso sostenuto

Pieces

Play TWO pieces, one to be chosen from each list.

List A

(see General Notes p.210)

From the *Boosey Woodwind Method, clarinet book 1*   (B&H M060112904)

York & Marks.......Image, p.60

From the *Boosey Woodwind Method, clarinet book 2*   (B&H M060112935)

Trad.....................Lannigan's Ball, p.17 [with CD track 18]

Marks ....Tiger Leap, p.26

Trad.....................The College Hornpipe, p.49

Stadler..................Marcia di Camelo, p.52

Brahms, arr.
Davies & Reade ...Andante, No.22 (First Book of Clarinet Solos)   (Faber 0571504507)

Fauré, arr.
Lyons ....Berceuse (Useful Clarinet Solos)   (Useful Music U5)

Gritton, arr.
Davies &
Harris ....Rêverie, No.5 (Second Book of Clarinet Solos)   (Faber 0571510930)

German, arr.
Wastall ....Romance, No.1 (First Repertoire Pieces for Clarinet)   (B&H M060040757)

Grieg, arr.
Harrison ....Gavotte from *Holberg Suite*
                     (Amazing Solos for Clarinet)   (B&H M060084690)

Mozart, ed.
King ....Il Mio Tesoro from *Don Giovanni*, No.1
                     (Clarinet Solos Vol.1)   (Chester/Music Sales CH55089)

Arne, arr. Davies
& Reade ....When Daisies Pied, No.27
                     (First Book of Clarinet Solos)   (Faber 0571504507)

Purcell, arr.
Lyons ....The Moor's Revenge, Rondo (Useful Clarinet Solos)   (Useful Music U5)

List B

> (see General Notes p.210)
>
> From the *Boosey Woodwind Method, clarinet book 1*   (B&H M060112904)
>
> *Barratt* ....Quirk, p.60 [either part, with *either* the clarinet duet part *or*
>   CD accompaniment]
>
> *Norton* ....Club Soda, p.59 [clarinet 1 part]
>
> From the *Boosey Woodwind Method, clarinet book 2*   (B&H M060112935)
>
> *Trad.* ....Hero's Farewell, p.28
>
> *Weiss &*
> *Shearing* ....Lullaby of Birdland, p.27 [with CD track 28]
>
> *Barratt* ....Italian Connection, p.16
>
> *Jenkins* ....La la la koora, p.41 [with CD track 46]

Ferguson, arr.
Wastall ....Prelude from *Four Short Pieces*, No.8
                     (First Repertoire Pieces for Clarinet)   (B&H M060040757)

Gershwin ....Nice Work If You Can Get It (Easy Gershwin for Clarinet)   (OUP N6678)

Norton ....Shoehorn Blues (The Microjazz Clarinet Collection 2)   (B&H M060110610)

Pilling ....Tyrolean Dance (Seven Simple Pieces)   (Forsyth FPD08)

Pogson ....Picnic (The Way to Rock)   (B&H M060087288)

Vinter, arr.
Wastall ....First Song, No.12 (First Repertoire Pieces for Clarinet) (B&H M060040757)

Cowles ....Waltzing Lil the Pterodactyl (Dancing Dinosaurs)　　(De Haske F645)

Harris ....Dancing Bears, No.3 (Summer Sketches)　　(B&H M060081699)

Finzi ....Carol (Five Bagatelles)　　(B&H M060030253)

Lyons ....Today Nothing Happened (Useful Clarinet Solos)　　(Useful Music U5)

Harris ....Affair in Manhattan, p.56 (Clarinet Basics)　　(Faber 0571518141)

Wilson ....Helen (Girl Names)　　(Camden Music CM063)

List C: Study

Play ONE study, to be chosen from the list below.

(see General Notes p.210)

From the *Boosey Woodwind Method, clarinet book 2*　　(B&H M060112935)

Barratt ....Sit up and Beg!, p.35

Trad. ....The Parson's Farewell, p.38

Marks ....Flying Away, p.20

Marks ....Chromatic Cheesecake, p.26

Baermann, arr.
Weston ....No.6, p.7 (50 Classical Studies for Clarinet)　　(De Haske F111)

Demnitz, arr.
Davies &
Harris ....No.22, p.7 (80 Graded Studies for Clarinet Bk.1)　　(Faber 0571509517)

Demnitz, arr.
Davies &
Harris ....No.27, p.9 (80 Graded Studies for Clarinet Bk.1)　　(Faber 0571509517)

Klosé, arr.
Weston ....No.10, p.9 (50 Classical Studies for Clarinet)　　(De Haske F111)

Rae ....In the Beginning, No.12
　　　　　　　　　(40 Modern Studies for Solo Clarinet)　　(Universal UE19735)

Rae ....Forever, No.10 (40 Modern Studies for Solo Clarinet)　　(Universal UE19735)

Wastall ....Study No.1, Unit 17, p.42 (Learn As You Play Clarinet) (B&H M060029271)

Gumbley ....In the Small Hours, p.5 (Cool School for Clarinet)　　(Brass Wind 1318)

Rose ....Arietta [unaccompanied]
　　　　　　　　　(A Miscellany for Clarinet Bk.I)　　(ABRSM 185472 502 5)

Wilson ....Green Constancy (Colour Studies)　　(Camden Music CM180)

Sight-reading (see p.209)

Aural Tests *or* **Initiative Tests** (see p.207)

Musicianship Questions (see p.208)

Grade 4

Warm-ups

Warm-ups do not form part of the examination, but it is highly recommended that candidates prepare by using warm-up exercises immediately before entering the examination room. See page 6.

The Examination

Facility Exercises

* Play a long note *mf* for a prescribed number of beats (8 – 12 at ♩ = 60).
  The examiner will specify the note and the number of beats and will set the pulse.
* Exercise

Scales and Arpeggios

(See Notes on Scales and Arpeggios page 198)

To be played from memory. All scales and arpeggios should be prepared with the specifications listed in the grey box on the following page. The examiner will request *one only* (e.g. one rhythm *or* one articulation *or* one character) when requesting each scale/arpeggio.

Range

Note Centres

Candidates should prepare the following note centre: C (two octaves).

The following should be prepared:

- the major scale
- the major arpeggio
- the natural minor scale
- the melodic minor scale
- the minor arpeggio
- the pentatonic major scale
- the whole tone scale
- the chromatic scale

Rhythms	i) ♪s grouped in 3s or 4s as appropriate. ii) as given in Ex.3 (see p.204) (major and minor scales only) Candidates may if they wish devise their own rhythms for pentatonic, whole tone and chromatic scales.
Dynamics	Within the range $mp - f$, 1) sustaining a level throughout; ii) cresc.; iii) decresc.
Tempi	Scales ♩= 72 – 84 Arpeggios ♩= 60 – 66
Articulations	i) Tongued; ii) slurred; Arpeggios tongued only
Character	i) Staccato and light; ii) Heavy and accented; iii) Douce et très passioné

Candidates may pause between individual scales and arpeggios.

Pieces

Play TWO pieces, one to be chosen from each list.

List A

Baermann, arr.
Davies &
Harris ....Schlummerlied, No.8
(Second Book of Clarinet Solos)   (Faber 0571510930)

Fauré, arr.
Salter ....Après un Rêve
(Jack Brymer Clarinet Series Easy Bk.2)   (Weinberger/Elkin JW157)

German, arr.
Wastall ....Andante, No.16 (First Repertoire Pieces for Clarinet)   (B&H M060040757)

Labor, arr.
King ....Allegretto (Clarinet Solos Vol.1)   (Chester/Music Sales CH55089)

Mendelssohn, arr.
King ....Andante from *Konzertstück in D minor Op.114*, No.3
(Clarinet Solos Vol.2)   (Chester/Music Sales CH55093)

Mozart, arr.
Dobree...................Divertimento No.2, K439b, 1st Movt: Allegro   (Chester/Music Sales CH55335)

Reger, arr.
Wastall ....Romance, No.13 (First Repertoire Pieces for Clarinet) (B&H M060040757)

Gade, arr.
Wastall ....Fantasy Piece, Op.43/1, No.10
                       (First Repertoire Pieces for Clarinet)   (B&H M060040757)

Mozart, arr.
King ....Minuet and Trio from E♭ Serenade
                       (Clarinet Solos Vol.1)   (Chester/Music Sales CH55089)

Rimsky–Korsakov,
arr. King ....Andante (Clarinet Solos Vol.2)   (Chester/Music Sales CH55093)

Weber, arr.
Klosé ....Petite Fantasie, No.10
                       (Second Book of Clarinet Solos)   (Faber 0571510930)

Lefevre, arr.
Davies &
Harris ....Sonata No.3, 3rd Movt: Allegro
                       (Five Sonatas for Clarinet and Piano)   (OUP N7551)

Ravel, arr.
Harris ....Pavane of the Sleeping Beauty
                       (Music Through Time Bk.3)   (OUP N7186)

Shostakovich,
arr. Cowles ....Romance from The Gadfly Op.97   (De Haske F689)

Mozart, arr. Benoy
& Bryce ....Voi che sapete from The Marriage of Figaro (Two Arias)   (OUP N7838)

Purcell, arr.Harris
& Reade ....Rondeau, No.19 (First book of Clarinet Solos)   (Faber 0571504507)

List B

Cowles ....Peg Leg Stegosauras Polka (Dancing Dinosaurs)   (De Haske F645)

Ferguson, arr.
Wastall ....Pastorale from Four Short Pieces, No.2
                       (First Repertoire Pieces for Clarinet)   (B&H M060040757)

Gershwin ....It Ain't Necessarily So (Easy Gershwin for Clarinet)   (OUP N6678)

Harris ....No.5: Allegro con fuoco (Suite in Five)   (Ricordi LD735)

Joplin, arr.
Cowles ....Figleaf Rag (Joplin Ragtime)   (De Haske F636)

Norton ....Stick Together or Intercity Stomp
                       (The Microjazz Clarinet Collection 2)   (B&H M060110610)

Pogson ....Jumpin' Jack (The Way to Rock)   (B&H M060087288)

Wilson ....Katie *or* Emma (Girl Names)   (Camden Music CM063)

Wedgwood ....Hot on the Line, No.1
                   (Jazzin' About for Clarinet and Piano)   (Faber 0571512739)

Harris ....Donkey Ride, No.7 (Summer Sketches)   (B&H M060081699)

Parker ....Soldier, Soldier (The Music of Jim Parker for Clarinet)   (Brass Wind 1317)

Dickinson ....Lullaby from the Unicorns   (Novello NOV120648)

Frith ....Queen Mary's Rest (A Garland for the Queen)   (Camden Music CM085)

List C: Study

Play ONE study, to be chosen from the list below.

Demnitz, arr.
Weston..................No.17, p.13 (50 Classical Studies for Clarinet)   (De Haske F111)

Harris ....Study, p.55
                   (Cambridge Clarinet Tutor)   (Cambridge University Press 0521283507)

Klosé, arr.
Weston..................No.18, p.14 (50 Classical Studies for Clarinet)   (De Haske F111)

Demnitz, arr.
Davies &
Harris ....No.33, p.11 (80 Graded Studies for Clarinet Bk.1)   (Faber 0571509517)

Demnitz, arr.
Davies & Harris...No.35, p.11 (80 Graded Studies for Clarinet Bk.1)   (Faber 0571509517)

Rae No.62, p.16
                   (Progressive Jazz Studies for Clarinet Easy Level)   (Faber 057151359X)

Rae ....Tumbledown Blues, No.11
                   (40 Modern Studies for Solo Clarinet)   (Universal UE19735)

Wastall ....Unit 23, Study No.4, p.54 (Learn As You Play Clarinet) (B&H M060029271)

Wilson ....Violet Enchantment (Colour Studies)   (Camden Music CM180)

Lyons ....No.33 (Clarinet Studies)   (Useful Music U30)

Sight-reading (see p.209)

Aural Tests *or* Initiative Tests (see p.207)

Musicianship Questions (see p.208)

Grade 5

Warm-ups

Warm-ups do not form part of the examination, but it is highly recommended that candidates prepare by using warm-up exercises immediately before entering the examination room. See page 6.

The Examination

Facility Exercises

* Play a long note *mf* for a prescribed number of beats (8 – 12 at ♩ = 60).
  The examiner will specify the note and the number of beats and will set the pulse.

* Exercise

Scales and Arpeggios

(See Notes on Scales and Arpeggios page 198)

To be played from memory. All scales and arpeggios should be prepared with the specifications listed in the grey box below. The examiner will request *one only* (e.g. one rhythm *or* one articulation *or* one character) when requesting each scale/arpeggio.

Range

Note Centres

Candidates should prepare the following note centre: F (two and a half octaves, except where specified).

The following should be prepared:

* the major scale
* the major arpeggio
* the natural minor scale
* the melodic minor scale

Rhythms	♪ s grouped in 3s or 4s as appropriate. Candidates may if they wish devise their own rhythms for pentatonic, whole tone, chromatic and blues scales.
Dynamics	Within the range *mp – f,* i) sustaining a level throughout; ii) cresc.; iii) decresc.
Tempi	Scales ♩ = 72 – 84; Arpeggios ♩ = 60 – 66
Articulations	i) Tongued; ii) slurred
Character	i) Sehr ruhig; ii) Rasch und feuerig; iii) Trotzig; iv) Lebhaft und mit wut

- the harmonic minor scale
- the minor arpeggio
- the pentatonic major scale (two octaves)
- the whole tone scale (two octaves)
- the chromatic scale (two octaves)
- the blues scale (two octaves)

Candidates may pause between individual scales and arpeggios.

Pieces

Play TWO pieces, one to be chosen from each list.

List A

Gade ....Allegro Vivace, No.2 (Phantasiestücke, Op.43) (Hansen/Music Sales WH03537)

Mendelssohn ....Sonata in E♭ Major, 2nd Movt: Andante
[cut piano bars 31-43]   (Bärenreiter BA8151)

Nielsen ....Fantasy   (Hansen/Music Sales WH29642)

Weber, arr.
Weston..................Theme and Variation I from *Variations, Op.33*
(New Weber Edition)   (De Haske F618)

Schumann ....Fantasy Pieces for A or B♭ Clarinet,
Op.73, No.1: Zart und mit Ausdruck   (Peters P2366)

Brahms.................Sonata in F Minor, Op.120, No.1
3rd Movt: Allegretto grazioso (Simrock/B&H EE607 or Wiener Urtext/Universal UT500515)

Lefevre, arr.
Davies & Harris...Sonata, 1st Movt: Allegro moderato, No.3
(Five Sonatas for Clarinet and Piano)   (OUP N7551)

Mozart, arr.
Dobree..................Divertimento No.2, last Movt: Rondo   (Chester/Music Sales CH55335)

Mozart.................Minuet and 2nd Trio from *Quintet,*
K581 [B♭/A Clarinet]   (Peters P19b/P19c)

List B

Cowles ....Archaeopteryx Mix (Dancing Dinosaurs)   (De Haske F645)

Kelly ....Aries (Zodiac for Clarinet and Piano, SET 1) (Weinberger/Elkin JW431)

Norton ....Puppet Theatre, No.9 *or* Carthorse Rag, No.11
(The Microjazz Clarinet Collection 2)   (B&H M060110610)

Templeton ....Pocket sized Sonata No.2, 1st Movt:
Moderato (and mellow)   (Shawnee/Music Sales SP16819)

Both ....Santa Monica Blues (Dancing Clarinet)   (Schott ED8484)

Arnold..................Sonatina, 2nd Movt: Andantino (Lengnick/Elkin AL1000)

Finzi....................Forlana *or* Romance (Five Bagatelles) (B&H M060030253)

Lutoslawski..........Andante, No.4 (Dance Preludes) (Chester/Music Sales CH55171)

Frith ....Carillon *and* Royal Pageant
(A Garland for the Queen) (Camden Music CM085)

Reade..................Summer, No.5
(Suite from *The Victorian Kitchen Garden*) (Weinberger/Elkin JW485)

Binge ....The Watermill (Weinberger/Elkin JW416)

Harris ....Clarinetwise (Camden Music CM153)

List C: Study

Play ONE study, to be chosen from the list below.

Baermann, arr.
Weston..................No.26, p.21 (50 Classical Studies) (De Haske F111)

Baermann, arr.
Weston..................No.31, p.26 (50 Classical Studies) (De Haske F111)

Cavallini, arr.
Weston..................No.33, p.18 (50 Melodious Studies) (De Haske F500)

Kell ....No.1 (17 Staccato Studies for Clarinet) (IMC/Universal 1554)

Rae ....Windy Ridge, No.19 (40 Modern Studies for Clarinet) (Universal UE19735)

Stark, arr Davies
& Harris ....No.50, p.19 (80 Graded Studies Bk.1) (Faber 0571509517)

Wiedmann, arr.
Davies & Harris...No.48, p.18 (80 Graded Studies Bk.1) (Faber 0571509517)

Demnitz, arr. Davies
& Harris ....No.52, p.2 (80 Graded Studies Bk.2) (Faber 0571509525)

Rose ....Invention [unaccompanied]
(A Miscellany for Clarinet Bk.II) (ABRSM 185472 503 3)

Lyons ....No.35 (Clarinet Studies) (Useful Music U30)

Wilson ....Yellow Radiance (Colour Studies) (Camden Music CM180)

Sight-reading (see p.209)

Aural Tests *or* Initiative Tests (see p.207)

Musicianship Questions (see p.208)

Grade 6

Warm-ups

Warm-ups do not form part of the examination, but it is highly recommended that candidates prepare by using warm-up exercises immediately before entering the examination room. See page 6.

The Examination

Facility Exercises

- Play a long note *mf* for a prescribed number of beats (4 – 10 at ♩ = 60).
  The examiner will specify the note and the number of beats and will set the pulse.
- Play a long note *f* for a prescribed number of beats (4 – 6 at ♩ = 60).
  The examiner will specify the note and the number of beats and will set the pulse.
- Exercise

Scales and Arpeggios

(See Notes on Scales and Arpeggios page 198)

To be played from memory. All scales and arpeggios should be prepared with the specifications listed in the grey box opposite. The examiner will request *two only* (e.g. one rhythm *and* one dynamic *or* one articulation *and* one character) when requesting each scale/exercise.

Range

Note Centres

Candidates should prepare the following note centres: G, E♭ *and* B (all two octaves).

When the examiner names a note centre the candidate will play:

- the scale/arpeggio exercise on p.203
- the pentatonic major scale
- the whole tone scale
- the blues scale

Candidates may pause between individual scales and arpeggios.

Rhythms	Scale/arpeggio exercise as written; other scales ♪ s grouped in 3s or 4s as appropriate. Candidates may if they wish devise their own rhythms for pentatonic, whole tone and blues scales.
Dynamics	Within the range *pp – ff*, i) sustaining a level throughout; ii) cresc. throughout each scale /arpeggio; iii) decresc. throughout each scale /arpeggio
Tempi	♩ = 94+
Articulations	i) Tongued; ii) slurred Candidates may if they wish offer additional articulation patterns of their own.
Character	Candidates to offer a selection of at least four of their own contrasting choices which may include familiar Italian/German terms of expression or terms from any other language provided an explanation can be given.

Pieces

Play TWO pieces, one to be chosen from each list. Candidates may offer the Bass Clarinet piece as their List A choice.

List A

Baermann ....Adagio   (Breitkopf & Härtel EB4884)

Saint-Saëns ....Sonata, 1st Movt: Allegretto   (Chester/Music Sales CH55238)

Hurlstone ....Croon Song (Four Characteristic Pieces)   (Emerson E97)

Horovitz ....Sonatina, 2nd Movt: Lento, quasi andante   (Novello NOV120541)

Weber ....Concerto No.1, 2nd Movt: Adagio ma non troppo   (Peters P8789)

Reade ....Prelude, No.1
           (Suite from *The Victorian Kitchen Garden*)   (Weinberger/Elkin JW485)

Schumann, arr.
Ettlinger ....Three Romances, Op.94 for A/B♭
           Clarinet, No.1: Nicht schnell   (Stainer & Bell R7851)

Delibes, ed.
Lyle.....................Andante quasi allegretto (French Clarinet Encores Bk.2)   (Pan PEM92)

Ibert ....Aria   (Leduc/UMP19856)

Bullard ....Meditative Blues, No.2 (Three Blues)   (Harlequin Music 21701)

Bass Clarinet

Scriabin................Etude   (Forberg/Emerson)

List B

Debussy................Petite Piece   (Durand/UMP 0790500)

Finzi...................Prelude, No.1 (Five Bagatelles)   (B&H M060030253)

Lloyd, C.H ...."Bon Voyage!"   (Lazarus M708007043)

Stamitz, arr.
Drucker................Concerto No.3 in B♭, 3rd Movt: Rondo   (IMC/Universal 2287)

Gade ....Fantasy Pieces Op.43, 4th Movt:
Allegro molto Vivace   (Hansen/Music Sales WH03537)

Satie, arr.
Weston.................Jack in the Box, 3rd Movt: Finale   (Universal UE19093)

Vaughan
Williams...............Six Studies on English Folk Song, 6th Movt:
Allegro Vivace [B♭ Clarinet version]   (Stainer & Bell H51)

Lutoslawski ....Dance Preludes, 1st Movt: Allegro molto   (Chester/Music Sales CH55171)

Banks ....Prologue, Night Piece and Blues
for Two, 1st Movt: Prologue   (Schott 11092)

Ferguson...............Four Short Pieces, 1st Movt:
Prelude - non troppo Allegro
and 4th Movt: Burlesque – con spirito   (B&H M060019999)

List C: Study

Play ONE study, to be chosen from the list below. An option is given for Bass Clarinet. N.B. The Bass Clarinet option may only be chosen if the candidate offers a Clarinet piece as their List A choice.

Bach, arr.
Giampieri.............Bourée, p.4, No.2 (21 Pieces)   (Ricordi ER2621)

Harris, arr. Davies
& Harris ....No.60 (80 Graded Studies Bk.2)   (Faber 0571509525)

Wiedemann, arr.
Davies & Harris...No.64 (80 Graded Studies Bk.2)   (Faber 0571509525)

Baermann, arr.
Weston.................No.41 (50 Classical Studies for Clarinet)   (De Haske F111)

Klosé, arr.
Weston.................No.35 (50 Classical Studies for Clarinet)   (De Haske F111)

Ferling/Rose, arr.
Mauz .... Andante Cantabile, p.32 (The Finest Etudes for Clarinet) (Schott ED8906)

Ferling/Rose, arr.
Mauz .... Moderato assai, p.20 (The Finest Etudes for Clarinet)　(Schott ED8906)

Ferling/Rose, arr.
Mauz .... Andante sostenuto quasi Adagio, p.10
      (The Finest Etudes for Clarinet)　 (Schott ED8906)

Rae .... Latin Jive, No.32
      (40 Modern Studies for Solo Clarinet)　 (Universal UE19735)

Rae .... Helix, No.29 (40 Modern Studies for Solo Clarinet)　 (Universal UE19735)

Rae .... Meditation, No.35
      (40 Modern Studies for Solo Clarinet)　 (Universal UE19735)

Wilson .... Black Shadows (Colour Studies)　 (Camden Music CM180)

Bass Clarinet

Bach, J.S,
arr. Bontoux .... Sarabande from Suite No.2　 (Fuzeau/Emerson)

Sight-reading (see p.209)

Aural Tests *or* Initiative Tests (see p.207)

Musicianship Questions (see p.208)

Grade 7

Warm-ups

Warm-ups do not form part of the examination, but it is highly recommended that
candidates prepare by using warm-up exercises immediately before entering the
examination room. See page 6.

The Examination

Facility Exercises

- Play a long note *p/mf* for a prescribed number of beats (4 – 12 at ♩ = 60).
  The examiner will specify the note and the dynamic, choose the number of beats
  and set the pulse.
- Play a long note *f* for a prescribed number of beats (4 – 8 at ♩ = 60).
  The examiner will specify the note and the number of beats and will set the pulse.

- Chromatic exercise for finger co-ordination

Scales and Arpeggios

(See Notes on Scales and Arpeggios page 198)

To be played from memory. All scales and arpeggios should be prepared with the specifications listed in the grey box below. The examiner will request *two only* (e.g. one rhythm *and* one dynamic *or* one articulation *and* one character) when requesting each scale/exercise.

Range

Note Centres

Candidates should prepare the following note centres: A, D, A♭ and F♯ (all two octaves). (The starting pitch for the F♯ note centre is at candidate's choice.)

When the examiner names a note centre the candidate will play:

- the scale/arpeggio exercise on p.203
- the whole tone scale
- the diminished scales (both forms)
- the blues scale

Candidates may pause between individual scales and arpeggios.

Rhythms	Scale/arpeggio exercise as written; other scales ♪s grouped in 3s or 4s as appropriate. Candidates may if they wish devise their own rhythms for whole tone, diminished and blues scales.
Dynamics	Within the range *pp – ff*, i) sustaining a level throughout; ii) cresc. iii) decresc.
Tempi	♩= 94+
Articulations	i) Tongued; ii) slurred Candidates may if they wish offer additional articulation patterns of their own.
Character	Candidates to offer a selection of at least four of their own contrasting choices which may include familiar Italian/German terms of expression or terms from any other language provided an explanation can be given.

Pieces

Play TWO pieces, one to be chosen from each list. Candidates may offer the Bass Clarinet piece as their List A choice.

List A

Hurlstone ....No.1 (Four Characteristic Pieces)   (Emerson E97)

Poulenc ....Sonata, 2nd Movt: Romanza   (Chester/Music Sales CH61763)

Bliss ....Pastoral   (Novello NOV120509)

Stanford ....Sonata, 2nd Movt: Caoine   (Stainer & Bell H44)

Brahms ....Sonata in F minor, Op.120, No.1, 2nd Movt:
Andante un poco Adagio   (Simrock/B&H EE607 or Wiener Urtext/Universal UT500515)

Lefanu ....Lullaby for A Clarinet   (Novello NOV361053)

Weber ....Concerto No.2 in E♭, 2nd Movt:
Romanze Andante [with cadenza]   (B&H M060029486)

Schumann, arr.
Ettlinger ....Three Romances, Op.94 for A/B♭
Clarinet No.2: Einfach, innig   (Stainer & Bell R7851)

Schumann ....Fantasy Pieces Op.73 for
A or B♭ Clarinet, No.2: Lebhaft, leicht   (Peters P2366)

Busoni ....Elegie   (Breitkopf & Härtel EB5188)

Bass Clarinet

Zanielli ....Peg Leg Pete   (B&H M051020041)

List B

Krommer ....Concerto in E♭ Major, Op.36,
1st Movt: Allegro   (Supraphon/Bärenreiter H888)

Pierné ....Canzonetta, Op.19   (Leduc/UMP AL8206)

Weber ....Concerto No.1 in F Minor, 1st Movt: Allegro   (Peters P8789)

Finzi ....Fughetta, No.5 (Five Bagatelles)   (B&H M060030253)

Gomez ....Lorito Caprice   (Lazarus M708007012)

Horovitz ....Sonatina, 1st Movt: Allegro calmato   (Novello NOV120541)

Tartini, arr.
Jacob ....Concertino, 3rd Movt: Adagio
and 4th Movt: Allegro Risoluto   (B&H M060027833)

McCabe ....Nocturne, No.1 *and* Improvisation,
No.2 (Three Pieces for Clarinet)   (Novello NOV120135)

Chapple ....No.1 *and* No.5 (A Bit of a Blow)   (Bosworth/Music Sales BOE005035)

Banks ....1st Movt: Prologue *and* 3rd Movt: Blues
for Two (Prologue, Night Piece and Blues
for Two for Clarinet and Piano)   (Schott ED11092)

List C: Study

Play ONE study, to be chosen from the list below. An option is given for Bass Clarinet. N.B. The Bass Clarinet option may only be chosen if the candidate offers a Clarinet piece as their List A choice.

Bach, arr.
Giampieri.............Corrente, No.5, p.8 (21 Pieces) (Ricordi ER2621)

Harris, arr. Davies
& Harris ....No.67 (80 Graded Studies Bk.2) (Faber 0571509525)

Baermann, arr.
Davies & Harris...No.73 (80 Graded Studies Bk.2) (Faber 0571509525)

Blatt, arr
Weston..................No.46 (50 Classical Studies for Clarinet) (De Haske F111)

Uhl........................No.6 (48 Etüden für Klarinette) (Schott KLB12)

Uhl........................No.3 (48 Etüden für Klarinette) (Schott KLB12)

Ferling/Rose, arr.
Mauz...................Adagio non troppo, p.16
(The Finest Etudes for Clarinet) (Schott ED8906)

Ferling/Rose, arr.
Mauz...................Moderato assai (The Finest Etudes for Clarinet) (Schott ED8906)

Jacob ....Waltz, No.2 *and* Homage to J.S.Bach, No.3
(Five Pieces for Clarinet) (OUP N7368)

Wilson..................Red Flame (Colour Studies) (Camden Music CM180)

Bass Clarinet

Bach, J.S,
arr. Bontoux ....Gigue from Suite No.2 (Fuzeau/Emerson)

Sight-reading (see p.209)

Aural Tests *or* Initiative Tests (see p.207)

Musicianship Questions (see p.208)

Grade 8

Warm-ups

Warm-ups do not form part of the examination, but it is highly recommended that candidates prepare by using warm-up exercises immediately before entering the examination room. See page 6.

The Examination

Facility Exercises

- Play a long note *pp/p/mf* for a prescribed number of beats (4 – 16 at ♩ = 60).
  The examiner will specify the note and the dynamic, choose the number of beats and set the pulse.
- Play a long note *f* for a prescribed number of beats (4 – 10 at ♩ = 60).
  The examiner will specify the note and the number of beats and will set the pulse.
- Exercise

- Legato octave exercise for embouchure flexibility, dynamic and intonation control

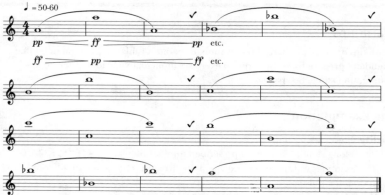

The examiner will choose the starting dynamic.

Scales and Arpeggios

(See Notes on Scales and Arpeggios page 198)

To be played from memory. All scales and arpeggios should be prepared with the specifications listed in the grey box on the opposite page. The examiner will request *two only* (e.g. one rhythm *and* one dynamic *or* one articulation *and* one character) when requesting each scale/exercise.

Range

Note Centres

Candidates should prepare the following note centres: C♯ (two octaves, except where specified), B♭ (two octaves, except where specified), E (three octaves, except where specified) *and* F (three octaves, except where specified).

When the examiner names a note centre the candidate will play:

- the scale/arpeggio exercise on p.203 (two octaves)
- the whole tone scale
- the diminished scales (both forms)
- the blues scale
- the crabwise major scale (one octave, starting either on the note centre or on C – candidate's choice)

Rhythms	Scale/arpeggio exercise as written; crabwise as written (see p.199); other scales ♪s grouped in 3s or 4s as appropriate. Candidates may if they wish devise their own rhythms for whole tone, diminished and blues scales.
Dynamics	Within the range $pp - ff$, i) sustaining a level throughout; ii) cresc. throughout each scale/arpeggio; iii) decresc. throughout each scale/arpeggio.
Tempi	♩= 94+
Articulations	i) tongued; ii) slurred Candidates may if they wish offer additional articulation patterns of their own.
Character	Candidates to offer a selection of at least four of their own contrasting choices which may include familiar Italian/German terms of expression or terms from any other language provided an explanation can be given.

Candidates may pause between individual scales and arpeggios. Where there is more than one starting pitch within the range (e.g. scale/arpeggio exercise for E note centre), the starting pitch is at candidate's choice.

Pieces and studies for Grade 8

Options are given for B♭ Clarinet, Bass Clarinet and E♭ Clarinet in the lists below. Candidates may offer one piece/study on the Bass Clarinet *or* E♭ Clarinet, but must offer at least TWO choices on the B♭ Clarinet.

Pieces

Play TWO pieces, one to be chosen from each list. Options are given for B♭ Clarinet, Bass Clarinet and E♭ Clarinet.

List A

Brahms.................Sonata in E♭, Op.120, No.2 1st Movt: Allegro Amabile   (Wiener Urtext/Universal UT50016)

Brahms................Sonata in F Minor, Op.120, No.1, 1st Movt:
Allegro Appassionata   (Simrock/B&H EE607 or Wiener Urtext/Universal UT50015)

Finzi...................Concerto, 2nd Movt: Adagio   (B&H M060030161)

Bowen................Sonata, Op.109, 1st Movt: Allegro moderato   (Emerson E166)

Weber.................Introduction, Theme and Variations [complete]   (IMC/Universal 1742)

Burgmüller..........Duo in E♯ for Clarinet
and Piano, Op.15 [complete]   (Simrock/B&H 221113184)

Martinů..............Sonatine [complete]   (Leduc/UMP AL21698)

Weber.................Concertino in E♭ [complete]   (Peters PET8755)

Mozart................Concerto, 3rd Movt: Rondo (Clarinet in A only)   (Peters PET9821)

Crusell, arr.
Weston................Concerto in F Minor, 1st Movt: [with cadenza]   (Universal UE19084)

Bass Clarinet

Zander................Ballade   (Simrock/B&H)

E♭ Clarinet

Shiskov................Grotesque Dance   (Edition Musicus/Emerson)

List B

Options are given for B♭ Clarinet only.

Stanford ....Three Intermezzi, Op.13, 2nd Movt: Allegro
Agitato *and* 3rd Movt: Allegretto Scherzando   (Chester/Music Sales CH55205)

McCabe...............Fantasy, No.3 (Three Pieces for Clarinet)   (Novello NOV120135)

Horovitz ....Sonatina, 3rd Movt: Con brio   (Novello NOV120541)

Poulenc...............Sonata, 3rd Movt: Allegro con Fuoco   (Chester/Music Sales CH61763)

Milhaud...............Duo Concertant [complete]   (Heugel/UMP HE31564)

Pierné ....Andante Scherzo [complete]   (Billaudot/UMP CC2421)

Penderecki ....3 Miniatures for Clarinet and Piano [complete]   (Maecenas BW100492)

Weiner.................Recruiting Dance from Pereg [complete]   (EMB/B&H M080004609)

Tate......................Prelude-Aria-Interlude-Finale, 3rd Movt:
Interlude *and* 4th Movt: Finale   (OUP N9030)

Chapple................No.2 *and* No.3 (A Bit of a Blow)   (Bosworth/Music Sales BOE005035)

List C: Study

Play ONE study, to be chosen from the list below. Options are given for B♭ Clarinet, Bass Clarinet and E♭ Clarinet.

Arnold...................Fantasy [unaccompanied]   (Faber 0571500293)

Bennett ....Sonatina, 1st Movt: Con fuoco [unaccompanied]   (Novello NOV120549)

Stravinsky............No.3 (Three Pieces)   (Chester/Music Sales CH01551)

Gershwin, arr.
Harvey.................It Ain't Necessarily So, No.3
                              (Three Etudes on Themes from Gershwin)   (Emerson 177)

Bach, arr.
Giampieri.............Corrente, No.8, p.12 (21 Pieces)   (Ricordi ER2621)

Uhl.......................No.14 (48 Etüden)   (Schott KLB12)

Wiedemann, arr.
Davies & Harris...No.75 (80 Graded Studies Bk.2)   (Faber 0571509525)

Ferlin/Rose, arr.
Mauz ....Allegretto con moto, p.33
                              (The Finest Etudes for Clarinet)   (Schott ED8906)

Berkley ....Flighting   (OUP N5476)

Penderecki ....Prelude for Solo Clarinet   (Schott ED7567)

Bass Clarinet

Bach, J.S,
arr. Bontoux ....Allemande from Suite No.4   (Fuzeau/Emerson)

E♭ Clarinet

Lecail ....Fantasie Concertante   (Rubank/Emerson)

Sight-reading (see p.209)

Aural Tests *or* Initiative Tests (see p.207)

Musicianship Questions (see p.208)

JAZZ CLARINET

Grade 1

Warm-ups

Warm-ups do not form part of the examination, but it is highly recommended that candidates prepare by using warm-up exercises immediately before entering the examination room. See page 6.

The Examination

Facility Exercise

Play a long note with full tone for a prescribed number of beats (6 – 8 at ♩ = 60). The examiner will specify the note and the number of beats and will set the pulse.

Scales and Arpeggios (Chord Shapes)

(See Notes on Scales and Arpeggios page 198)

To be played from memory. All scales and arpeggios should be prepared with the specifications listed in the grey box below. The examiner will request *one only* (e.g. one rhythm *or* one articulation *or* one character) when requesting each scale/arpeggio.

Range

Rhythms	♪ s grouped in 3s or 4s as appropriate. i) straight; ii) medium swing
Dynamics	With a confident and consistent full tone
Tempi	♩ = 72+
Articulations	Scales i) tongued; ii) legato Arpeggios tongued only Swing ♫♫♪
Character	i) Spiky and angry (when tongued) ii) Relaxed and laid back (when legato)

Creative Exercise

Choose one of the scales or arpeggios from the list for this Grade and perform a creative version using elements chosen from the menu on page 205 and/or from the grey box for this Grade.

Candidates may notate their creative exercise and read from this or simply improvise a version. In either case the same exercise should be performed twice so as to clarify the musical intentions. Candidates will be rewarded for adventure and invention.

Note Centres

Candidates should prepare the following note centre: G (one octave).

The following should be prepared:

- the major scale followed by the major seventh arpeggio
- the dorian scale followed by the minor seventh arpeggio

Candidates may pause between pairs of scales and arpeggios.

Improvisation

Module 1, either A, B, or C (candidate's choice), from the GSMD publication *Jazz Improvisation*. See p.210 for details and for further useful publications.

Pieces

Play TWO pieces, one to be chosen from each list.

List A

(see General Notes p.210)

From the *Boosey Woodwind Method, clarinet book 1*   (B&H M060112904)

Wine/Bayer Sager.A Groovy Kind of Love, p. 36 [with CD track 56 *or* 57]

Marks ....Rambling Man, p. 26

Cohan, arr.
Goldstein &
Agay.....................Give My Regards to Broadway, No.11
             (The Joy of Clarinet)   (York Town/Music Sales YK21038)

Martini, arr.
Goldstein &
Agay.....................Plaisir d'Amour, No.14 (The Joy of Clarinet)   (York Town/Music Sales YK21038)

Trad., arr.
Wilson.................Swing Low (Face to Face) [play top line]   (Camden Music CM093)

Kosma, arr.
Ledbury ....Autumn Leaves (All Jazzed Up for Clarinet)   (Brass Wind 0303)

Mancini, arr.
Ledbury ....Moon River (All Jazzed Up for Clarinet)   (Brass Wind 0303)

Wilson.................Gospel Joe (Creative Variations Vol.1)   (Camden Music CM181)

List B

> (see General Notes p.210)
>
> From the *Boosey Woodwind Method, clarinet book 1*   (B&H M060112904)
>
> *Marks* ....The Clarinet Rap, p. 37
>
> *Trad.*....................When the Saints go Marching in, p. 26

Harvey................Blackwood Rock, No.1 *or* Offbeat,
          No.2 *or* Shorty, No.4 (Easy Jazzy Clarinet)   (Universal UE 19214)

Miles....................Arriving Home (Creative Variations Vol.1)   (Camden Music CM181)

Lewin ....Table Talk (Up Front Album for Clarinet)   (Brass Wind 0306)

Norton ....Tall Tale, Big Hat *or* Soldier Boy *or* Head for the Hills
          (The Microjazz Clarinet Collection 1)   (B&H M060109096)

List C: Study

Play ONE study, to be chosen from the list below.

Rae ....No. 44 *or* No.45 *or* No.46
          (Progressive Jazz Studies for Clarinet Easy Level)   (Faber 057151359X)

Rae ....Sad Dance *or* In the Wings
          (40 Modern Studies for Solo Clarinet)   (Universal UE19735)

Wastall ....Corumba, p.17 (Learn As You Play Clarinet)   (B&H M060029271)

Wilson..................Swing Scale *or* G Rock (Times Ten)   (Camden Music CM152)

Sight-reading (see p.209)

Aural Tests *or* Initiative Tests (see p.207)

Musicianship Questions (see p.208)

Grade 2

Warm-ups

Warm-ups do not form part of the examination, but it is highly recommended that candidates prepare by using warm-up exercises immediately before entering the examination room. See page 6.

The Examination

Facility Exercise

Play a long note with full tone for a prescribed number of beats (6 – 8 at ♩ = 60). The examiner will specify the note and the number of beats and will set the pulse.

Scales and Arpeggios (Chord Shapes)

(See Notes on Scales and Arpeggios page 198)

To be played from memory. All scales and arpeggios should be prepared with the specifications listed in the grey box below. The examiner will request *one only* (e.g. one rhythm *or* one articulation *or* one character) when requesting each scale/arpeggio.

Range

Rhythms	♪s grouped in 3s or 4s as appropriate. i) straight; ii) medium swing
Dynamics	With a confident and consistent full tone
Tempi	♩ = 72+
Articulations	i) tongued; ii) legato Swing ♫♫♩
Character	i) Medium 'up' and dance-like; ii) Bluesy and dragging

Creative Exercise

Choose one of the scales or arpeggios from the list for this Grade and perform a creative version using elements chosen from the menu on page 205 and/or from the grey box for this Grade.

Candidates may notate their creative exercise and read from this or simply improvise a version. In either case the same exercise should be performed twice so as to clarify the musical intentions. Candidates will be rewarded for adventure and invention.

Note Centres

Candidates should prepare the following note centre: D (one octave).

The following should be prepared:

- the major scale followed by the major seventh arpeggio
- the dorian scale followed by the minor seventh arpeggio
- the mixolydian scale followed by the dominant seventh arpeggio (starting and finishing on the note centre)

Candidates may pause between pairs of scales and arpeggios.

Improvisation

Module 2, either A, B, or C (candidate's choice), from the GSMD publication *Jazz Improvisation*. See p.210 for details and for further useful publications.

Pieces

Play TWO pieces, one to be chosen from each list.

List A

(see General Notes p.210)

From the *Boosey Woodwind Method, clarinet book 1*   (B&H M060112904)

Oliviero................I'll Set my Love to Music, p.46 [clarinet 1 part]

From the *Boosey Woodwind Method, clarinet book 2*   (B&H M060112935)

Norton ....Off the Rails, p.12 [clarinet 1 part, with CD track 9 *or* 10]

Davenport, arr.
Long ....Fever [no repeats except DC al fine]
                (Blues for Clarinet)   (Wise/Music Sales AM952006)

Hilliard, arr.
Long ....Our Day will come (Blues for Clarinet)   (Wise/Music Sales AM952006)

Anon, arr. Goldstein
& Agay ....When The Saints Come Marchin' In, No.15
                (The Joy of Clarinet)   (Yorktown/Music Sales YK21038)

Wilson.................J's Dream (Creative Variations Vol.1)   (Camden Music CM181)

Gershwin, arr.
Gout.....................'S wonderful (Play Gershwin B♭/E♭)   (Faber 0571517544)

Kander.................Cabaret (Play Cabaret B♭/E♭)   (Faber 0571510183)

List B

(see General Notes p.210)

From the *Boosey Woodwind Method, clarinet book 1*   (B&H M060112904)

Norton ....Tragic Consequences, p. 63

Marks ....Blue 4 U, p.47 [with CD track 72 *or* 73]

From the *Boosey Woodwind Method, clarinet book 2*   (B&H M060112935)

Norton ....Long Shadows, p.10

Norton ....Calypso Facto, p.55

Norton ....Miller's Crossing, p.21

Bennett ....Bad Hair Day (Jazz Club Clarinet)		(IMP 7531A)
Harvey................Swinging Quavers, No.3 *or* Hunkafunk, No.5 *or*		
The Groveller, No.6 (Easy Jazz Clarinet)		(Universal UE19214)
Hamer.................Brynglas Bounce [CD track 18] *or* Easy Going		
[CD track 30] (Play It Cool)		
[piano accompaniment also available]		(Spartan Press SP561)
Miles...................Abigail's Song (Creative Variations Vol.1)		(Camden Music CM181)
Cole.....................Granite (Learn As You Play Clarinet)		(B&H M060029271)
Norton ....Tread Softly (The Microjazz Clarinet Collection 2)		(B&H M060110610)

List C: Study

Play ONE study, to be chosen from the list below.

Bennett ....Early Doors (Jazz Club Clarinet)		(IMP 7531A)
Lyons ....Swing Style No.9 (Clarinet Studies)		(Useful Music U30)
Rae ....Jumpin' *or* Backtrack		
(40 Modern Studies for Solo Clarinet)		(Universal UE19735)
Wilson ....Round Dorian *or* High and Low (Times Ten)		(Camden Music CM152)
Rae ....No.47 *or* No.51 *or* No.52		
(Progressive Jazz Studies for Clarinet Easy Level)		(Faber 057151359X)

Sight-reading (see p.209)

Aural Tests *or* Initiative Tests (see p.207)

Musicianship Questions (see p.208)

Grade 3

Warm-ups

Warm-ups do not form part of the examination, but it is highly recommended that candidates prepare by using warm-up exercises immediately before entering the examination room. See page 6.

The Examination

Facility Exercise

Play a long note with full tone for a prescribed number of beats (6 – 12 at ♩ = 60).
The examiner will specify the note and the number of beats and will set the pulse.

Scales and Arpeggios (Chord Shapes)

(See Notes on Scales and Arpeggios page 198)

To be played from memory. All scales and arpeggios should be prepared with the
specifications listed in the grey box below. The examiner will request *one only* (e.g.
one rhythm *or* one articulation *or* one character) when requesting each
scale/arpeggio.

Range

Creative Exercise

Choose one of the scales or
arpeggios from the list for this
Grade and perform a creative
version using elements chosen
from the menu on page 205
and/or from the grey box for this
Grade.

Rhythms	♪s grouped in 3s or 4s as appropriate. i) straight; ii) medium swing
Dynamics	With a confident and consistent full tone
Tempi	♩ = 72+
Articulations	Scales i) tongued; ii) legato Swing ♫♫♩
Character	i) Latin 'feel'; ii) Rock groove; ii) like a ballad i.e melodic and sensitive

Candidates may notate their creative exercise and read from this or simply improvise
a version. In either case the same exercise should be performed twice so as to clarify
the musical intentions. Candidates will be rewarded for adventure and invention.

Note Centres

Candidates should prepare the following note centre: A (two octaves).

The following should be prepared:

- the major scale followed by the major seventh arpeggio
- the dorian scale followed by the minor seventh arpeggio
- the mixolydian scale followed by the dominant seventh arpeggio (starting and
  finishing on the note centre)
- the pentatonic major scale

Candidates may pause between pairs of scales and arpeggios.

Improvisation

Module 3, either A, B, or C (candidate's choice), from the GSMD publication *Jazz Improvisation*. See p.210 for details and for further useful publications.

Pieces

Play TWO pieces, one to be chosen from each list.

List A

(see General Notes p.210)

From the *Boosey Woodwind Method, clarinet book 1*   (B&H M060112904)

York/Marks ....Image, p. 60

From the *Boosey Woodwind Method, clarinet book 2*   (B&H M060112935)

Trad. ....Yellow Bird, p.19

Weiss & Shearing ..Lullaby of Birdland, p.27 [with CD track 28]

Carmichael, arr.
Long ....The Nearness of You (Blues for Clarinet)   (Wise/Music Sales AM952006)

Waller, arr.
Long ....Ain't Misbehavin' (Classic Jazz for Clarinet)   (Wise/Music Sales AM937046)

Howard, arr.
Long ....Fly me to the Moon (Classic Jazz for Clarinet)   (Wise/Music Sales AM937046)

Wilson, J..............Joe's New Words (Creative Variations Vol.1)   (Camden Music CM181)

Auric....................Where is your Heart (Play Cabaret B♭/E♭)   (Faber 0571510183)

Gershwin, arr.
Gout....................They can't take that away from me
                              (Play Gershwin B♭/E♭)   (Faber 0571517544)

List B

(see General Notes p.210)

From the *Boosey Woodwind Method, clarinet book 1*   (B&H M060112904)

Norton ....Club Soda, p.59 [clarinet 1 part]

From the *Boosey Woodwind Method, clarinet book 2*   (B&H M060112935)

Norton ....Crayfish, p.34 [clarinet 1 part]

Norton ....Cover Up, p.28

Norton ....Feeling Sunny, p.42 [clarinet 1 part]

Bennett ....The Hungry Blues *or* Nestor Leaps In (Jazz Club Clarinet)   (IMP 7531A)

Hamer..................Casa Mia [CD track 25] (Play it Cool)
[piano accompaniment also available]   (Spartan Press SP561)

Wilson, A..............Chicago Sidewalk *or* Las Vegas Casino
(American Jazz and More)   (Spartan Press SP568)

Miles....................Who's Got The Answer? (Creative Variations Vol.1)   (Camden Music CM181)

Wilson ....Helen (Girl Names)   (Camden Music CM063)

Norton ....Shoehorn Blues *or* Inter-city Stomp
(The Microjazz Clarinet Collection 2)   (B&H M060110610)

Norton ....It Takes Two (The Microjazz Clarinet Collection 1)   (B&H M060109096)

List C: Study

Play ONE study, to be chosen from the list below.

Lyons ....Ragtime, No.21 (Clarinet Studies)   (Useful Music U30)

Rae ....No.55 *or* No.56
(Progressive Jazz Studies for Clarinet Easy Level)   (Faber 057151359X)

Rae ....Passing Time *or* Forever
(40 Modern Studies for Solo Clarinet)   (Universal UE19735)

Wilson ....Minor Feel *or* Latin (Times Ten)   (Camden Music CM152)

Sight-reading (see p.209)

Aural Tests *or* Initiative Tests (see p.207)

Musicianship Questions (see p.208)

Grade 4

Warm-ups

Warm-ups do not form part of the examination, but it is highly recommended that candidates prepare by using warm-up exercises immediately before entering the examination room. See page 6.

The Examination

Facility Exercise

Play a long note *mf* for a prescribed number of beats (8 – 12 at ♩ = 60).
The examiner will specify the note and the number of beats and will set the pulse.

Scales and Arpeggios (Chord Shapes)

(See Notes on Scales and Arpeggios page 198)

To be played from memory. All scales and arpeggios should be prepared with the
specifications listed in the grey box below. The examiner will request *one only* (e.g.
one rhythm *or* one articulation *or* one character) when requesting each
scale/arpeggio.

Range

Creative Exercise

Choose one of the scales or
arpeggios from the list for this
Grade and perform a creative
version using elements chosen
from the menu on page 205
and/or from the grey box for this
Grade.

Rhythms	♪s grouped in 3s or 4s as appropriate. i) straight; ii) medium swing
Dynamics	Within the range *mp – f,* i) sustaining a level throughout; ii) cresc.; iii) decresc.
Tempi	♩ = 96+
Articulations	i) tongued; ii) legato Swing ♫ ♫♪
Character	i) Staccato and light; ii) Heavy and accented

Candidates may notate their creative exercise and read from this or simply improvise
a version. In either case the same exercise should be performed twice so as to clarify
the musical intentions. Candidates will be rewarded for adventure and invention.

Note Centres

Candidates should prepare the following note centre: C (two octaves except where
specified).

The following should be prepared:

- the major scale (extended down to lowest G of range) followed by the major
  seventh arpeggio
- the dorian scale followed by the minor seventh arpeggio
- the mixolydian scale followed by the dominant seventh arpeggio (starting and
  finishing on the note centre)
- the melodic *or* harmonic minor scale (candidate's choice) followed by the minor
  arpeggio with the major seventh

- the pentatonic major scale
- the chromatic scale

Candidates may pause between pairs of scales and arpeggios.

Improvisation

Module 4, either A, B, or C (candidate's choice), from the GSMD publication *Jazz Improvisation*. See p.210 for details and for further useful publications.

Pieces

Play TWO pieces, one to be chosen from each list.

List A

Williams, arr.
Long ....Basin Street Blues (Blues For Clarinet)   (Wise/Music Sales AM952006)

Monk, arr.
Long ....Blue Monk (Blues For Clarinet)   (Wise/Music Sales AM952006)

Carmichael, arr.
Long ....Lazy River (Classic Jazz For Clarinet)   (Wise/Music Sales AM937046)

Shearing, arr.
Long ....Lullaby of Birdland (Classic Jazz For Clarinet)   (Wise/Music Sales AM937046)

Wilson ....Hey Joe....Let's Meet (Creative Variations Vol.1)   (Camden Music CM181)

Porter..................Anything Goes (Play Cabaret B♭/E♭)   (Faber 0571510183)

Gershwin, arr.
Gout.....................Let's call the whole thing off (Play Gershwin B♭/E♭)   (Faber 0571517544)

List B

Miles...................Three Views of Orford (Creative Variations Vol.1)   (Camden Music CM181)

Wilson ....Emma (Girl Names)   (Camden Music CM063)

Martin ....A Touch of Blues (The Joy of Clarinet)   (Yorktown/Music Sales YK21038)

Pogson ....Jumping Jack (The Way to Rock)   (B&H M060087288)

Ledbury ....One Over the Eight (All Jazzed Up for Clarinet)   (Brass Wind 0303)

Sands ....Beginners Blues (Jazzy Clarinet 1)   (Universal UE 18826)

Norton ....Stick Together *or* Swing Out Sister
                              (The Microjazz Clarinet Collection 2)   (B&H M060110610)

Norton ....Show-Stopper (The Microjazz Clarinet Collection 1)   (B&H M060109096)

List C: Study

Play ONE study, to be chosen from the list below.

Lyons ....Calypso no.23 (Clarinet Studies) (Useful Music U30)

Rae ....No.57 *or* No.60
(Progressive Jazz Studies for Clarinet Easy Level) (Faber 057151359X)

Rae ....Tumbledown Blues *or* Ted's Shuffle
(40 Modern Studies for Solo Clarinet) (Universal UE19735)

Wilson ....Rock Lick's *or* Swing Waltz (Times Ten) (Camden Music CM152)

Sight-reading (see p.209)

Aural Tests *or* Initiative Tests (see p.207)

Musicianship Questions (see p.208)

Grade 5

Warm-ups

Warm-ups do not form part of the examination, but it is highly recommended that candidates prepare by using warm-up exercises immediately before entering the examination room. See page 6.

The Examination

Facility Exercise

Play a long note *mf* for a prescribed number of beats (8 – 12 at $\downarrow$ = 60).
The examiner will specify the note and the number of beats and will set the pulse.

Scales and Arpeggios (Chord Shapes)

(See Notes on Scales and Arpeggios p.198)

To be played from memory. All scales and arpeggios should be prepared with the specifications listed in the grey box on the following page. The examiner will request *one only* (e.g. one rhythm *or* one articulation *or* one character) when requesting each scale/arpeggio.

Range

Creative Exercise

Choose one of the scales or arpeggios from the list for this Grade and perform a creative version using elements chosen from the menu on page 205 and/or from the grey box for this Grade.

Rhythms	♪s grouped in 3s or 4s as appropriate. i) straight; ii) medium swing
Dynamics	Within the range *mp – f,* i) sustaining a level throughout; ii) cresc.; iii) decresc.
Tempi	♩= 96+
Articulations	i) tongued; ii) legato Swing ♫♫♪
Character	i) Earthy and soulful; ii) restrained and gentle

Candidates may notate their creative exercise and read from this or simply improvise a version. In either case the same exercise should be performed twice so as to clarify the musical intentions. Candidates will be rewarded for adventure and invention.

Note Centres

Candidates should prepare ONE of the following note centres: E (two octaves except where specified) *or* F (two octaves except where specified).

For the chosen note centre, the following should be prepared:

- the major scale (two and a half octaves) followed by the major seventh arpeggio
- the dorian scale followed by the minor seventh arpeggio
- the mixolydian scale followed by the dominant seventh arpeggio (starting and finishing on the note centre)
- the melodic *or* harmonic minor scale (candidate's choice) followed by the minor arpeggio with the major seventh
- the pentatonic major scale
- the pentatonic minor scale
- the blues scale
- the chromatic scale

Candidates may pause between pairs of scales and arpeggios.

Improvisation

Module 5, either A, B, or C (candidate's choice), from the GSMD publication *Jazz Improvisation*. See p.210 for details and for further useful publications.

Pieces

Play TWO pieces, one to be chosen from each list.

List A

Hagen, arr.
Long ....Harlem Nocturne (Blues for Clarinet)   (Wise/Music Sales AM952006)

Ellington, arr.
Long ....Prelude To A Kiss (Blues for Clarinet)   (Wise/Music Sales AM952006)

Brubeck, arr.
Long ....It's A Raggy Waltz
           (Classic Jazz for Clarinet)   (Wise/Music Sales AM937046)

Wilson ....Blues for Joseph (Creative Variations Vol.1)   (Camden Music CM181)

Desmond, arr.
Rae ....Take Five (Take Ten for Clarinet and Piano)   (Universal UE19736)

Ellington, arr.
Rae ....Sophisticated Lady (Take Ten for Clarinet and Piano)   (Universal UE19736)

Gershwin, arr.
Gout.....................Bess, you is my woman now (Play Gershwin B♭/E♭)   (Faber 0571517544)

List B

Miles ....Bathwater Blues (Creative Variations Vol.1)   (Camden Music CM181)

Pogson ....South Sea Bubble (Way To Rock)   (B&H M060087288)

Harvey.................Stomping Stella (Jazzy Clarinet 2)   (Universal UE19361)

Blackford, arr.
Power ....Jam Session (All That Jazz For Clarinet)   (Arrensdorff/Music Sales PM1942100)

Gorb.....................Side Street Blues (Up Front Album for Clarinet)   (Brass Wind 0306)

Gumbley...............Heading West (Cops, Caps and Cadillacs)   (Saxtet Publications 006)

Norton ....Hot Potato *or* Puppet Theatre
           (The Microjazz Clarinet Collection 2)   (B&H M060110610)

Wilson ....12 Bar *or* Swing 8 (Jazz Album)   (Camden Music CM097)

List C: Study

Play ONE study, to be chosen from the list below.

Lyons ....Swing Style No.36 (Clarinet Studies)   (Useful Music U30)

Holcombe..............Goin' To See The Man *or* Neon Nights
           (12 Intermediate Jazz Studies)   (Musicians Publications/Studio Music JE007)

Rae ....Flying Overland *or* Windy Ridge   (Universal UE19735)

Wilson ....Blue Funk *or* Sevenths in Swing (Times Ten)   (Camden Music CM152)

Rae ....No.58 *or* No.61 *or* No.62 *or* No.63
                    (Progressive Jazz Studies for B♭ Clarinet)   (Faber 057151359X)

Sight-reading (see p.209)

Aural Tests *or* Initiative Tests (see p.207)

Musicianship Questions (see p.208)

Grade 6

Warm-ups

Warm-ups do not form part of the examination, but it is highly recommended that candidates prepare by using warm-up exercises immediately before entering the examination room. See page 6.

The Examination

Facility Exercises

* Play a long note *mf* for a prescribed number of beats (4 – 10 at ♩ = 60).
  The examiner will specify the note and the number of beats and will set the pulse.
* Play a long note *f* for a prescribed number of beats (4 – 6 at ♩ = 60).
  The examiner will specify the note and the number of beats and will set the pulse.

Scales and Arpeggios (Chord Shapes)
(See Notes on Scales and Arpeggios p.198)

To be played from memory. All scales and arpeggios should be prepared with the specifications listed on the opposite page. The examiner will request *two only* (e.g. one rhythm *and* one dynamic *or* one articulation *and* one character) when requesting each scale/arpeggio.

Range

Creative Exercise

Choose one of the scales or
arpeggios from the list for this
Grade and perform a creative
version using elements chosen
from the menu on page 205
and/or from the grey box for this
Grade.

Candidates may notate their
creative exercise and read from
this or simply improvise a version. In either case the same exercise should be
performed twice so as to clarify the musical intentions. Candidates will be rewarded
for adventure and invention.

Rhythms	♪s grouped in 3s or 4s as appropriate. i) straight; ii) medium swing
Dynamics	Within the range *pp – ff,* i) sustaining a level throughout; ii) cresc.; iii) decresc.
Tempi	♩= 132+
Articulations	i) tongued; ii) legato Swing ♫♫♩
Character	Candidates to offer a selection of at least four of their own contrasting choices which reflect the jazz idiom, provided an explanation can be given.

Note Centres

Candidates should prepare the following note centres: G (two octaves, with major
scale two and a half octaves) *and* C♯/D♭ (two octaves, with major scale extended down
to lowest A♭ of range).

When the examiner names a note centre the candidate will play:

- the major scale followed by the major seventh arpeggio
- the dorian scale followed by the minor seventh arpeggio
- the mixolydian scale followed by the dominant seventh arpeggio (starting and
finishing on the note centre)
- the melodic minor scale
- the harmonic minor scale
- the minor arpeggio with the major seventh
- the blues scale
- the chromatic scale

Candidates may pause between pairs of scales and arpeggios.

Improvisation

Play once through then improvise two choruses of a modal tune, e.g., *Cantaloupe Island, Maiden Voyage, Impressions, Footprints, Little Sunflower, Milestones,* or a similar modal tune.

Or

Play once through then improvise two choruses of an original modally-based composition.

Candidates must provide a legible copy of the composition for the examiner's use.

Pieces

Play TWO pieces, one to be chosen from each list.

List A

Robin, arr.
Brown..................Love Is Just Around The Corner (Jazz Clarinet 1)   (IMP 09827)

Rodgers & Hart, arr.
Fairhead...............Blue Moon (Cascade Woodwind Series)   (Cascade CM10)

Wilson..................After Charlie…Joe (Creative Variations Vol.2)   (Camden Music CM182)

Joplin, arr.
Rae ....The Favorite (Five Scott Joplin Rags)   (Universal UE19661)

Gershwin, arr.
Brown..................Liza (Jazz Clarinet 1)   (IMP 09827)

Koffman, arr.
Ledbury ....Swinging Shepherd Blues (Jazzed Up Too for Clarinet)   (Brass Wind 1306)

Legrand, arr.
Coe.......................What are you doing for the rest of your life?
                              (Jazzed Up Too for Clarinet)   (Brass Wind 1307)

Trad., arr.
Power ....Bill Bailey (All That Jazz For Clarinet)   (Arrensdorff/Music Sales PM1942100)

List B

Miles....................Candlelight (Creative Variations Vol.2)   (Camden Music CM182)

Wilson.................Jazz Waltz (Jazz Album)   (Camden Music CM097)

Rae ....Situation Comedy (Take Ten for Clarinet and Piano)   (Universal UE19736)

Thompson.............Something Blue   (Studio Music 008200)

Harvey.................Wayward Waltz (Jazzy Clarinet 2)   (Universal UE19361)

Mower ....This Should Be Fun
　　　　　　　　(Not The Boring Stuff)　　　　　(Itchy Fingers Publications/B&H M708010296)

Vizzutti ....Nickle Blues *or* Bluebird *or* Havana
　　　　　　　　(Clarinet Play-a-long Jazz Solos)　　　　(De Haske 1001924)

List C: Study

Play ONE study, to be chosen from the list below.

Holcombe..............D Minor Etude, p.7 *or* D Major Etude, p.29
　　　　　　　　(24 Jazz Etudes For Clarinet)　　　(Musicians Publications/Studio Music JE013)

Lyons ....Swing Style, No.38 (Clarinet Studies)　　　　(Useful Music U30)

Rae ....Catch It *or* Dai's Surprise (40 Modern Studies)　　　(Universal UE19735)

Wilson ....No.2 (Three Jazz Studies)　　　　(Camden Music CM098)

Sight-reading (see p.209)

Aural Tests *or* Initiative Tests (see p.207)

Musicianship Questions (see p.208)

Grade 7

Warm-ups

Warm-ups do not form part of the examination, but it is highly recommended that
candidates prepare by using warm-up exercises immediately before entering the
examination room. See page 6.

The Examination

Facility Exercises

* Play a long note *p/mf* for a prescribed number of beats (4 – 12 at $\quarternote$ = 60).
  The examiner will specify the note and the dynamic, choose the number of beats
  and set the pulse.
* Play a long note *f* for a prescribed number of beats (4 – 8 at $\quarternote$ = 60).
  The examiner will specify the note and the number of beats and will set the pulse.

Scales and Arpeggios (Chord Shapes)
(See Notes on Scales and Arpeggios p.198)

To be played from memory. All scales and arpeggios should be prepared with the specifications listed in the grey box below. The examiner will request *two only* (e.g. one rhythm *and* one dynamic *or* one articulation *and* one character) when requesting each scale/arpeggio.

Range

Rhythms	♪s grouped in 3s or 4s as appropriate. i) straight; ii) medium swing
Dynamics	Within the range *pp – ff,* i) sustaining a level throughout; ii) cresc.; iii) decresc.
Tempi	♩= 132+
Articulations	i) tongued; ii) legato Swing ♫♫♪
Character	Candidates to offer a selection of at least four of their own contrasting choices which reflect the jazz idiom, provided an explanation can be given.

Creative Exercise
Choose one of the scales or arpeggios from the list for this Grade and perform a creative version using elements chosen from the menu on page 205 and/or from the grey box for this Grade.

Candidates may notate their creative exercise and read from this or simply improvise a version. In either case the same exercise should be performed twice so as to clarify the musical intentions. Candidates will be rewarded for adventure and invention.

Note Centres
Candidates should prepare the following note centres: F (three octaves) *and* B (two octaves, with major scale extended up to highest F♯ and down to lowest F♯).

When the examiner names a note centre the candidate will play:

- the major scale followed by the major seventh arpeggio
- the dorian scale followed by the minor seventh arpeggio
- the mixolydian scale followed by the dominant seventh arpeggio (starting and finishing on the note centre)
- the harmonic minor *or* melodic minor *or* jazz melodic minor *or* Spanish Phrygian minor scale (candidate's choice) followed by the minor arpeggio with the major seventh
- the blues scale
- the chromatic scale

Candidates may pause between pairs of scales and arpeggios.

The following should also be prepared:

- the whole tone scale, three octaves, starting on E
- the whole tone scale, three octaves, starting on F
- the augmented arpeggio, three octaves, starting on E
- the augmented arpeggio, three octaves, starting on F

Improvisation

Play once through then improvise two choruses of a blues-based tune, e.g., *Now's the Time, Billie's Bounce, Tenor Madness, Blue Monk, Watermelon Man, West Coast Blues,* or a similar blues-based tune.

Or

Play once through then improvise two choruses of an original blues-based composition.

Candidates must provide a legible copy of the composition for the examiner's use.

Pieces

Play TWO pieces, one to be chosen from each list.

List A

Gershwin, arr.
Fairhead...............Summertime (Cascade Woodwind Series)   (Cascade CM32)

Wilson..................Just a Ballad for Joseph (Creative Variations Vol.2)   (Camden Music CM182)

Goodman..............Tattletale *or* Flying Home *or* Grand Slam
                        (Benny Goodman Composer/Artist)   (Regent Music/Music Sales AM942337)

Trad., arr.
Brown..................Down by the Riverside (Jazz Clarinet 2)   (IMP 09973)

Stewart, arr.
Brown..................Morning Thunder (Jazz Clarinet 2)   (IMP 09973)

Gershwin, arr.
Brown..................S'Wonderful (Jazz Clarinet 2)   (IMP 09973)

Joplin, arr.
Rae......................Easy Winners (5 Scott Joplin Rags)   (Universal UE19661)

List B

Chapple ....No.1 *and* No.5 (A Bit Of A Blow)   (Bosworth/Music Sales BOE005035)

Templeton, arr.
Johnson ....Pocket-sized Sonata No.1, In Rhythm
                    (Encore: Emma Johnson)   (Chester CH61037)

Miles ....Sideways On (Creative Variations Vol.2)   (Camden Music CM182)

Wilson ....Bebop (Jazz Album)   (Camden Music CM097)

Coe ....La Colina del Tejon *or* Some Other Autumn
                    (Jazzed Up Too for Clarinet)   (Brass Wind 1307)

Thompson ....Boogie Bounce (Boogie and Blues)   (Studio Music 03290)

Harvey ....Teasing Tango (Jazzy Clarinet 2)   (Universal UE19361)

List C: Study

Play ONE study, to be chosen from the list below.

Holcombe ....G Minor Etude, p.9 *or* E♭ Minor Etude, P.19
                    or B Major Etude, p.20 *or* G♯ Minor Etude, p.21
                    (24 Jazz Etudes for Clarinet)   (Musicians Publications/Studio Music JE013)

Lyons ....Swing Style, No.42 (Clarinet Studies)   (Useful Music U30)

Rae ....Now Hear This! (40 Modern Studies)   (Universal UE19735)

Wilson ....No.1 (Three Jazz Studies)   (Camden Music CM098)

Sight-reading (see p.209)

Aural Tests *or* Initiative Tests (see p.207)

Musicianship Questions (see p.208)

Grade 8

Warm-ups

Warm-ups do not form part of the examination, but it is highly recommended that candidates prepare by using warm-up exercises immediately before entering the examination room. See page 6.

The Examination

Facility Exercises

- Play a long note *pp/p/mf* for a prescribed number of beats (4 – 16 at ♩ = 60).
  The examiner will specify the note and the dynamic, choose the number of beats and set the pulse.
- Play a long note *f* for a prescribed number of beats (4 – 10 at ♩ = 60).
  The examiner will specify the note and the number of beats and will set the pulse.

Scales and Arpeggios (Chord Shapes)

(See Notes on Scales and Arpeggios p.198)

To be played from memory. All scales and arpeggios should be prepared with the specifications listed in the grey box below. The examiner will request *two only* (e.g. one rhythm *and* one dynamic *or* one articulation *and* one character) when requesting each scale/arpeggio.

Range

Creative Exercise

Choose one of the scales or arpeggios from the list for this Grade and perform a creative version using elements chosen from the menu on page 205 and/or from the grey box for this Grade.

Candidates may notate their creative exercise and read from this or simply improvise a version. In either case the same exercise should be performed twice so as to clarify the musical intentions. Candidates will be rewarded for adventure and invention.

Rhythms	♪s grouped in 3s or 4s as appropriate. i) straight; ii) fast swing
Dynamics	Within the range *pp – ff*, i) sustaining a level throughout; ii) cresc.; iii) decresc.
Tempi	♩ = 132+
Articulations	i) tongued; ii) legato Swing ♫♫♪
Character	Candidates to offer a selection of at least four of their own contrasting choices which reflect the jazz idiom, provided an explanation can be given.

Note Centres

Candidates should prepare the following note centres:

E (three octaves, except where specified), A♭/G♯ (two octaves, except where specified, with major scale two and a half octaves) *and* C (two octaves, except where specified, with major scale two and a half octaves).

When the examiner names a note centre the candidate will play:

- the major scale followed by the major seventh arpeggio
- the dorian scale followed by the minor seventh arpeggio
- the mixolydian scale followed by the dominant seventh arpeggio (starting and finishing on the note centre)
- the harmonic minor *or* Spanish Phrygian minor scale (candidate's choice)
- the melodic minor *or* jazz melodic minor scale (candidate's choice)
- the minor arpeggio with the major seventh
- the blues scale
- the chromatic scale (starting on lowest note of range and extended to cover the whole range for this Grade)

Candidates may pause between pairs of scales and arpeggios.

The following should also be prepared:

- the whole tone scale, three octaves, starting on E
- the whole tone scale, three octaves, starting on F
- the augmented arpeggio, three octaves, starting on E
- the augmented arpeggio, three octaves, starting on F

Improvisation

Play once through then improvise two choruses of a 32-bar song form, e.g., *Autumn Leaves, Whisper Not, Fly me to the Moon, Take the A Train, Stella by Starlight*, or a similar 32-bar song form.

Or

Play once through then improvise two choruses of a 'rhythm changes' tune, e.g. *I've got Rhythm, Oleo, Anthropology, Moose the Mooche, Lester Leaps in*, or a similar 'rhythm changes' tune.

Or

Play once through then improvise two choruses of an original 32-bar song form or 'rhythm changes' composition.

Candidates must provide a legible copy of the composition for the examiner's use.

Pieces

Play TWO pieces, one to be chosen from each list.

List A

Wilson ....Funky Joe (Creative Variations Vol.2)　　　(Camden Music CM182)

Goodman ....Paganini Caprice *or* Slipped Disk *or* Mission To Moscow
　　　　　　　(Benny Goodman Composer/Artist)　　(Regent Music/Music Sales AM942337)

Gershwin, arr.
Brown ....The Man I Love, p.27 (Jazz Clarinet 2)　　　(IMP 09973)

Seitz, arr.
Brown ....The World Is Waiting For The Sunrise, p.36
　　　　　　　(Jazz Clarinet 2)　　　　　　　　　　　(IMP 09973)

Desenne, arr.
Fairhead ....Brigitte (Cascade Woodwind Series)　　　　(Cascade CM26)

List B

Chapple ....No.2 *and* No.3 (A Bit Of A Blow)　　(Bosworth/Music Sales BOE005035)

Miles ....Struttin' in the Barbican
　　　　　　　(Creative Variations Vol.2)　　　　　(Camden Music CM182)

Coe ....Blue September (Jazzed Up Too for Clarinet)　　(Brass Wind 1307)

Thompson ....Models in Blue (Boogie and Blues)　　　(Studio Music 03290)

Horovitz ....Sonatina for Clarinet and Piano, 3rd Movt: Con Brio　(Novello NOV120541)

List C: Study

Play ONE study, to be chosen from the list below.

Holcombe ....C Major Etude, p.2 *or* G♭ Major Etude, p.18
　　　　　　　or E Major Etude, p.22
　　　　　　　(24 Jazz Etudes for Clarinet)　　(Musicians Publications/Studio Music JE013)

Rae ....Blue Tarantella, No.8 (12 Modern Etudes)　　(Universal UE18790)

Harvey ....Any Etude from –
　　　　　　　(Three Etudes On Themes of Gershwin)　　(Emerson E177)

Wilson ....No.3 (Three Jazz Studies)　　　　　　(Camden Music CM098)

Sight-reading (see p.209)

Aural Tests *or* Initiative Tests (see p.207)

Musicianship Questions (see p.208)

SAXOPHONE

Grade 1

Warm-ups

Warm-ups do not form part of the examination, but it is highly recommended that candidates prepare by using warm-up exercises immediately before entering the examination room. See page 6.

The Examination

Facility Exercise

Play a long note with full tone for a prescribed number of beats (6 – 8 beats at $\downarrow$ = 60). The examiner will specify the note and the number of beats and will set the pulse.

Scales and Arpeggios

(See Notes on Scales and Arpeggios page 198)

To be played from memory. All scales and arpeggios should be prepared with the specifications listed in the grey box below. The examiner will request *one only* (e.g. one rhythm *or* one articulation *or* one character) when requesting each scale/arpeggio.

Range

Scales
G major (one octave)
G natural minor (one octave)

Arpeggios
G major (one octave)
G minor (one octave)

Rhythms	i) $\downarrow$ s grouped in 3s or 4s as appropriate. ii) As given in Ex.1 (see p.204) (scales only)
Dynamics	With a confident and consistent full tone
Tempi	$\downarrow$ = 56 – 62
Articulations	Scales i) tongued; ii) slurred; arpeggios tongued only
Character	i) Spiky and angry (when tongued) i) Smooth and calm (when slurred)

Alto/Baritone Pieces

Play TWO pieces, one to be chosen from each list.

List A

(see General Notes p.210)

From the *Boosey Woodwind Method, saxophone book 1*   (B&H M060112911)

Trad.....................Dona, dona, p.24

Barratt.................Centre Stage, p.24

Trad.....................Land of the Silver Birch, p.31

Wine &
Bayer Sager ....A Groovy Kind of Love, p.33

Brahms, arr.
Harle ....Sunday (Classical Album for Saxophone)   (Universal UE17772)

Byrd, arr.
Goldstein/Agay .....The Carman's Whistle
                (The Joy of Saxophone)   (Yorktown/Music SalesYK21541)

Denver, arr.
Lanning ....Annie's Song (Making the Grade, Grade 2)   (Chester/Music Sales CH60098)

Foster, arr.
De Smet ....Beautiful Dreamer   (De Haske WA6001)

Gretry, arr.
Wastall ....Air (Learn As You Play Saxophone)   (B&H M060063794)

Harris ....Champagne Jig
                (Seven Easy Dances for Saxophone and Piano)   (B&H M060071492)

Monckton, arr.
Davies & Harris...Come to the Ball
                (The Really Easy Saxophone Book)   (Faber 0571510361)

Harris ....Dance of the Clown
                (Seven Easy Dances for Saxophone and Piano)   (B&H M060071492)

Swann, arr.
Davies & Harris...The Hippopotamus
                (The Really Easy Saxophone Book)   (Faber 0571510361)

Harris ....Evening Mood
                (Seven Easy Dances for Saxophone and Piano)   (B&H M060071492)

Haydn, arr.
Harle ....Minuet (Classical Album for Saxophone)   (Universal UE17772)

Prichard, arr.
Lawton ....Hyfrodol (The Young Saxophone Player)   (OUP N7512)

Tchaikovsky, arr.
Harle ....Old French Song (Classical Album for Saxophone)   (Universal UE17772)

Trad., arr.
Isacoff...................Scarborough Fair *or* Amazing Grace
                        or Morning Has Broken
                        (Skill Builders for Alto Saxophone)   (Schirmer/Music Sales GS33481)

Trad., arr.
Goldstein/Agay .....Red River Valley (The Joy of Saxophone)   (Yorktown/Music Sales YK21541)

Trad., arr.
Lawton ....Drink To Me Only (The Young Saxophone Player)   (OUP N7512)

List B

(see General Notes p.210)

From the *Boosey Woodwind Method, saxophone book 1*   (B&H M060112911)

Trad.....................Kalinka, p.28

Naplan................Hine ma tov, p.35

Marks ....The Saxophone Rap, p.36

Trad.....................When the Saints Go Marching in, p.25

Beswick ....Farewell for a Fox (Six for Sax)   (Universal UE17973)

Cowles, arr.
Wastall ....Tri-Time (Learn As You Play Saxophone)   (B&H M060063749)

Dodgson ....Sledgehammer
                        (Up Front Album for B♭/E♭ Saxophone)   (Brass Wind 0307)

Gershwin, arr.
Harris ....Love Walked In (Easy Gershwin for Saxophone)   (OUP N6679)

Gorb....................Valentine (Up Front Album for B♭/E♭ Saxophone)   (Brass Wind 0307)

Hyde, arr.
Wastall ....Soliloquy (Learn As You Play Saxophone)   (B&H M060063794)

Lewin ....Heat Haze [with repeat]
                        (Up Front Album for B♭/E♭ Saxophone)   (Brass Wind 0307)

Lyons ....Rock Steady *or* Laura's Lament
                        (New Alto Sax Solos Bk.1)   (Useful Music U7)

Strauss, arr.
Goldstein/Agar .....Roses from the South
                        (The Joy of Saxophone)   (Yorktown/Music Sales YK21541)

Street ....Lazy Afternoon *or* Reflections *or* Attention Please!
      (Streetwise for Alto Sax and Piano)   (B&H M060079276)

Trad., arr.
Lanning ....Country Gardens
      (Making the Grade, Grade 1)   (Chester/Music Sales CH60080)

Soprano/Tenor Pieces

Play TWO pieces, one to be chosen from each list.

List A

Beethoven, arr.
Mason ....Theme from the Choral Symphony
       (Pop Go the Classics for Tenor Saxophone)   (Cramer 90480)

Brahms, arr.
Harle ....Sunday (Classical Album for Saxophone)   (Universal UE17772)

Cowles, arr.
Wastall ....Tri-Time (Learn As You Play Saxophone)   (B&H M060063794)

Haydn, arr.
Harle ....Minuet (Classical Album for Saxophone)   (Universal UE17772)

Hyde, arr.
Wastall ....Soliloquy (Learn As You Play Saxophone)   (B&H M060063794)

Schein, arr.
Both ....Allemande or Tripla
      (Classical Pieces for Tenor or Soprano Sax)   (Schott ED7330)

Tchaikovsky, arr.
Harle ....Old French Song (Classical Album for Saxophone)   (Universal UE17772)

List B

Dodgson ....Sledgehammer
      (Up Front Album for B♭/E♭ Saxophone)   (Brass Wind 0307)

Jackman ....Chinese Night Music or Honeysuckle Blues
      (Six Easy Pieces for B♭ Saxophone)   (Novello NOV120674)

Lewin ....Heat Haze [with repeat]
      (Up Front Album for B♭/E♭ Saxophone)   (Brass Wind 0307)

Lyons ....Wheels Within Wheels *or* Soft Song *or* Laura's
      Lament *or* Rock Steady (New Tenor Sax Solos Bk.1)   (Useful Music U9)

Mouret, arr.
Thompson ....Musette Vol.1
      (Dances from the French Operas for Tenor Sax)   (Studio Music 033363)

List C: Study

Play ONE study, to be chosen from the list below.

(see General Notes p.210)

From the *Boosey Woodwind Method, saxophone book 1*   (B&H M060112911)

Marks ....Wave Machine, p.34

Purcell.................Minuet, p.39

Bach, J.S., arr.
Wastall ....Chorale, p.19 (Learn As You Play Saxophone)   (B&H M060063794)

Chinese Trad., arr.
Harrison ....Bamboo Flute, No.25
                    (Amazing Studies for Saxophone)   (B&H M060103872)

Diabelli, arr.
Wastall ....Serenade, p.19 (Learn As You Play Saxophone)   (B&H M060063794)

Hampton..............Down the road, p.24 (Saxophone Basics)   (Faber 0571519725)

Hampton..............G force, p.27 (Saxophone Basics)   (Faber 0571519725)

Hampton..............Blue call, p.33 (Saxophone Basics)
                    [No repeats except D.C.]   (Faber 0571519725)

Garnier, ed. Davies
& Harris ....No.8 (80 Graded Studies for Saxophone Bk.1)   (Faber 0571510477)

Demnitz, ed. Davies
& Harris ....No.9 (80 Graded Studies for Saxophone Bk.1)   (Faber 0571510477)

Harris, ed. Davies
& Harris ....No.10 (80 Graded Studies for Saxophone Bk.1)   (Faber 0571510477)

Lacour.................No.1 (50 Etudes Faciles et Progressives Vol.1)   (Billaudot/UMP G15491B)

Gariboldi, arr.
Harle ....No.1 (Easy Classical Studies)   (Universal UE17770)

Sight-reading (see p.209)

Aural Tests *or* Initiative Tests (see p.207)

Musicianship Questions (see p.208)

Grade 2

Warm-ups

Warm-ups do not form part of the examination, but it is highly recommended that candidates prepare by using warm-up exercises immediately before entering the examination room. See page 6.

The Examination

Facility Exercises

- Play a long note with full tone for a prescribed number of beats (6 – 8 at ♩ = 60). The examiner will specify the note and the number of beats and will set the pulse.
- Articulation study

Scales and Arpeggios

(See Notes on Scales and Arpeggios page 198)

To be played from memory. All scales and arpeggios should be prepared with the specifications listed in the grey box below. The examiner will request *one only* (e.g. one rhythm *or* one articulation *or* one character) when requesting each scale/arpeggio.

Range

Note Centres

Candidates should prepare the following note centre: D (two octaves).

Rhythms	i) ♪s grouped in 3s or 4s as appropriate. ii) As given in example below (scales only)
Dynamics	With a confident and consistent full tone
Tempi	♩ = 56 – 62
Articulations	Scales i) tongued; ii) slurred; arpeggios tongued only
Character	i) Happy and bright ii) Sad and dragging

The following should be prepared:

- the major scale
- the major arpeggio
- the natural minor scale
- the minor arpeggio
- the dorian scale

Candidates may pause between individual scales and arpeggios.

Alto/Baritone Pieces

Play TWO pieces, one to be chosen from each list.

List A

(see General Notes p.210)

From the *Boosey Woodwind Method, saxophone book 1*   (B&H M060112911)

Oliviero................I'll Set my Love to Music, p.48 [saxophone 1 part]

Trad......................I Love My Love, p.62 [saxophone 1 part]

Jenkins ....Cantilena, p.46

Trad......................Scarborough Fair, p.47

From the *Boosey Woodwind Method, saxophone book 2*   (B&H M060112942)

Trad......................On the Waves of Lake Balaton, p.8

Norton ....Off the Rails, p.11 [saxophone 1 part, with CD track 9 *or* 10]

Trad......................Dance of Displeasure, p.14

Bach, J.S., arr.
Rae ....Minuet in G
                    (Take Ten for Alto Saxophone and Piano)   (Universal UE18836)

Beethoven, arr.
Cowles ....Shepherd's Hymn (Ten Easy Tunes for Sax and Piano)   (De Haske F462)

Byrd, arr.
Harvey.................Pavane for the Earl of Salisbury
        (Saxophone Solos Vol.1, Alto)   (Chester/Music Sales CH55120)

Delangle...............No.16 *and* No.17 (Premier Voyage Vol.1)   (Lemoine/UMP 25046)

Elgar, arr.
Lanning...............Pomp and Circumstance March No.1
        (The Classic Experience)   (Cramer 90524)

Haydn, arr.
Harle ....Allemande (Classical Album for Saxophone)   (Universal UE17772)

McLean, arr.
Lanning...............Vincent (Making the Grade, Grade 2)   (Chester/Music Sales CH60098)

Purcell, arr.
Rae ....Air (Take Ten for Alto Saxophone and Piano)   (Universal UE18836)

Ribault.................Barcarolle   (Martin/UMP 2208)

Tchaikovsky, arr.
Harle ....Chanson Triste (Classical Album for Saxophone)   (Universal UE17772)

Trad., arr.
Lanning...............Greensleeves *or* The Gift to be Simple *or* Skye Boat Song
        (Making the Grade, Grade 2)   (Chester/Music Sales CH60098)

List B

(see General Notes p.210)

From the *Boosey Woodwind Method, saxophone book 1*   (B&H M060112911)

attrib. Henry VIII,
arr. Barratt.............Hélas madame, p.55 [top part, with sax duet part *or* CD track 84]

Trad......................Athol Highlanders' Jig, p.56

Trad.....................Dodi Li, p.58 [with CD track 90]

From the *Boosey Woodwind Method, saxophone book 2*   (B&H M060112942)

Gervaise...............Pavan, p.6 *or* Galliard, p.7

Marks ....Long Shadows, p.10

Norton ....Regretfully Yours, p.10

De Smet ....Dixie   (De Haske WA6015)

Dodgson ....Meadowsweet
        (Up Front Album for B♭/E♭ Saxophone)   (Brass Wind 0307)

Foster ....Old Folks at Home
(Elementary Solos for Alto Saxophone)   (Frederick Harris / Elkin)

Gershwin, arr.
Harris ....Love is Here to Stay (Easy Gershwin for Saxophone)   (OUP N6679)

Isacoff...................Turkey in the Straw [with repeats]
(Skill Builders for Alto Saxophone)   (Schirmer/Music Sales GS33481)

Ledbury ....Takin' it Easy (All Jazzed Up for Alto Saxophone)   (Brass Wind 0302)

Norton ....Young at Heart
(The Microjazz Alto Saxophone Collection 2)   (B&H M060110566)

Offenbach, arr.
Both ....Barcarolle (Classical Pieces for Alto Saxophone)   (Schott ED7331)

Schubert, arr.
Goldstein/Agay .....The Trout (The Joy of Saxophone)   (Yorktown/Music Sales YK21541)

Street ....Let's Get Away [with repeat]
(Streetwise for Alto Saxophone and Piano)   (B&H M060079276)

Wastall ....Midnight in Tobago (Learn As You Play Saxophone)   (B&H M060063794)

Soprano/Tenor Pieces

Play TWO pieces, one to be chosen from each list.

List A

Couperin, arr.
Both ....Gavotte (Classical Pieces for Tenor or Soprano Sax)   (Schott ED7330)

Haydn, arr.
Harle ....Allemande or Minuet
(Classical Album for Saxophone)   (Universal UE17772)

Lully ....Sarabande et Gavotte
(Les Classiques des Saxophones Si♭, No.115)   (Leduc/UMP AL25145)

Mozart.................Menuet from Divertissement
(Les Classiques des Saxophones Si♭, No.116)   (Leduc/UMP AL25146)

Offenbach, arr.
Both ....Barcarolle (Classical Pieces for Tenor or Soprano Sax)   (Schott ED7330)

Tchaikovsky, arr.
Harle ....Chanson Triste *or* Old French Song
(Classical Album for Saxophone)   (Universal UE17772)

List B

Bazelaire, arr.
Londeix ....Chanson d'Alsace (Suite Francaise)   (Schott SF9261)

Fauré, arr.
Siebert ....Pavane (Classical Album for B♭ Instruments Bk.2)   (Studio Music 036548)

Hanmer ....Aria 1, No.2 *or* Preludio, No.1
(Saxophone Sample for B♭ Saxophone)   (Studio Music 000003)

Jackman ....Hint of Boogie (Six Easy Pieces for B♭ Saxophone)   (Novello NOV120674)

Trad., arr.
Both ....The Londonderry Air
(Classical Pieces for Tenor or Soprano Sax)   (Schott ED7330)

Wastall ....Midnight in Tobago (Learn As You Play Saxophone)   (B&H M060063794)

List C: Study

Play ONE study, to be chosen from the list below.

(see General Notes p.210)

From the *Boosey Woodwind Method, saxophone book 1*   (B&H M060112911)

Morgan ....Imaginary Dancer, p.45

Marks ....Upstairs, Downstairs, p.42

Marks ....Step by Step, p.41

From the *Boosey Woodwind Method, saxophone book 2*   (B&H M060112942)

Trad. ....Ghana Alleluia, p.17 [play one of the three 'Calls' (candidate's choice), followed by the top part of the 'Response']

Anon., arr.
Harrison ....Medieval Dance Tune, No.13
(Amazing Studies for Saxophone)   (B&H M060103872)

Baermann, ed.
Davies & Harris...No.12 *or* No.17
(80 Graded Studies for Saxophone Bk.1)   (Faber 0571510477)

Chedeville, arr.
Wastall ....Gavotte, p.33 (Learn As You Play Saxophone)   (B&H M060063794)

Trad., arr.
Hampton ....Greensleeves, p.35 (Saxophone Basics)   (Faber 0571519725)

Lacour.................No.2 *or* No.3
          (50 Etudes Faciles et Progressives Vol.1)   (Billaudot/UMP G15491B)

Popp, arr.
Harle ....No.10 *or* No.24
          (Easy Classical Studies for Saxophone)   (Universal UE17770)

Trad., arr.
Lawrence ....The Ash Grove (Winners Galore for Saxophone)   (Brass Wind 0316)

Sight-reading (see p.209)

Aural Tests *or* Initiative Tests (see p.207)

Musicianship Questions (see p.208)

Grade 3

Warm-ups

Warm-ups do not form part of the examination, but it is highly recommended that candidates prepare by using warm-up exercises immediately before entering the examination room. See page 6.

The Examination

Facility Exercises

*   Play a long note with full tone for prescribed number of beats (6 – 12 at $\quarternote$ = 60).
    The examiner will specify the note and the number of beats and will set the pulse.
*   Articulation study

Scales and Arpeggios

(See Notes on Scales and Arpeggios page 198)

To be played from memory. All scales should be prepared with the specifications listed in the grey box below. The examiner will request *one only* (e.g. one rhythm *or* one articulation *or* one character) when requesting each scale/arpeggio.

Range

Rhythms	i) ♪ s grouped in 3s or 4s as appropriate; ii) As given in Ex.2 (see p.204) (major and minor scales only)
Dynamics	With a confident and consistent full tone
Tempi	♩ = 56 – 62
Articulations	i) Tongued; ii) slurred
Character	i) Vivace; ii) Pesante; iii) Dolce; iv) Maestoso sostenuto

Note Centres

Candidates should prepare the following note centre: A (a twelfth, except where specified).

The following should be prepared:

* the major scale
* the major arpeggio
* the natural minor scale
* the minor arpeggio
* the pentatonic major scale (one octave)
* the whole tone scale (one octave)
* the chromatic scale (one octave)

Candidates may pause between individual scales and arpeggios.

Alto/Baritone Pieces

Play TWO pieces, one to be chosen from each list.

List A

(see General Notes p.210)
From the *Boosey Woodwind Method, saxophone book 1*   (B&H M060112911)
York & Marks.......Image, p.60
From the *Boosey Woodwind Method, saxophone book 2*   (B&H M060112942)
Marks ....Tiger Leap, p.26
Trad.....................Jewish Wedding Song, p.48
Stadler..................Marcia di Camelo, p.52
Trad.....................Lannigan's Ball, p.16 [with CD track 18]
Trad.....................The College Hornpipe, p.49

Bach, J.S., arr.
Lawton ....Bist Du Bei Mir? (The Young Saxophone Player)   (OUP N7512)

Dvořák, arr.
Lanning...............Largo from *The New World Symphony*
(The Classic Experience)   (Cramer 90524)

Fauré, arr.
Cowles ....Pavane (10 Easy Tunes for Saxophone and Piano)   (De Haske F462)

Gershwin, arr.
Gout....................Summertime (Play Gershwin B♭/E♭)   (Faber 0571517552)

Handel, arr.
Harle ....Bourée (Classical Album for Saxophone)   (Universal UE17772)

Haydn, arr.
Harle ....Serenade (Classical Album for Saxophone)   (Universal UE17772)

Ilyinsky, arr.
Wastall ....Berceuse (First Repertoire Pieces for Alto Saxophone) (B&H M060071454)

Joplin, arr.
Lanning...............The Entertainer
(Making the Grade, Grade 3)   (Chester/Music Sales CH60106)

Rimsky-Korsakov,
arr. Cowles ....Scheherezade (10 Easy Tunes for Saxophone and Piano) (De Haske F462)

Rubenstein, arr.
Wastall ....Melody (First Repertoire Pieces for Alto Saxophone)   (B&H M060071454)

Schubert, arr.
Wastall ....Serenade
(First Repertoire Pieces for Alto Saxophone)   (B&H M060071454)

Schumann, arr.
Brodie ....Träumerei (Elementary Solos for Alto Saxophone)   (Frederick Harris / Elkin)

Wystraete..............Alphonic   (Leduc/UMP AL27127)

List B

(see General Notes p.210)

From the *Boosey Woodwind Method, saxophone book 1*   (B&H M060112911)

Barratt ....Quirk, p.60 [either part, with *either* the sax duet part *or* CD
                                accompaniment]

Norton ....Club Soda, p.59 [saxophone 1 part]

From the *Boosey Woodwind Method, saxophone book 2*   (B&H M060112942)

Trad. ....A Hero's Farewell, p.28

Jenkins ....La la la koora, p.41 [with CD track 47]

Weiss &
Shearing...............Lullaby of Birdland, p.27 [with CD track 29]

Barratt ....Italian Connection, p.15

Bernstein, arr.
Lanning ....America [with repeat]
                                (Making the Grade, Grade 3)   (Chester/Music Sales CH60106)

Beswick ....Song for a Scarecrow (Six for Sax)   (Universal UE17973)

Bizet, arr.
De Smet ....Toreador's Song   (De Haske WA6016)

Finzi, arr.
Wastall ....Carol (Learn As You Play Saxophone)   (B&H M060063794)

Harris, arr.
Wastall ....Foxtrot from *Seven Easy Dances*
                                (First Repertoire Pieces for Alto Saxophone)   (B&H M060071454)

Hazell ....Ho-Hoe-Down
                                (Up Front Album for B♭/E♭ Saxophone)   (Brass Wind 0307)

Lennon/McCartney,
arr. Lanning........Yesterday (Making the Grade, Grade 3)   (Chester/Music Sales CH60106)

Norton ....Latin (The Microjazz Alto Saxophone Collection 2)   (B&H M060110566)

Satie, arr.
Rae ....Gnossienne, No.3 (Erik Satie Album for Alto Sax)   (Universal UE18508L)

Street ....By The Lake (Streets Ahead)   (Saxtet Publications 008)

Trad., arr.
Lanning ....El Condor Pasa (If I Could)
                                (Making the Grade, Grade 3)   (Chester/Music Sales CH60106)

Soprano/Tenor Pieces

Play TWO pieces, one to be chosen from each list.

List A

Bach, arr.
Rascher ....Gavotte (Gavotte and Bourrée)   (Maecenas FDS00168)

Bach, arr.
Londeix ....Scherzetto
              (Les Classiques des Saxophones Si♭, No.111)   (Leduc/UMP AL25141)

De Fesch, arr.
Kalman ....Canzonetta   (Spratt/Elkin)

Gershwin ....Summertime (Play Gershwin B♭/E♭)   (Faber 0571517552)

Handel, arr.
Harle ....Bourée (Classical Album for Saxophone)   (Universal UE17772)

Haydn, arr.
Harle ....Serenade (Classical Album for Saxophone)   (Universal UE17772)

Illyinsky, arr.
Wastall ....Berceuse
              (First Repertoire Pieces for Tenor Saxophone)   (B&H M060071522)

Leclair.................Musette (Les Classiques des Saxophones Si♭, No.76)   (Leduc/UMP AL19757)

Schubert, arr.
Wastall ....Serenade
              (First Repertoire Pieces for Tenor Saxophone)   (B&H M060071522)

List B

Bach, arr.
Both ....Air (Classical Pieces for Tenor or Soprano Saxophone)   (Schott ED7330)

Finzi, arr.
Wastall ....Carol (Learn As You Play Saxophone)   (B&H M060063794)

Hanmer...............Aria II, No.4 *or* Valse, No.3
              (Saxophone Samples for B♭ Saxophones)   (Studio Music 000003)

Harris, arr.
Wastall ....Foxtrot from *Seven Easy Dances*
              (First Repertoire Pieces for Tenor Saxophone)   (B&H M060071522)

Rodney Bennett,
arr. Harle ....Tender is the Night
              (Nicole's Theme) (Encore!)   (Chester/Music Sales CH61090)

Rubenstein, arr.
Both ....Melodie
              (Classical Pieces for Tenor or Soprano Saxophone)   (Schott ED7330)

List C: Study

Play ONE study, to be chosen from the list below.

(see General Notes p.210)

From the *Boosey Woodwind Method, saxophone book 2*   (B&H M060112942)

Barratt.................Sit up and Beg!, p.35

Barratt.................Bird of Paradise, p.40

Trad......................The Parsons Farewell, p.38

Marks ....Flying Away, p.16

Marks ....Chromatic Cheesecake, p.26

Anon., arr.
Harrison ....Song, No.17 (Amazing Studies for Saxophone)   (B&H M060103872)

Bach, J.S., arr.
Harrison ....Bourrée, No.15 (Amazing Studies for Saxophone)   (B&H M060103872)

Briard, arr.
Westall..................Study No.1, p.42 (Learn As You Play Saxophone)   (B&H M060063794)

Briard, arr.
Westall..................Study No.3, p.50 (Learn As You Play Saxophone)   (B&H M060063794)

Fenwick, arr.
Harrison ....The Flower Among Them All, No.47 [no repeat]
                   (Amazing Studies for Saxophone)   (B&H M060103872)

Garnier, ed.
Davies & Harris...No.21 (80 Graded Studies for Saxophone Bk.1)   (Faber 0571510477)

Hampton..............Tell me about it, p.46 (Saxophone Basics)   (Faber 0571519725)

Hampton..............I'm late for school!, p.48 [with repeat]
                   (Saxophone Basics)   (Faber 0571519725)

Kohler, arr.
Harle ....No.20 *or* No. 26
                   (Easy Classical Studies for Saxophone)   (Universal UE17770)

Lacour..................No.9 *or* No.19
                   (50 Etudes Faciles et Progressives Vol.1)   (Billaudot/UMP G15491B)

Lacour..................No.11 (50 Etudes Faciles et Progressives Vol.1)   (Billaudot/UMP G15491B)

Sight-reading (see p.209)

Aural Tests *or* **Initiative Tests** (see p.207)

Musicianship Questions (see p.208)

Grade 4

Warm-ups

Warm-ups do not form part of the examination, but it is highly recommended that candidates prepare by using warm-up exercises immediately before entering the examination room. See page 6.

The Examination

Facility Exercises

- Play a long note *mf* for a prescribed number of beats (8 – 12 at ♩ = 60).
  The examiner will specify the note and the number of beats and will set the pulse.
- Tone study

Scales and Arpeggios

(See Notes on Scales and Arpeggios page 198)

To be played from memory. All scales should be prepared with the specifications listed in the grey box on the following page. The examiner will request *one only* (e.g. one rhythm *or* one articulation *or* one character) when requesting each scale/arpeggio.

Range

Note Centres

Candidates should prepare the following note centre: C (two octaves).

The following should be prepared:

- the major scale
- the major arpeggio
- the natural minor scale
- the melodic minor scale
- the minor arpeggio
- the pentatonic major scale
- the whole tone scale
- the chromatic scale

Rhythms	i) ♪s grouped in 3s or 4s as appropriate; ii) as given in Ex.3 (see p.204) (major and minor scales only); Candidates may if they wish devise their own rhythms for pentatonic, whole tone and chromatic scales.
Dynamics	Within the range *mp – f*, i) sustaining a level throughout; ii) cresc.; iii) decresc.
Tempi	Scales: ♩= 72 – 84 Arpeggios: ♩= 60 – 66
Articulations	i) tongued; ii) slurred
Character	i) Staccato and light; ii) Heavy and accented; iii) Douce et très passioné

Candidates may pause between individual scales and arpeggios.

Pieces

Play TWO pieces, one to be chosen from List A and one from List B.

List A (Alto/Baritone)

Bach, arr.
Wastall ....Musette (First Repertoire Pieces for Alto Saxophone)   (B&H M060071454)

Bach, arr.
Lawton ....Sicilienne (The Young Saxophone Player)   (OUP N7512)

Blyton, arr.
Harvey.................In Memoriam Scott Fitzgerald
                     (Saxophone Solos Vol.1, Alto)   (Chester/Music Sales CH55120)

Chopin, arr.
Goldstein/Agay .....Nocturne (The Joy of the Saxophone)   (Yorktown/Music Sales YK21541)

Dvořák, arr.
Teal......................Romantic Piece
                     (Solos for the Alto Saxophone Player)   (Schirmer/Music Sales GS33058)

Elgar, arr.
Lawton ....Variation IX (Nimrod) (An Elgar Saxophone Album) (Novello NOV120742)

Handel, arr.
Rae ....Siciliana and Allegro
(Take Ten for Alto Saxophone and Piano) (Universal UE18836)

Lesieur ....Rondo (Prelude and Rondo) (Billaudot/UMP MRB1037)

Maltby, arr.
Wastall ....Heather on the Hill
(First Repertoire Pieces for Alto Saxophone) (B&H M060071454)

Mussorgsky, arr.
Harvey.................The Old Castle (Saxophone Solos Vol.1, Alto) (Chester/Music Sales CH55120)

Mozart, arr.
Harle ....Minuet and Trio (Classical Album for Saxophone) (Universal UE17772)

Puccini, arr.
Lanning ....Nessun Dorma (The Classic Experience) (Cramer 90524)

Rachmaninov, arr.
Harle ....Romance (John Harle's Saxophone Album) (B&H M060069572)

Satie, arr.
Harle ....Je te Veux (Encore!) (Chester/Music Sales CH61090)

Telemann, arr.
Londeix ....Sonata in C Minor, 1st Movt: Siciliana – Andante (Leduc/UMP AL25008)

Trad., arr.
Cowles ....The Harmonious Blacksmith
(10 Easy Tunes for Saxophone and Piano) (De Haske F462)

List B (Alto/Baritone)

Benjamin, arr.
Wastall ....Jamaican Rumba (Learn As You Play Saxophone) (B&H M060063794)

Blemant, arr.
Wastall ....Petit Jeu (First Repertoire Pieces for Alto Saxophone) (B&H M060071454)

Debussy, arr.
Rae ....Jimbo's Lullaby or Le Petit Negre or Petite Piece
(Debussy Saxophone Album) (Universal UE17777)

Gorb.....................Habenera (Up Front Album for B♭/E♭ Saxophone) (Brass Wind 0307)

Gregson ....Stepping Out Towards the Blue Horizon
(Up Front Album for B♭/E♭ Saxophone) (Brass Wind 0307)

Heath ....Reflections (Studio Music 03326-4)

Lyons ....Morning Glory or Set Free (New Alto Sax Solos Bk.2) (Useful Music U8)

Norton ....Elegance
(The Microjazz Alto Saxophone Collection 2) (B&H M060110566)

Rossignol ....Manege (Billaudot/UMP 4434)

Street ....Cruisin' (Streets Ahead) (Saxtet Publications 008)

List A (Soprano/Tenor)

Bach, arr.
Leonard................Sonata in E♭, 2nd Movt: Siciliano (Presser PR2237)

Bach, arr.
Wastall ....Musette
  (First Repertoire Pieces for Tenor Saxophone) (B&H M060071522)

Corelli, arr.
Both ....Pastorale
  (Classical Pieces for Tenor or Soprano Saxophone) (Schott ED7330)

Cowles, arr.
Harvey.................Bala Ballade (Saxophone Solos Vol.2, Tenor) (Chester/Music Sales CH55208)

Dowland, arr.
Harle ....Flow My Tears (Lachrimae) (Encore!) (Chester/Music Sales CH61090)

Dvořák, arr.
Stent ....Larghetto (Simply Sax for Tenor) (De Haske F488)

Elgar, arr.
Lawton ....Variation IX (Nimrod) (An Elgar Saxophone Album) (Novello NOV120742)

Maltby, arr.
Wastall ....Heather on the Hill
  (First Repertoire Pieces for Tenor Saxophone) (B&H M060071522)

Mozart, arr.
Harle ....Minuet and Trio (Classical Album for Saxophone) (Universal UE17772)

Rameau, arr.
Mule ....Tambourin (Les Classiques du Saxophone No.81) (Leduc/UMP AL19765)

Telemann, arr.
Londeix................Sonata in C Minor, 1st Movt: Siciliana – Andante (Leduc/UMP AL25864)

List B (Soprano/Tenor)

Beethoven, arr.
Teal.......................Scherzo
  (Solos for the Tenor Saxophone Player) (Schirmer/Music SalesGS33057)

Benjamin, arr.
Wastall ....Jamaican Rumba (Learn As You Play Saxophone) (B&H M060063794)

Blemant, arr.
Wastall ....Petit Jeu
  (First Repertoire Pieces for Tenor Saxophone) (B&H M060071522)

Blyton, arr.
Harvey.................Mock Joplin (Saxophone Solos Vol. 1, Tenor) (Chester/Music Sales CH55207)

Borodin ....Polovtsian Dance for B♭ Saxophone (Rubank 04476699)

Gregson ....Stepping Out Towards the Blue Horizon
(Up Front Album for B♭/E♭ Saxophone)   (Brass Wind 0307)

Ibert......................Melopee   (Lemoine/UMP 2444)

Lyons ....Morning Glory *or* Set Free
(New Tenor Sax Solos Vol.2)   (Useful Music U10)

Mozart, arr.
Both ....Divertimento No.12
(Classical Pieces for Tenor or Soprano Saxophone)   (Schott ED7330)

Norton ....Pulling No Punches (Microjazz for Tenor Saxophone) (B&H M060085635)

List C: Study

Play ONE study, to be chosen from the list below.

Anon., arr.
Harrison ....La Rotta, No.14 (Amazing Studies for Saxophone)   (B&H M060103872)

Baermann, ed.
Davies & Harris...No.32 (80 Graded Studies for Saxophone Bk.1)   (Faber 0571510477)

Gariboldi, arr.
Harle ....No.42 (Easy Classical Studies for Saxophone)   (Universal UE17770)

Harrison, arr.
Harrison ....Calypso Collapso, No.19
(Amazing Studies for Saxophone)   (B&H M060103872)

Haydn, arr.
Harrison ....Allegro, No.46 (Amazing Studies for Saxophone)   (B&H M060103872)

Lacour...................No.18 *or* No.23
(50 Etudes Faciles et Progressives Vol.1)   (Billaudot/UMP G15491B)

Rae ....Turn About, No.1
(20 Modern Studies for Solo Saxophone)   (Universal UE18820)

Street ....A Little Piece, No.4 (Street Beats)   (Saxtet Publications 120)

Van Eyck, arr.
Harrison ....Malle Symen, No.39
(Amazing Studies for Saxophone)   (B&H M060103872)

Sight-reading (see p.209)

Aural Tests *or* Initiative Tests (see p.207)

Musicianship Questions (see p.208)

Grade 5

Warm-ups

Warm-ups do not form part of the examination, but it is highly recommended that candidates prepare by using warm-up exercises immediately before entering the examination room. See page 6.

The Examination

Facility Exercises

- Play a long note *mf* for a prescribed number of beats (8 – 12 at ♩ = 60).
  The examiner will specify the note and the number of beats and will set the pulse.

- Breath support/tone/dynamic control study

Scales and Arpeggios

(See Notes on Scales and Arpeggios page 198)

To be played from memory. All scales and arpeggios should be prepared with the specifications listed in the grey box on the following page. The examiner will request *one only* (i.e. one rhythm *or* one articulation *or* one character) when requesting each scale/arpeggio.

Range

Note Centres

Candidates should prepare ONE of the following note centres: E (two octaves) *or* F (two octaves).

For the chosen note centre, the following should be prepared:

- the major scale
- the major arpeggio
- the natural minor scale
- the melodic minor scale
- the harmonic minor scale
- the minor arpeggio
- the pentatonic major scale
- the whole tone scale
- the chromatic scale
- the blues scale

Rhythms	i) ♪s grouped in 3s or 4s as appropriate; ii) as given in Ex.3 (see p.204) (major and minor scales only); iii) as given in Ex.4 (see p.204) (major and minor scales only); Candidates may if they wish devise their own rhythms for pentatonic, whole tone, chromatic and blues scales.
Dynamics	Within the range *mp – f*, i) sustaining a level throughout; ii) cresc.; iii) decresc.
Tempi	Scales: ♩= 72 – 84 Arpeggios: ♩= 60 – 66
Articulations	i) tongued; ii) slurred
Character	i) Sehr ruhig; ii) Rasch und feuerig; iii) Trotzig; iv) Lebhaft und mit Wut.

Candidates may pause between individual scales and arpeggios.

Pieces

Play TWO pieces, one to be chosen from List A and one from List B.

List A (Alto/Baritone)

Bach, arr.
Mule ....Badinerie (Les Classiques du Saxophone No.1)   (Leduc/UMP AL19511)

Beethoven, arr.
Mule ....Petit Valse (Les Classiques du Saxophone No.2)   (Leduc/UMP AL19512)

Bizet, arr.
Harvey.................L'Arlesienne (Saxophone Solos Vol.1, Alto)   (Chester/Music Sales CH55120)

Debussy, arr.
Rae ....The Little Shepherd *or* Golliwog's Cakewalk *or* Le Fille aux Cheveux de Lin (Debussy Saxophone Album)   (Universal UE17777)

Dowland, arr.
Harle ....Flow My Tears (Lachrimae) (Encore!)   (Chester/Music Sales CH61090)

Elgar, arr.
Lawton ....Salut d'Amour (An Elgar Saxophone Album)   (Novello NOV120742)

Gates ....Wonderland (Mood Music)   (Camden Music CM061)

Mendelssohn, arr.
Mule ....Chanson de Printemps
                    (Les Classiques du Saxophone No.7)   (Leduc/UMP AL19752)

Telemann, arr.
Londeix ....Sonata in C Minor, 3rd Movt:
                    Andante *and* 4th Movt: Vivace   (Leduc/UMP AL25008)

Wolf-Ferrari, arr.
Wastall ....Strimpellata
                    (First Repertoire Pieces for Alto Saxophone)   (B&H M060071454)

List B (Alto/Baritone)

Albéniz, arr.
Staber ....Tango   (Schott BSS33749)

Braga ....La Serenata   (Durand/UMP 1203300)

Cowles ....King Arthur and Sir Lancelot *or* Guinevere
                    (The Legends of Avalon)   (Ricordi LD929)

Crepin ....Celine Mandarine   (Lemoine/UMP 25244)

Damase ....Note a Note   (Billaudot/UMP 4950B)

Dvořák, arr.
Teal ....Larghetto
                    (Solos for the Alto Saxophone Player)   (Schirmer/Music Sales GS33058)

Harvey, arr.
Harvey ....Caprice Anglaise
                    (Saxophone Solos Vol. 2, Alto)   (Chester/Music Sales CH55121)

Lantier ....Sicilienne   (Leduc/UMP AL20261)

Lyons ....Butterfly Waltz (New Alto Sax Solos Bk.2)   (Useful Music U8)

Lyons ....Uncle Samba (New Alto Sax Solos Bk.3)   (Useful Music U26)

Norton ....Set Piece
                    (The Microjazz Alto Saxophone Collection 2)   (B&H M060110566)

Prokofiev, arr.
Maganini ....Kije's Wedding
                    (Lieutenant Kije Suite) [E♭ Edition]   (Musicus/Schauer M695)

Street ....All Because of You   (Saxtet Publications 001)

List A (Soprano/Tenor)

Bach, J.S., arr.
Teal......................Bourrée I and II
(Solos for the Tenor Saxophone Player) (Schirmer/Music Sales GS33057)

Bazelaire, arr.
Londeix................Suite Francaise, 1st Movt: Bourrée d'Auvergne (Schott SF9261)

Bouillon, arr.
Wastall.................Valse-Fantasie
(First Repertoire Pieces for Tenor Saxophone) (B&H M060071522)

Dvořák, arr.
Teal......................Lament
(Solos for the Tenor Saxophone Player) (Schirmer/Music Sales GS33057)

Elgar, arr.
Lawton.................Salut D'Amour (An Elgar Saxophone Album) (Novello NOV120742)

Gounod, arr.
Stent....................The Entry of the Nubian Slaves *or*
Moderato Con Moto (Simply Sax for Tenor) (De Haske F488)

Granados, arr.
Harvey.................Andaluza (Saxophone Solos Vol.1, Tenor) (Chester/Music Sales CH55207)

Machaut, arr.
Harle...................Qui n'Aroit Autre Deport (Encore!) (Chester/Music Sales CH61090)

Mendelssohn, arr.
Mule....................Chanson de Printemps
(Les Classiques du Saxophone No.7) (Leduc/UMP AL19752)

Telemann, arr.
Loudeix................Sonata in C Minor, 3rd Movt:
Andante *and* 4th Movt: Vivace (Leduc/UMP AL25864)

Wolf-Ferrari, arr.
Wastall.................Strimpellata
(First Repertoire Pieces for Tenor Saxophone) (B&H M060071522)

List B (Soprano/Tenor)

Bariller................Fan Jazz (Leduc/UMP AL23209)

Cowles................King Arthur and Sir Lancelot *or* Guinevere
(The Legends of Avalon) (Ricordi LD929)

Fiocco, arr.
Frackenpohl..........Aria and Rondo (Kendor/Elkin)

Gurewich, arr.
Wastall.................Czardas
(First Repertoire Pieces for Tenor Saxophone) (B&H M060071522)

Hanmer................Finale, No.5
                  (Saxophone Samples for B♭ Saxophone)   (Studio Music 000003)

Lyons ....Butterfly Waltz (New Tenor Sax Solos Bk.2)   (Useful Music U10)

Lyons ....Uncle Samba (New Tenor Sax Solos Bk.3)   (Useful Music U27)

Norton ....Puppet Theatre (Microjazz for Tenor Saxophone)   (B&H M060085635)

Norton ....Hot Potato (Microjazz for Tenor Saxophone)   (B&H M060085635)

Nyman, arr.
Harle & Davies ....Lost and Found (Encore!)   (Chester/Music Sales CH61090)

Rodney Bennett,
arr. Harle ....Tender is the Night
                  (Rosemary's Waltz) (Encore!)   (Chester/Music Sales CH61090)

Schumann, arr.
Teal......................Romance
                  (Solos for the Tenor Saxophone Player)   (Schirmer/Music Sales GS33057)

Street ....All Because of You   (Saxtet Publications 001)

Strimer................Serenade [tenor saxophone only]   (Leduc/UMP AL18118)

List C: Study

Play ONE study, to be chosen from the list below.

Anon, arr.
Harrison ....Trotto, No.51 (Amazing Studies for Saxophone)   (B&H M060103872)

Bach, J.S., arr.
Harrison ....Gigue, No.16 (Amazing Studies for Saxophone)   (B&H M060103872)

Gariboldi, arr.
Harrison ....Study, No.11 (Amazing Studies for Saxophone)   (B&H M060103827)

Gariboldi, arr.
Harle ....No.55 (Easy Classical Studies for Saxophone)   (Universal UE17770)

Baermann, ed.
Davies &
Harris ....No.38 (80 Graded Studies for Saxophone Bk.1)   (Faber 0571510477)

Harris, ed.
Davies & Harris...No.44 (80 Graded Studies for Saxophone Bk.1)   (Faber 0571510477)

Lacour..................No.26 (50 Etudes Faciles et Progressives Vol.2) (Billaudot/UMP G15492B)

Lacour..................No.29 (50 Etudes Faciles et Progressives Vol.2) (Billaudot/UMP G15492B)

Lacour..................No.30 (50 Etudes Faciles et Progressives Vol.2) (Billaudot/UMP G15492B)

Presser..................Sad Song, No.V (Eight Brevities)   (Tenuto 49401723)

Presser..................Waltz, No.VIII (Eight Brevities)   (Tenuto 49401723)

Sight-reading (see p.209)

Aural Tests *or* Initiative Tests (see p.207)

Musicianship Questions (see p.208)

Grade 6

Warm-ups

Warm-ups do not form part of the examination, but it is highly recommended that candidates prepare by using warm-up exercises immediately before entering the examination room. See page 6.

The Examination

Facility Exercises

- Play a long note *mf* for a prescribed number of beats (4 – 10 at ♩ = 60).
  The examiner will specify the note and the number of beats and will set the pulse.
- Play a long note *f* for a prescribed number of beats (4 – 6 at ♩ = 60).
  The examiner will specify the note and the number of beats and will set the pulse.
- Tone study

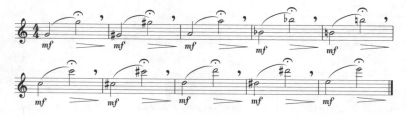

Scales and Arpeggios

(See Notes on Scales and Arpeggios page 198)

To be played from memory. All scales and arpeggios should be prepared with the specifications listed in the grey box below. The examiner will request *two only* (e.g. one rhythm *and* one dynamic *or* one articulation *and* one character) when requesting each scale/exercise.

Range

Note Centres

Candidates should prepare ONE of the following groups of note centres:

i) C (two octaves) *and* G (one octave);

ii) C (two octaves) *and* A (one octave).

For the chosen note centres, the following should be prepared:

- the scale/arpeggio exercise on p.203 (C note centre only)
- the pentatonic major scale
- the whole tone scale
- the blues scale

Candidates may pause between individual scales and arpeggios.

Rhythms	Scale/arpeggio exercise as written; other scales ♪ s grouped in 3s or 4s as appropriate; Candidates may if they wish devise their own rhythms for pentatonic, whole tone and blues scales.
Dynamics	Within the range *pp – ff*, i) sustaining a level throughout; ii) cresc. throughout each scale/arpeggio; iii) decresc. throughout each scale/arpeggio
Tempi	♩ = 94+
Articulations	i) tongued; ii) slurred Candidates may if they wish offer additional articulation patterns of their own.
Character	Candidates to offer a selection of at least four of their own contrasting choices which may include familiar Italian/German terms of expression or terms from any other language provided an explanation can be given.

Pieces

Play TWO pieces, one to be chosen from List A and one from List B.

List A (Alto/Baritone)

Bizet ....Intermezzo, No. 3 (Minuetto)
(Les Soli de L'Arlesienne) (Choudens/UMP AC20036)

Casinière ....Ronde (Les Contemporains Écrivent Vol.2) (Billaudot/UMP 6183)

Couperin, arr.
Mule ....Musette de Taverny (Pieces Classiques Célèbres) (Leduc/UMP AL25707)

Debussy, arr.
Rae ....Arabesque, No.1 (Debussy Saxophone Album) (Universal UE17777)

Elgar, arr.
Lawton ....Chanson de Matin *or* Chanson de Nuit
(An Elgar Saxophone Album) (Novello NOV120742)

Handel, arr.
Mule ....Sonata No. 6, Op.1/15, 1st Movt: Adagio *and* 2nd Movt: Allegro
(Les Classiques du Saxophone No.90) (Leduc/UMP AL20830)

Koechlin ....Etude No.5 (15 Etudes pour Saxophone Alto et Piano) (EFM/UMP 1008)

Koechlin ....Etude No.11 (15 Etudes pour Saxophone Alto et Piano) (EFM/UMP 1008)

Mozart, arr.
Teal......................Minuet (Solos for the Alto Saxophone Player) (Schirmer/Music Sales GS33058)

Planel...................Chanson Triste (Suite Romantique) (Leduc/UMP AL20248)

Rachmaninov,
arr. Harle ....Vocalise (John Harle's Sax Album) (B&H M060069572)

Vaughan Williams,
arr. Harvey ....Dance of Job's Comforters
(Saxophone Solos Vol. 2, Alto) (Chester/Music Sales CH55121)

Albinoni, arr.
Kynaston ....Concerto in D Minor, Op.9, No.2, 1st Movt:
Allegro e non presto *or* 3rd Movt: Allegro (Advance/Studio Music 07042)

Vaughan
Williams...............Six Studies in English Folk-Song,
No. 5 and No.6 or No.4 and No.6 (Stainer & Bell H173)

Ravel, arr.
Viard....................Pièce en Forme de Habanera [E♭ Edition] (Leduc/UMP AL17680)

List B (Alto/Baritone)

Binge ....Concerto for Alto Saxophone,
2nd Movt: Romance (Weinberger/Elkin JW062)

Bozza...................Aria (Leduc/UMP AL19714)

Carpenter, arr.
Harle ....Chorinho Carinhoso (John Harle's Sax Album) (B&H M060069572)

Cowles ....Across the Waters (The Legends of Avalon) (Ricordi LD929)

Delibes, arr.
Harvey.................Barcarolle (Saxophone Solos Vol.1, Alto) (Chester/Music Sales CH55120)

Dukas ....Alla Gitana (Leduc/UMP AL19995)

Ibert, arr.
Mule ....Le Petit Ane Blanc (Leduc/UMP AL19847)

Jacques ....Rondino (Ricordi LD802)

Krein .... Serenade   (New Wind Music Co./Emerson NWM103)

Lyons .... The Quick Brown Fox (New Alto Sax Solos Bk.2)   (Useful Music U8)

Trainer .... Bicycle Kicks (Unbeaten Tracks)   (Faber 0571518648)

Sondheim, arr.
Bennett .... Night Waltz, No.1 *or* You Must Meet My Wife, No.3
                 (Three Sondheim Waltzes)   (Novello NOV120799)

Cowles .... Scherzino   (Studio Music 033295)

Bullard .... Agile Blues, No.3
                 (Three Blues for Alto Sax and Piano)   (Harlequin Music 19701)

Ullrich .... Rondó Furlán   (Trio/Harlequin Music HK050)

List A (Soprano/Tenor)

Bach, arr.
Both, ... Sinfonia in B♭, 2nd Movt: Andante *and* 3rd Movt: Presto
                 (Classical Pieces for Tenor or Soprano Saxophone)   (Schott ED7331)

Clerisse .... Prelude and Divertissement   (Billaudot/UMP AF0049)

Cowan .... Shadows   (B&H M051680405)

Debussy, arr.
Teal .... Sarabande
                 (Solos for the Tenor Saxophone Player)   (Schirmer/Music Sales GS33057)

Elgar, arr.
Lawton .... Chanson de Matin *or* Chanson de Nuit
                 (An Elgar Saxophone Album)   (Novello NOV120742)

Fiocco, arr.
Harvey .... Arioso (Saxophone Solos Vol 2, Tenor)   (Chester/Music Sales CH55208)

German, arr.
Voxham .... Pastorale and Bourrée   (Rubank 04477543)

Gretry/Bazelaire ... Suite Rococo, 1st Movt: Chasse *or* 2nd Movt:
                 Ariete *or* 4th Movt: Tambourin   (Schott SF9259)

Handel, arr.
Londeix .... Sonata No. 1, 1st Movt: Adagio *and* 2nd Movt: Allegro
                 (Les Classiques des Saxophones Si♭ No.113)   (Leduc/UMP AL25143)

Ravel, arr.
Harvey .... Bolero (Saxophone Solos Vol.2, Tenor)   (Chester/Music Sales CH55208)

Ravel, arr.
Viard .... Piece en Forme de Habanera [B♭ Edition]   (Leduc/UMP AL17679)

Saint-Saens, arr.
Teal......................Allegro Apassionato
(Solos for the Tenor Saxophone Player)   (Schirmer/Music Sales GS33057)

Singelee ....Adagio et Rondo Op.63   (Roncorp USA/Emerson)

Tchaikovsky, arr.
Teal......................Sleigh Ride
(Solos for the Tenor Saxophone Player)   (Schirmer/Music Sales GS33057)

Albinoni, arr.
Kynaston ....Concerto in D Minor, Op.9, No.2, 1st Movt:
Allegro e non presto *or* 3rd Movt: Allegro   (Advance/Studio Music 07041)

Mendelssohn, arr.
Teal......................Song Without Words
(Solos for the Tenor Saxophone)   (Schirmer/Music Sales GS33057)

List B (Soprano/Tenor)

Cowles ....Across the Waters (The Legends of Avalon)   (Ricordi LD929)

Cowles, arr.
Harvey.................Bala Breeze and Bala Bounce
(Saxophone Solos Vol. 2, Tenor)   (Chester/Music Sales CH55208)

Granados, arr.
Amaz ....Rondalla Aragonesa (Danza Espanola)   (UME/Music Sales UME21472: Archive)

Joplin, arr.
Ferguson/
Wehage .... Palm Leaf Rag   (Lemoine/UMP 25143)

Lyons ....The Quick Brown Fox (New Tenor Sax Solos Bk.2)   (Useful Music U10)

Meriot.................Grisaille   (Combre/UMP C5027)

Moszkowski, arr.
Teal......................Spanish Dance
(Solos for the Tenor Saxophone Player)   (Schirmer/Music Sales GS33057)

Norton ....Riff Laden *and* Slow Boogie
(Microjazz for Tenor Saxophone)   (B&H M060085635)

Schmitt.................Song de Coppelius   (Lemoine/UMP 24443)

Tomasi ....Chant Corse   (Leduc/UMP AL18132)

Wilson ....Tango in D   (Camden Music CM065)

Bennett, arr.
Harle & Davies ....Rosemary's Waltz from
Tender is the Night (Encore!)   (Chester/Music Sales CH61090)

Nyman, arr.
Harle & Davies ....Lost and Found (Encore!)   (Chester/Music Sales CH61090)

Turnage ....Elegy No.2, 3rd Movt (Two Elegies Framing a Shout)   (Schott ED12492)

Cowan ....Shadows   (B&H M051680405)

Granados, arr.
Teal......................Playera (Solos for the Tenor Sax Player)   (Schirmer/Music Sales GS33057)

List C: Study

Play ONE study, to be chosen from the list below.

Ferling, arr.
Mule ....No. 18 (48 Etudes d'Après Ferling)   (Leduc/UMP AL20402)

Gariboldi, arr.
Harle ....No. 65 (Easy Classical Studies for Saxophone)   (Universal UEI7770)

Gariboldi, arr.
Harle ....No.66 (Easy Classical Studies for Saxophone)   (Universal UEI7770)

Lacour...................No. 33 (50 Etudes Faciles et Progressives Vol.2)   (Billaudot/UMP G15492B)

Mazas, arr.
Davies &
Harris ....No. 64 (80 Graded Studies for Saxophone Bk.2)   (Faber 0571510485)

Pietzsch, arr.
Harle ....No. 67 (Easy Classical Studies for Saxophone)   (Universal UE17770)

Rae ....Latin Jive, No.10 (20 Modern Studies for Saxophone) (Universal UEI8820)

Street ....Spic and Spanish, No. 5 (Street Beats)   (Saxtet Publications 120)

Street ....Like it or Not?, No.6 (Street Beats)   (Saxtet Publications 120)

Rae ....Staccato Prelude, No.4 *or* If Only....., No.7
      (12 Modern Etudes)   (Universal UE18795)

Dubois ....Sarabande (Suite Française)   (Leduc/UMP AL23138)

Lyons ....No.21 (24 Melodic Studies)   (Useful Music U55)

Allen ....No.16 (Saxophone Studio)   (Hunt Edition HE40)

Sight-reading (see p.209)

Aural Tests *or* Initiative Tests (see p.207)

Musicianship Questions (see p.208)

Grade 7

Warm-ups

Warm-ups do not form part of the examination, but it is highly recommended that candidates prepare by using warm-up exercises immediately before entering the examination room. See page 6.

The Examination

Facility Exercises

- Play a long note *p/mf* for a prescribed number of beats (4 – 12 at ♩ = 60). The examiner will specify the note and the dynamic, choose the number of beats and will set the pulse.
- Play a long note *f* for a prescribed number of beats (4 – 8 at ♩ = 60). The examiner will specify the note and the number of beats and will set the pulse.
- Tone study

Hold each note for 8 – 12 beats.

Pause for a similar amount of time between notes.

Whilst playing, aim for a constant airstream and a controlled embouchure.

Each note should have a constant dynamic and a constant pitch.

Scales and Arpeggios

(See Notes on Scales and Arpeggios page 198)

To be played from memory. All scales and arpeggios should be prepared with the specifications listed in the grey box on the opposite page. The examiner will request *two only* (e.g. one rhythm *and* one dynamic *or* one articulation *and* one character) when requesting each scale/exercise.

Range

Note Centres

Candidates should prepare the following note centres: D, F, E, and B♭ (all two octaves).

When the examiner names a note centre the candidate will play:

- scale/arpeggio exercise on p.203
- the whole tone scale
- the diminished scales (both forms)
- the blues scale

Candidates may pause between individual scales and arpeggios.

Rhythms	Scale/arpeggio exercise as written; other scales ♪s grouped in 3s or 4s as appropriate; Candidates may if they wish devise their own rhythms for whole tone, diminished and blues scales.
Dynamics	Within the range *pp – ff,* i) sustaining a level throughout; ii) cresc. throughout each scale/arpeggio; iii) decresc. throughout each scale/arpeggio
Tempi	♩= 94+
Articulations	i) tongued; ii) slurred Candidates may if they wish offer additional articulation patterns of their own.
Character	Candidates to offer a selection of at least four of their own contrasting choices which may include familiar Italian/German terms of expression or terms from any other language provided an explanation can be given.

Pieces

Play TWO pieces, one to be chosen from List A and one from List B.

List A (Alto/Baritone)

Bach, arr.
Mule ....Sonata No. 6, 2nd Movt: Allegro *and* 3rd Movt:
             Siciliano (Les Classiques des Saxophones, No.92)   (Leduc/UMP AL20832)

Berthelot...............Adage et Arabesque   (Leduc/UMP AL24562)

Debussy, arr.
Rae ....Danse Bohemienne (Debussy Saxophone Album)   (Universal UE17777)

Eccles ....Sonata in G Minor
             [any *two* contrasting movements]   (Elkan-Vogel/UMP 16400047)

Gallois-
Montbrun ....Lied, No.4 *and* Finale, No.6
             (Six Pièces Musicales d'Etude)   (Leduc/UMP AL21131)

Handel, arr.
Mule ....Sonata No.1 (Op. 1, No.1a), 1st Movt:
             Grave *and* 2nd Movt: Allegro   (Leduc/UMP20827)

Haydn, arr.
Teal......................Gypsy Rondo
               (Solos for the Alto Saxophone Player)   (Schirmer/Music Sales GS33058)

Jacob ....Variations on a Dorian Theme   (Emerson E5)

Joly ....Cantilene et Danse   (Leduc/UMP AL20698)

Koechlin ....Etude No.1 *or* Etude No.13
               (15 Etudes pour Saxophone Alto et Piano)   (EFM/UMP 1008)

Vinci, arr.
Harle ....Adagio and Allegro (John Harle's Sax Album)   (B&H M060069572)

Bach, arr.
Kynaston ....Sonata No.6, 1st Movt: Allegro ma non troppo
               or 2nd Movt: Allegro (Classics for Saxophone)   (Advance/Studio Music 07044)

Handel, arr.
Mule ....Allegro, Largo and Final
               (Les Classiques des Saxophones, No.95)   (Leduc/UMP AL20835)

Pierné ....Canzonetta   (Leduc/UMP AL18879)

Wiedoeft ....Valse Vanite   (Hunt Edition HE33)

List B (Alto/Baritone)

Beaucamp ....Tarentelle   (Leduc/UMP AL20466)

Binge ....Concerto for Alto Saxophone, 1st Movt: Allegro
               spiritoso *or* 3rd Movt: Rondo – Allegro giocoso   (Weinberger/Elkin JW062)

Bonneau ....Suite, Danse des Demons *and* Plainte   (Leduc/UMP AL20303)

Casterede ....Pastorale   (Leduc/UMP AL26092)

Cowles, arr.
Harvey.................Tolmer's Village (Saxophone Solos Vol.2, Alto) (Chester/Music Sales CH55121)

Frackenpohl ....Dorian Elegy   (Kendor/Elkin KD11310)

Maurice...............Tableaux de Provence, La Bohemienne
               and des Alyscamps l'Ame Soupire   (Lemoine/UMP 23953)

Planel...................Suite Romantique, Danseuses   (Leduc/UMP AL20247)

Richardson ....No.1 (Three Pieces Op.22)   (Emerson E68b)

Wilson.................Day for Baritone or Alto Saxophone and Piano   (Camden Music CM062)

Albeniz, I, arr.
Bayer ....Puerta de Tierra (Bolero)   (UME/Music Sales UME21434: Archive)

Johnson ....Nightsong for Alto Sax and Orchestra
               (Alto Sax and Piano Reduction)   (Schirmer/Music Sales GS82586)

Bennett ....Three Piece Suite for Alto Sax and Piano,
               1st Movt: Samba Triste *or* 3rd Movt: Finale   (Novello NOV120804)

Daneels ....Aria et Valse Jazz   (Schott Frères SF9412)

Jacob ....Variations on a Dorian Theme   (Emerson E5)

Wilson ....Day for Baritone or Alto Sax and Piano)   (Camden Music CM062)

Nelson ....Sonata for Alto Sax and Piano,
                          2nd Movt: Largo   (Advance/Studio Music 07037A)

List A (Soprano/Tenor)

Bach, J.S. ....Sonata in E♭, 1st Movt:Allegro
                          moderato *and* 2nd Movt: Siciliano   (Presser PR2237)

Bonnard ....Sonata, 2nd Movt: Recitativo and Scherzo   (Billaudot/UMP 1703)

Fiocco/
Bazelaire ....Concerto, 3rd Movt: Lent et Très
                          expressif *and* 4th Movt: Très animé   (Schott SF9260)

Handel ....Sonata in G Minor Op1/6, 1st Movt:
                          Larghetto *and* 2nd Movt: Allegro
                          (Les Classiques des Saxophones Si♭ No.114)   (Leduc/UMP AL25144)

Harvey ....Contest Solo No.1   (Studio Music 033998)

Marcello, arr.
Joosen ....Concerto in C Minor, 2nd Movt:
                          Adagio *and* 3rd Movt: Adagio   (Molenaar/Elkin MN167)

Singelee ....4th Solo de Concert   (Molenaar/Elkin MN169)

Teleman, arr.
Voxman ....Sonata in C Minor [elaborated version],
                          any two contrasting movements   (Rubank 04471910)

Bach, arr.
Kynaston ....Sonata No.6, 1st Movt: Allegro ma non troppo
                          or 2nd Movt: Allegro (Classics for Saxophone)   (Advance/Studio Music 07043)

Bach, arr.
Nichols ....Sonata da Gamba No.2 in D,
                          1st Movt: Adagio *and* 2nd Movt: Allegro   (Saxtet Publications 014)

Singelee ....Caprice Op.80   (Roncorp USA/Emerson)

Albéniz, arr.
Amaz ....Mallorca *or* Puerta de Tierra (Bolero)   (UME/Music Sales 22468)

Brahms, arr.
Teal......................Hungarian Dance No.1
                          (Solos for the Tenor Saxophone Player)   (Schirmer/Music Sales GS33057)

List B (Soprano/Tenor)

Boccherini, arr.
Mule ....Adagio (Les Classiques des Saxophones Si♭ No.72)   (Leduc/UMP AL19758)

Hartley.................Poem for Tenor Saxophone and Piano   (Tenuto 49400049)

Harvey.................Rue Maurice-Berteau
(Saxophone Solos Vol.2, Tenor)   (Chester/Music Sales CH55208)

Joplin, arr.
Ferguson/
Wehage.................Elite Syncopations   (Lemoine/UMP 25143)

Lacour..................Belle Epoque (Evocation)   (Billaudot/UMP 4249)

Norton ....Home Blues *and* Rolling Stock
(Microjazz for Tenor Saxophone)   (B&H M060085635)

Gould ....Diversions for Tenor Sax and Orchestra, 2nd Movt:
Serenades and Airs *or* 4th Movt: Ballads and Lovenotes
(Tenor Sax and Piano Reduction)   (Schirmer/Music Sales GS82055)

Smith ....Sonata No.1, Hall of Mirrors, 4th Movt: Hologram   (Camden Music CM117)

Heath...................Gentle Dreams *and* Shiraz
(The Gerard McChrystal Saxophone Series)   (Camden Music CM115)

List C: Study

Play ONE study, one to be chosen from the list below.

Bach, arr.
Londeix.................Suite No.1, 2nd Movt: Allemande   (UMP)

Cowles ....Capriccio (My Love's an Arbutus)   (Studio Music 033455)

Cowles ....I Will Give My Love an Apple   (Studio Music 033479)

Cowles ....My Love She's but a Lassie Yet [with repeat]   (Studio Music 033486)

Ferling, arr.
Mule ....No.9 *and* No.10 (48 Etudes d' Apres Ferling)   (Leduc/UMP AL20402)

Ferling, arr.
Mule ....No.21 *and* No.22 (48 Etudes d' Apres Ferling)   (Leduc/UMP AL20402)

Harle ....No.76 *and* No.77
(Easy Classical Studies for Saxophone)   (Universal UE17770)

Harris ....No.72 (80 Graded Studies for Saxophone Bk.2)   (Faber 0571510485)

Harris ....No.73 (80 Graded Studies for Saxophone Bk.2)   (Faber 0571510485)

Lacour..................No.38 *and* No.40
(50 Etudes Faciles et Progressives Vol.2)   (Billaudot/UMP G15492B)

Morland...............Prelude *and* Burlesque II
          (Recitatives for Solo Saxophone)   (Broadbent & Dun 11210)

Street ....Reel Time, No.7 [no repeats, DC only]
          and Party Time, No.10 (Street Beats)   (Saxtet Publications 120)

Wilson ....Monody for Solo Saxophone   (Camden Music CM099)

Rae ....Point to Point, No.5 *or* Neat!,
          No.8 (12 Modern Etudes)   (Universal UE18795)

Dubois ....First Gavotte (Suite Française)   (Leduc/UMP AL23138)

Lyons ....No.23 (24 Melodic Studies)   (Useful Music U55)

Allen ....No.19 *and* No.21 (Saxophone Studio)   (Hunt Edition HE40)

Sight-reading (see p.209)

Aural Tests *or* Initiative Tests (see p.207)

Musicianship Questions (see p.208)

Grade 8

Warm-ups

Warm-ups do not form part of the examination, but it is highly recommended that candidates prepare by using warm-up exercises immediately before entering the examination room. See page 6.

The Examination

Facility Exercises

- Play a long note *pp/p/mf* for a prescribed number of beats (4 – 16 at ♩ = 60). The examiner will specify the note and the dynamic, choose the number of beats and set the pulse.
- Play a long note *f* for a prescribed number of beats (4 – 10 at ♩ = 60). The examiner will specify the note and the number of beats and will set the pulse.
- Dynamic control study

Play a long note for approximately 20 seconds. The note will be specified by the examiner.
Start with breath only, then make a smooth transition from breath to note (*ppp*).

Make a smooth increase in dynamic, to arrive at *fff* after approx. 10 seconds, then a controlled diminuendo to *ppp*.

End the note by smoothly changing back to breath only.

The embouchure should be controlled throughout – firm, but relaxed.

The diaphragm should work harder at a quieter dynamic.

Pitch should remain constant.

• Semitones exercise

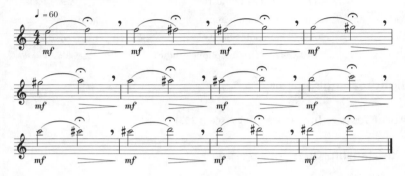

Scales and Arpeggios

(See Notes on Scales and Arpeggios page 198)

To be played from memory. All scales and arpeggios should be prepared with the specifications listed in the grey box on the opposite page. The examiner will request *two only* (e.g. one rhythm *and* one dynamic *or* one articulation *and* one character) when requesting each scale/exercise.

Range

Note Centres

Candidates should prepare the following note centres: B (two octaves, except where specified), C♯ (two octaves, except where specified), E♭ (two octaves, except where specified) *and* A♭ (one octave).

When the examiner names a note centre the candidate will play:

- the scale/arpeggio exercise on p.203 (except A♭ note centre)
- the whole tone scale
- the diminished scales (both forms)
- the blues scale
- the crabwise major scale (one octave, starting either on the note centre or on C – candidate's choice)

Rhythms	Scale/arpeggio exercise as written; crabwise as written (see p.199); other scales ♪ s grouped in 3s or 4s as appropriate; Candidates may if they wish devise their own rhythms for whole tone, diminished and blues scales.
Dynamics	Within the range *pp – ff,* i) sustaining a level throughout; ii) cresc. throughout each scale/arpeggio; iii) decresc. throughout each scale/arpeggio
Tempi	♩ = 94+
Articulations	i) Tongued; ii) slurred Candidates may if they wish offer additional articulation patterns of their own.
Character	Candidates to offer a selection of at least four of their own contrasting choices which may include familiar Italian/German terms of expression or terms from any other language provided an explanation can be given.

N.B. When the A♭ note centre is requested, the candidate should play the crabwise scale starting on C.

Candidates may pause between individual scales and arpeggios.

Pieces

Play TWO pieces, one to be chosen from List A and one from List B.

List A (Alto/Baritone)

Bach, J.S.,
arr.Mule...............Sonata No.4, 1st Movt: Andante – Presto *and* 2nd Movt: Allegro
(Les Classiques des Saxophones No.91)   (Leduc/UMP AL20831)

Bach, J.S., arr.
Harle ....Sonata in G Minor [any *two* contrasting movements]   (Universal UE17774)

Bedard ....Sonata, 1st Movt *and* 2nd Movt   (Doberman/Spanish Guitar Centre DO85)

Gallois-
Montbrun ....Six Pièces Musicales d'Etude,
             1st Movt: Ballade *and* 3rd Movt: Ronde   (Leduc/UMP AL21131)

Handel, arr.
Harvey................Allegro (Saxophone Solos Vol.2, Alto)   (Chester/Music Sales CH55121)

Jacob ....Miscellanies   (Emerson E66)

Jacob ....Rhapsody for Cor Anglais or Sax [complete]   (Stainer & Bell H187)

Koechlin ....Etude No.9 *or* Etude No.15
             (15 Etudes pour Saxophone Alto et Piano)   (EFM/UMP 1008)

Leclair, arr.
Mule ....Adagio, Allemande et Gigue
             (Les Classiques du Saxophone No.104)   (Leduc/UMP AL20844)

Milhaud ....Brazileira (Scaramouche for Alto Saxophone)   (Salabert/UMP EAS15280a)

Richardson ....No.2 *and* No.3 (Three Pieces Op.22)   (Emerson E68b)

Ameller ....Suite d'Après Rameau [complete]   (EMT/UMP TR001187)

Debussy, arr.
Rae ....La Plus que Lente, No.6 (Debussy Saxophone Album) (Universal UE17777)

Guilhaud, arr.
Voxman ....First Concertino [complete]   (Rubank/Studio Music 04477534)

List B (Alto/Baritone)

Bozza...................Fantasie Italienne   (Leduc/UMP AL21151)

Bozza...................Pulcinella   (Leduc/UMP AL20298)

Casterede ....Scherzo   (Leduc/UMP AL21374)

Demillac..............Jeux de Vagues   (Combre/UMP C04979)

Jolivet ....Fantasie Impromptu   (Leduc/UMP AL21321)

Tomasi ....Introduction et Danse   (Leduc/UMP AL24936)

Wood ....Schwarzer Tänzer   (Saxtet Publications 005)

Tcherepnin ....Sonatine Sportive, 2nd Movt:
             Mi-temps *and* 3rd Movt: Course   (Leduc/UMP AL20090)

Hold....................Tango (Tango and Charleston)   (Thames/Elkin 978357)

Nelson ....Sonata for Alto Sax and Piano, 1st Movt:
             Drammatico *or* 3rd Movt: With vigor   (Advance/Studio Music 07037A)

Grovlez................Sarabande et Allegro   (Leduc/UMP AL23218)

Grundman ....Concertante [complete]   (B&HM051680061)

Ridout.................Concertino for Alto Saxophone   (Emerson E145)

List A (Soprano/Tenor)

Bach, J.S., arr.
Gee........................Sonata No.4, Andante-Presto *and* Allegro (Southern Music/Valentine Music SS882)

Bach, J.S., arr.
Harle ....Sonata in G Minor
                   [any *two* contrasting movements] (Universal UE17774)

Bonnard ....Sonata, 1st Movt: Andante moderato (Billaudot/UMP 1703)

Fiocco/
Bazelaire, arr.
Londeix ....Concerto, 1st Movt: Allégre (Schott SF9260)

Handel, arr.
Gee........................Andante and Allegro (Southern Music/Valentine Music SS963)

Handel, arr.
Mule ....Sonata en Sol Mineur Op.1/6
                   (Les Classiques du Saxophone No.14) (Leduc/UMP AL25144)

Marcello, arr.
Joosen ....Concerto in C Minor (Molenaar/Elkin MN167)

Millars, arr.
Harvey.................Andante and Rondo
                   (Saxophone Solos Vol.2, Tenor) (Chester/Music Sales CH55208)

Yuste ....Solo de Concurso (UME 87793)

Guilhaud, arr.
Voxman ....First Concertino (Rubank 04477534)

Villa-Lobos...........Fantasia for Soprano or Tenor
                   Saxophone, 1st Movt: Animé (Peer-Southern/Elkin PS305)

Martin ....Ballade (1940) for Tenor Saxophone (Universal UE11250)

Tuthill..................Sonata Op.56, 2nd Movt:
                   Andante *and* 3rd Movt: Fast (Southern Music/Valentine Music SS867)

List B (Soprano/Tenor)

Addison ....Harlequin for Soprano Saxophone (Emerson E236)

Clerisse.................A l'Ombre du Clocher (Leduc/UMP AL24774)

Cowles ....Of Spain (Studio Music 033394)

Cowles ....Five for a Tenor (Studio Music 033387)

Di Pasquale ....Sonata, 2nd Movt *and* 3rd Movt (Southern Music/Valentine Music SS761)

Fischer ....Kephas a Antioche: 1st Movt *and* 2nd Movt   (Billaudot/UMP 3880)

Joplin, arr.
Ferguson/
Wehange ....Bethena – A Concert Waltz   (Lemoine/UMP 25143)

Singelee, arr.
Voxman ....Solo de Concert Op.83   (Rubank 04477549)

Tuthill.................Sonata, Op.56, 1st Movt
                    and 2nd Movt: Andante   (Southern Music/Valentine Music SS867)

Bennett ....Sonata for Soprano Sax and Piano
                    [any single movement]   (Novello NOV120760)

Gould ....Diversions for Tenor Sax and Orchestra 3rd Movt:
                    Rags and Waltzes *or* 5th Movt: Quicksteps and
                    Trios (Tenor Sax and Piano Reduction)   (Schirmer/Music Sales GS82055)

Heath ....Out of the Cool for Soprano Sax and Piano   (Chester/Music Sales CH60422)

Wood ....Schwarzer Tänzer   (Saxtet Publications 005)

Morland...............No.III (Parallels for Tenor Saxophone & Piano)   (Broadbent & Dunn 11203)

Smith ....Sonata No.1, Hall of Mirrors,
                    2nd Movt: The Looking Glass   (Camden Music CM117)

List C: Study

Play ONE study, to be chosen from the list below.

Bach, C.P.E., arr.
Harle ....No.80 (Easy Classical Studies for Saxophone)   (Universal UE17770)

Debussy, arr.
Londeix ....Syrinx   (Jobert/UMP JJ001103)

Ferling, arr.
Mule ....No.23 *and* No.24 (48 Etudes d'Apres Ferling)   (Leduc/UMP AL20402)

Harris, ed.
Davies & Harris...No.79 (80 Graded Studies for Saxophone Bk.2)   (Faber 0571510485)

Hummel ....Tre Pezzi Fur Saxophon
                    Solo Op.81e, 1st Movt: Monolog   (Advance/Studio Music 07052)

Lacour.................No. 48 *and* No.49
                    (50 Etudes Faciles et Progressives Vol.2)   (Billaudot/UMP G15492B)

Wilson ....I Sleep at Waking   (Camden Music CM135)

Rae ....Grand Etude, No.12 (12 Modern Studies)   (Universal UE18795)

Dubois ....Gigue (Suite Française)   (Leduc/UMP AL23138)

Sight-reading (see p.209)

Aural Tests *or* **Initiative Tests** (see p.207)

Musicianship Questions (see p.208)

JAZZ SAXOPHONE

Grade 1

Warm-ups

Warm-ups do not form part of the examination, but it is highly recommended that candidates prepare by using warm-up exercises immediately before entering the examination room. See page 6.

The Examination

Facility Exercise

Play a long note with full tone for a prescribed number of beats (6 - 8 at ♩ = 60). The examiner will specify the note and the number of beats and will set the pulse.

Scales and Arpeggios (Chord Shapes)

(See Notes on Scales and Arpeggios page 198)

To be played from memory. All scales and arpeggios should be prepared with the specifications listed in the grey box below. The examiner will request *one only* (e.g. one rhythm *or* one articulation *or* one character) when requesting each scale/arpeggio.

Range

Rhythms	♪ s grouped in 3s or 4s as appropriate; i) straight; ii) medium swing
Dynamics	With a confident and consistent full tone
Tempi	♩ = 72+
Articulations	Scales i) tongued; ii) legato; Arpeggios tongued only; Swing ♫♫♪
Character	i) Spiky and angry (when tongued); ii) Relaxed and laid back (when legato)

Creative Exercise

Choose one of the scales or arpeggios from the list for this Grade and perform a creative version using elements chosen from the menu on page 205 and/or from the grey box for this Grade.

Candidates may notate their creative exercise and read from this or simply improvise a version.

In either case the same exercise should be performed twice so as to clarify the musical intentions. Candidates will be rewarded for adventure and invention.

Note Centres

Candidates should prepare the following note centre: G (one octave).

The following should be prepared:

- the major scale followed by the major seventh arpeggio
- the dorian scale followed by the minor seventh arpeggio

Candidates may pause between pairs of scales and arpeggios.

Improvisation

Module 1, either A, B, or C (candidate's choice) from the official GSMD publication *Jazz Improvisation*. See p.210 for details and for further useful publications.

Alto/Baritone Pieces

Play TWO pieces, one to be chosen from each list.

List A

> (see General Notes p.210)
>
> From the *Boosey Woodwind Method, saxophone book 1*   (B&H M060112911)
>
> *Wine/Bayer*
> *Sager* ....A Groovy Kind of Love, p.33
> *Marks*...................Rambling Man, p.29

Shilkret, arr.
Long......................The Lonesome Road
                    (Classic Jazz for Saxophone)   (Wise/Music Sales AM937068)

Wilson ....Gospel Joe (Creative Variations Vol.1)   (Camden Music CM183)

Mancini, arr.
Ledbury................Moon River (All Jazzed Up for Saxophone)   (Brass Wind 0302)

Ellington ....Solitude
                    (Jazz and Blues Greats for Saxophone)   (Wise/Music Sales AM82298)

Hebb......................Sunny (Jazz and Blues Greats for Saxophone)   (Wise/Music Sales AM82298)

Trad. ....Bill Bailey
                    (Jazz and Blues Greats for Saxophone)   (Wise/Music Sales AM82298)

Harris...................Midnight Air (First Repertoire for
                    Alto Saxophone)   (Faber 519032)

List B

> (see General Notes p.210)
>
> From the *Boosey Woodwind Method, saxophone book 1*   (B&H M060112911)
>
> *Marks* ....The Saxophone Rap, p. 36
>
> *Trad.* ....When the Saints go Marching in, p. 25

Bennett ....Cactus Music *or* Open Window (Jazz Club Alto Sax)   (IMP 7532A)

Boyle ....Fresh Air Waltz *or* Memories (Dances and Daydreams) (B&H M060079214)

Lyons ....Rock Steady (New Alto Sax Solos Bk.1)   (Useful Music U7)

Jackman ....Honeysuckle Blues (Six Easy Pieces for Saxophone)   (Novello NOV120674)

Street ....Reflections (Streetwise for Alto Sax and Piano)   (B&H M060079276)

Miles ....Arriving Home (Creative Variations Vol.1)   (Camden Music CM183)

Soprano/Tenor Pieces

Play TWO pieces, one to be chosen from each list.

List A

Shilkret, arr.
Long ....The Lonesome Road
　　　　　　　　　(Classic Jazz for Saxophone)   (Wise/Music Sales AM937068)

Ellington ....Solitude
　　　　　　　　　(Jazz and Blues Greats for Saxophone)   (Wise/Music Sales AM82298)

Young ....Sweet Sue – Just You
　　　　　　　　　(Jazz and Blues Greats for Saxophone)   (Wise/Music Sales AM82298)

Hebb ....Sunny (Jazz and Blues Greats for Saxophone)   (Wise/Music Sales AM82298)

Trad. ....Bill Bailey
　　　　　　　　　(Jazz and Blues Greats for Saxophone)   (Wise/Music Sales AM82298)

Gershwin, arr.
Stratford &
Hampton ....He Loves and She Loves
　　　　　　　　　(Play Jazztime B♭/E♭)   (Faber 0571519091)
　　　　　　　　　　　　　　(Tenor saxophone part: 0571564801)

Mancini ....Days of Wine and Roses (Saxmania Standards)   (Wise/Music Sales AM78262)

Wilson ....Gospel Joe (Creative Variations Vol.1)   (Camden Music CM183)

List B

Bennett ....Open Window *or* Cuban Taxi Ride (Jazz Club Tenor Sax)   (IMP 7533A)

Lyons ....Rock Steady *or* One Potato (New Tenor Sax Solos Bk.1)   (Useful Music U9)

Jackman ....Honeysuckle Blues (Six Easy Pieces for Saxophone)   (Novello NOV120674)

Miles ....Arriving Home (Creative Variations Vol.1)   (Camden Music CM183)

List C: Study

Play ONE study, to be chosen from the list below.

Lyons ....No.5 (24 Melodic Studies for Saxophone)   (Useful Music U55)

Dorsey ....Ex.1, p.36 (Jimmy Dorsey Saxophone Method)   (IMP 50308)

Evans, arr.
Wastall ....Sax-Appeal, p.25 (Learn As You Play Saxophone)   (B&H M060063794)

Niehaus ....Exercise No.1 (Basic Jazz Conception for
Saxophone Vol.1)   (Try/Elkin TRY001)

Rae ....Mayfair, No.1 *or* Powerplant, No.17
(Easy Studies in Jazz and Rock for Sax)   (Universal UE19392)

Rae ....No.44 *and* No.45 (Progressive Jazz Studies for Sax
Easy Level)   (Faber 0571513611)

Sight-reading (see p.209)

Aural Tests *or* Initiative Tests (see p.207)

Musicianship Questions (see p.208)

Grade 2

Warm-ups

Warm-ups do not form part of the examination, but it is highly recommended that candidates prepare by using warm-up exercises immediately before entering the examination room. See page 6.

The Examination

Facility Exercise

Play a long note with full tone for a prescribed number of beats (6 - 8 at $\rfloor$ = 60). The examiner will specify the note and the number of beats and will set the pulse.

Scales and Arpeggios (Chord Shapes)
(See Notes on Scales and Arpeggios page 198)

To be played from memory. All scales and arpeggios should be prepared with the specifications listed in the grey box below. The examiner will request *one only* (e.g. one rhythm *or* one articulation *or* one character) when requesting each scale/arpeggio.

Range

Creative Exercise
Choose one of the scales or arpeggios from the list for this Grade and perform a creative version using elements chosen from the menu on page 205 and/or from the grey box for this Grade.

Rhythms	♪s grouped in 3s or 4s as appropriate; i) straight; ii) medium swing
Dynamics	With a confident and consistent full tone
Tempi	♩ = 72+
Articulations	Scales i) tongued; ii) legato; Arpeggios tongued only Swing ♫♫♩
Character	i) Medium 'up' and dance-like; ii) Bluesy and dragging

Candidates may notate their creative exercise and read from this or simply improvise a version. In either case the same exercise should be performed twice so as to clarify the musical intentions. Candidates will be rewarded for adventure and invention.

Note Centres
Candidates should prepare the following note centre: D (two octaves).

The following should be prepared:

- the major scale followed by the major seventh arpeggio
- the dorian scale followed by the minor seventh arpeggio
- the mixolydian scale followed by the dominant seventh (starting and finishing on the note centre)

Candidates may pause between pairs of scales and arpeggios.

Improvisation
Module 2, either A, B, or C (candidate's choice), from the GSMD publication *Jazz Improvisation*. See p.210 for details and for further useful publications.

Alto/Baritone Pieces

Play TWO pieces, one to be chosen from each list.

List A

(see General Notes p.210)

From the *Boosey Woodwind Method, saxophone book 1* (B&H M060112911)

Oliviero ....I'll Set my Love to Music, p. 48 [saxophone 1 part]

From the *Boosey Woodwind Method, saxophone book 2* (B&H M060112942)

Norton ....Off the Rails, p. 11 [saxophone 1 part, with CD track 9 *or* 10]

Braham, arr.
Long ....Limehouse Blues (Blues for Saxophone) (Wise/Music Sales AM952028)

Hawkins ....Tuxedo Junction
             (Jazz and Blues Greats for Saxophone) (Wise/Music Sales AM82298)

Rogers ....Short Stop
             (Jazz and Blues Greats for Saxophone) (Wise/Music Sales AM82298)

Gershwin, arr.
Gout ....'S Wonderful (Play Gershwin Bb/Eb) (Faber 0571517552)

Wilson ....J's Dream (Creative Variations Vol.1) (Camden Music CM183)

Trad. ....Down By The Riverside (De Haske WA6010)

List B

(see General Notes p.210)

From the *Boosey Woodwind Method, saxophone book 1* (B&H M060112911)

Marks ....Blue 4 U, p.39 [with CD track 64 *or* 65]

Trad. ....Swing Low, Sweet Chariot, p.36 [with CD track 57 *or* 58]

From the *Boosey Woodwind Method, saxophone book 2* (B&H M060112942)

Marks ....Long Shadows, p. 10

Bennett ....Sweet Thing *or* Barbecue Blues *or*
             Arm's Length (Jazz Club Alto Sax) (IMP 7532A)

Street ....By The Lake (Streets Ahead) (Saxtet Publications 008)

Gumbley ....Oceanapolis (Cops, Caps and Cadillacs) (Saxtet Publications 006)

Miles ....Abigail's Song (Creative Variations Vol.1) (Camden Music CM183)

Lyons ....Wheels Within Wheels (New Alto Sax Solos Bk.1)   (Useful Music U7)

Hamer ....Brynglas Bounce [CD track 18] *or* Easygoing [CD track 30]
(Play It Cool) N.B. A piano accompaniment is also available.

(Spartan Press SP562)

Soprano/Tenor Pieces

Play TWO pieces, one to be chosen from each list.

List A

Braham, arr.
Long ....Limehouse Blues (Blues for Saxophone)   (Wise/Music Sales AM952028)

Hawkins ....Tuxedo Junction
(Jazz and Blues Greats for Saxophone)   (Wise/Music Sales AM82298)

Rogers ....Short Stop (Jazz and Blues Greats for Saxophone)   (Wise/Music Sales AM82298)

Gershwin ....'S Wonderful (Play Gershwin B♭/E♭)   (Faber 0571517552)

Wilson ....J's Dream (Creative Variations Vol.1)   (Camden Music CM183)

Johnston &
Burke, arr.
Stratford &
Hampton ....Pennies from Heaven (Play Jazztime B♭/E♭)   (Faber 0571519091)

(Tenor Saxophone part 0571564801)

List B

Hamer ....Brynglas Bounce [CD track 18] *or* Easygoing [CD track 30]
(Play It Cool) N.B. A piano accompaniment is also available.

(Spartan Press SP562)

Bennett ....Missed Chances *or* Blue Jay *or* My Dear Old Thing
(Jazz Club Tenor Sax)   (IMP 7533A)

Miles ....Abigail's Song (Creative Variations Vol.1)   (Camden Music CM183)

Lyons ....Wheels Within Wheels (New Tenor Sax Solos Bk.1)   (Useful Music U9)

Gumbley ....Oceanapolis (Cops, Caps and Cadillacs)   (Saxtet Publications 006)

List C: Study

Play ONE study, to be chosen from the list below.

Lyons ....No.7 (24 Melodic Studies for Sax)   (Useful Music U55)

Niehaus ....Exercise No.3 *or* Exercise No.4 *or* Exercise No.5
(Basic Jazz Conception for Saxophone Vol.1)   (Try/Elkin TRY001)

Rae ....Leapfrog, No.3 *or* Sir Neville, No.20
(Easy Studies in Jazz and Rock for Sax)   (Universal UE19392)

Dorsey ....Ex.2 *or* Ex.3, p.36 (Jimmy Dorsey Saxophone Method)   (IMP 50308)

Rae........................No.47 *or* No.51
                          (Progressive Jazz Studies for Sax Easy Level)   (Faber 0571513611)

Sight-reading (see p.209)

Aural Tests *or* Initiative Tests (see p.207)

Musicianship Questions (see p.208)

Grade 3

Warm-ups

Warm-ups do not form part of the examination, but it is highly recommended that candidates prepare by using warm-up exercises immediately before entering the examination room. See page 6.

The Examination

Facility Exercise

Play a long note with full tone for a prescribed number of beats (6 - 12 at ♩ = 60). The examiner will specify the note and the number of beats and will set the pulse.

Scales and Arpeggios (Chord Shapes)

(See Notes on Scales and Arpeggios page 198)

To be played from memory. All scales and arpeggios should be prepared with the specifications listed in the grey box on the following page. The examiner will request *one only* (e.g. one rhythm *or* one articulation *or* one character) when requesting each scale/arpeggio.

Range

Creative Exercise

Choose one of the scales or arpeggios from the list for this Grade and perform a creative version using elements chosen from the menu on page 205 and/or from the grey box for this Grade.

Rhythms	♪s grouped in 3s or 4s as appropriate; i) straight; ii) medium swing
Dynamics	With a confident and consistent full tone
Tempi	♩ = 72+
Articulations	i) tongued; ii) legato Swing ♫♫♪
Character	i) Latin 'feel'; ii) Rock groove; iii) Like a ballad i.e. melodic and sensitive

Candidates may notate their creative exercise and read from this or simply improvise a version. In either case the same exercise should be performed twice so as to clarify the musical intentions. Candidates will be rewarded for adventure and invention.

Note Centres

Candidates should prepare the following note centre: A (a twelfth, except where specified).

The following should be prepared:

- the major scale followed by the major seventh arpeggio
- the dorian scale followed by the minor seventh arpeggio
- the mixolydian scale followed by the dominant seventh (starting and finishing on the note centre)
- the pentatonic major scale (one octave)

Candidates may pause between pairs of scales and arpeggios.

Improvisation

Module 3, either A, B, or C (candidate's choice), from the GSMD publication *Jazz Improvisation*. See p.210 for details and for further useful publications.

Alto/Baritone Pieces

Play TWO pieces, one to be chosen from each list.

List A (Alto/Baritone)

> (see General Notes p.210)
>
> From the *Boosey Woodwind Method, saxophone book 1* (B&H M060112911)
>
> *York & Marks*.......Image, p.60
>
> From the *Boosey Woodwind Method, saxophone book 2* (B&H M060112942)
>
> *Trad.*...................Yellow Bird, p.18
>
> *Weiss & Shearing*..Lullaby of Birdland, p.27 [with CD track 29]

Koffman, arr.
Long.....................Swingin' Shepherd Blues
                   (Blues for Saxophone) (Wise/Music Sales AM952028)

Hamilton, arr.
Long.....................Cry Me A River (Classic Jazz for Saxophone) (Wise/Music Sales AM937068)

Wilson ....Joe's New Words (Creative Variations Vol.1) (Camden Music CM183)

Dennis ....Angel Eyes (Saxmania Standards) (Wise/Music Sales AM78262)

Tizol....................Perdido (Jazz and Blues Greats for Sax) (Wise/Music Sales AM82298)

Gershwin, arr.
Gout ....They can't take that away from me
                   (Play Gershwin Bb/Eb) (Faber 0571517552)

List B (Alto/Baritone)

> (see General Notes p.210)
>
> From the *Boosey Woodwind Method, saxophone book 1* (B&H M060112911)
>
> *Norton*.................Club Soda, p.59 [saxophone 1 part]
>
> From the *Boosey Woodwind Method, saxophone book 2* (B&H M060112942)
>
> *Norton*.................Crayfish, p.34 [saxophone 1 part]
>
> *Norton*.................Feeling Sunny, p.42 [saxophone 1 part]
>
> *Norton*.................Calypso Facto, p.55
>
> *Norton*.................Don't Wannabe, p.37

Wilson, A ....Californian Coast *or* Las Vegas Casino *or*
                   New York Subway (American Jazz and More) (Spartan Press SP569)

Street ....Take it easy *or* Strawberry Daquari (Streets Ahead) (Saxtet Publications 008)

Miles ....Who's got the Answer? (Creative Variations Vol.1) (Camden Music CM183)

Lyons....................Moonrock *or* Soft Song (New Alto Sax Solos Bk.1) (Useful Music U7)

Rae.......................Waltz for Emily (Blue Saxophone) (Universal UE19765)

Soprano/Tenor Pieces

Play TWO pieces, one to be chosen from each list.

List A

Koffman, arr.
Long ....Swingin' Shepherd Blues
               (Blues for Saxophone)   (Wise/Music Sales AM952028)

Hamilton, arr.
Long ....Cry Me A River (Classic Jazz for Saxophone)   (Wise/Music Sales AM937068)

Wilson ....Joe's New Words (Creative Variations Vol.1)   (Camden Music CM183)

Dennis ....Angel Eyes (Saxmania Standards)   (Wise/Music Sales AM78262)

Tizol ....Perdido (Jazz and Blues Greats for Sax)   (Wise/Music Sales AM82298)

Gershwin ....They can't take that away from me
               (Play Gershwin B♭/E♭)   (Faber 0571517552)

Gershwin, arr.
Stratford &
Hampton ....I Got Rhythm
               (Play Jazztime B♭/E♭)   (Faber 0571519091)
                         (Tenor Saxophone part: 0571564801)

List B

Wilson, A ....Californian Coast *or* Las Vegas Casino *or*
               New York Subway (American Jazz and More)   (Spartan Press SP569)

Lamont ....Blues for Hank (The Light Touch Bk.1)   (Stainer and Bell H387)

Miles ....Who's got the Answer? (Creative Variations Vol.1)   (Camden Music CM183)

Lyons ....Moonrock *or* Soft Song (New Tenor Sax Solos Bk.1)   (Useful Music U9)

Rae ....Waltz for Emily (Blue Saxophone)   (Universal UE19765)

Cole ....Hooligan Strain (First Repertoire Pieces for
               Tenor Sax)   (B&H M060071522)

List C: Study

Play ONE study, to be chosen from the list below.

Lyons ....No.11 (24 Melodic Studies for Sax)   (Useful Music U55)

Dorsey ....Ex.7, p.38 *or* Ex.8, p.39 (Jimmy Dorsey Saxophone Method) (IMP 50308)

Lewin ....Bermuda Breeze, p.14 (Starters for Saxophone)   (ABRSM 185472 421 5)

Niehaus ....Exercise No.3
               (Intermediate Jazz Conception for Saxophone)   (Try/Elkin TRY003)

Rae ....Freeway, No.4 *or* Overdrive, No.21
               (Easy Studies in Jazz and Rock for Saxophone)   (Universal UE19392)

Sight-reading (see p.209)

Aural Tests *or* Initiative Tests (see p.207)

Musicianship Questions (see p.208)

Grade 4

Warm-ups

Warm-ups do not form part of the examination, but it is highly recommended that candidates prepare by using warm-up exercises immediately before entering the examination room. See page 6.

The Examination

Facility Exercise

Play a long note *mf* for a prescribed number of beats (8 - 12 at ♩ = 60). The examiner will specify the note and the number of beats and will set the pulse..

Scales and Arpeggios (Chord Shapes)

(See Notes on Scales and Arpeggios page 198)

To be played from memory. All scales and arpeggios should be prepared with the specifications listed in the grey box below. The examiner will request *one only* (e.g. one rhythm *or* one articulation *or* one character) when requesting each scale/arpeggio.

Range

Creative Exercise

Choose one of the scales or arpeggios from the list for this Grade and perform a creative version using a combination of elements chosen from the menu on page 205 and/or from the grey box for this Grade.

Rhythms	♪s grouped in 3s or 4s as appropriate; i) straight; ii) medium up swing
Dynamics	Within the range *mp – f,* i) sustaining a level throughout; ii) cresc.; iii) decresc.
Tempi	♩ = 96+
Articulations	i) tongued; ii) legato Swing ♫♫♩
Character	i) Staccato and light; ii) Heavy and accented

Candidates may notate their creative exercise and read from this or simply improvise a version. In either case the same exercise should be performed twice so as to clarify the musical intentions. Candidates will be rewarded for adventure and invention.

Note Centres

Candidates should prepare the following note centre: C (two octaves, with major scale extended up to highest E).

The following should be prepared:

- the major scale followed by the major seventh arpeggio
- the dorian scale followed by the minor seventh arpeggio
- the mixolydian scale followed by the dominant seventh (starting and finishing on the note centre)
- the melodic *or* harmonic minor scale (candidate's choice) followed by the minor arpeggio with the major seventh
- the pentatonic major scale
- the chromatic scale

Candidates may pause between pairs of scales and arpeggios.

Improvisation

Module 4, either A, B, or C (candidate's choice), from the GSMD publication *Jazz Improvisation*. See p.210 for details and for further useful publications.

Pieces

Play TWO pieces, one to be chosen from List A and one from List B.

List A (Alto/Baritone)

Monk, arr.
Long .... Blue Monk (Blues for Saxophone)   (Wise/Music Sales AM952028)

Carmichael, arr.
Long .... Lazy River (Classic Jazz for Saxophone)   (Wise/Music Sales AM937068)

Wilson .... Hey Joe.... Let's Meet (Creative Variations Vol.1)   (Camden Music CM183)

Bechet .... Petite Fleur (Jazz and Blues Greats for Sax)   (Wise/Music Sales AM82298)

Gershwin, arr.
De Smet .... Fascinating Rhythm (Three Songs for Alto Sax and Piano) (De Haske F438)

Ellington, arr.
Harle .... In a Sentimental Mood (John Harle's
                       Saxophone Album)   (B&H M060065972)

List B (Alto/Baritone)

Harle .... Cradle Song (Encore)   (Chester/Music Sales CH61090)

Gumbley .... Cops, Caps and Cadillacs *or* Fast Food Funk
(Cops, Caps and Cadillacs)   (Saxtet Publications 006)

Holcombe .... Elegy *or* Midnight (Contemporary Alto Sax Solos in
Pop/Jazz Styles)   (Studio Music AS001)

Rae .... On the Edge *or* Cayenne (Latin Saxophone)   (Universal UE17364)

Miles .... Three Views of Orford (Creative Variations Vol.1)   (Camden Music CM183)

Wilson .... Dixie *or* Bossa (Jazz Album)   (Camden Music CM097)

Lyons .... Runway (New Alto Sax Solos Bk.1)   (Useful Music U7)

List A (Soprano/Tenor)

Monk, arr. Long .... Blue Monk (Blues for Saxophone)   (Wise/Music Sales AM952028)

Carmichael, arr.
Long .... Lazy River (Classic Jazz for Saxophone)   (Wise/Music Sales AM937068)

Wilson .... Hey Joe... Let's Meet (Creative Variations Vol.1)   (Camden Music CM183)

Bechet .... Petite Fleur (Jazz and Blues Greats for Sax)   (Wise/Music Sales AM82298)

Gershwin, arr.
Gout .... Let's call the whole thing off (Play Gershwin Bb/Eb)   (Faber 0571517552)

Mack &
Johnson, arr.
Stratford &
Hampton .... Charleston
(Play Jazztime Bb/Eb)   (Faber 0571519091)

(Tenor saxophone part: 0571564801)

List B (Soprano/Tenor)

Street .... All Because of You (Saxtet Series)   (Saxtet Publications 001)

Rae .... On the Edge *or* Cayenne (Latin Saxophone)   (Universal UE17364)

Miles .... Three Views of Orford (Creative Variations Vol.1)   (Camden Music CM183)

Wilson .... Dixie *or* Bossa (Jazz Album)   (Camden Music CM097)

Lyons .... Runway (New Tenor Sax Solos Bk.1)   (Useful Music U9)

Cowles, arr.
Wastall .... Myopic Mice (First Repertoire Pieces for Tenor Sax)   (B&H M060071522)

Ktomi .... Soul Track (First Repertoire Pieces for Tenor Sax)   (B&H M060071522)

List C: Study

Play ONE study, to be chosen from the list below.

Street .... A Little Piece, No.4 (Street Beats)   (Saxtet Publications 120)

Lyons .... No.14 (24 Melodic Studies for Sax)   (Useful Music U55)

Dorsey .... Ex.10, p.40 (Jimmy Dorsey Saxophone Method)   (IMP 50308)

Niehaus .... Exercise No.5 *or* Exercise No.7 (Intermediate
                    Jazz Conception for Saxophone)   (Try/Elkin TRY003)

Rae .... No.54 *or* No.58 (Progressive Jazz Studies for Sax
                    Easy Level)   (Faber 0571513611)

Rae .... Ted's Shuffle *or* No Return (Easy Studies in
                    Jazz and Rock for Saxophone)   (Universal UE19392)

Sight-reading (see p.209)

Aural Tests *or* Initiative Tests (see p.207)

Musicianship Questions (see p.208)

Grade 5

Warm-ups

Warm-ups do not form part of the examination, but it is highly recommended that candidates prepare by using warm-up exercises immediately before entering the examination room. See page 6.

The Examination

Facility Exercise

Play a long note *mf* for a prescribed number of beats (8 - 12 at $\downarrow$ = 60). The examiner will specify the note and the number of beats and will set the pulse.

Scales and Arpeggios (Chord Shapes)

(See Notes on Scales and Arpeggios page 198)

To be played from memory. All scales and arpeggios should be prepared with the specifications listed in the grey box on the opposite page. The examiner will request *one only* (e.g. one rhythm *or* one articulation *or* one character) when requesting each scale/arpeggio.

Range

Creative Exercise

Choose one of the scales or arpeggios from the list for this Grade and perform a creative version using elements chosen from the menu on page 205 and/or from the grey box for this Grade.

Rhythms	♪s grouped in 3s or 4s as appropriate; i) straight; ii) medium up swing
Dynamics	Within the range *mp – f*, i) sustaining a level throughout; ii) cresc.; iii) decresc.
Tempi	♩ = 96+
Articulations	i) tongued; ii) legato Swing ♫♫♩
Character	i) Earthy and soulful; ii) Restrained and gentle

Candidates may notate their creative exercise and read from this or simply improvise a version. In either case the same exercise should be performed twice so as to clarify the musical intentions. Candidates will be rewarded for adventure and invention.

Note Centres

Candidates should prepare ONE of the following note centres: E (two octaves, with major scale extended down to lowest B) *or* F (two octaves, with major scale extended down to lowest C).

For the chosen note centre the following should be prepared:

- the major scale followed by the major seventh arpeggio
- the dorian scale followed by the minor seventh arpeggio
- the mixolydian scale followed by the dominant seventh arpeggio (starting and finishing on the note centre)
- the melodic *or* harmonic minor scale (candidate's choice) followed by the minor arpeggio with the major seventh
- the pentatonic major scale
- the pentatonic minor scale
- the blues scale
- the chromatic scale

Candidates may pause between pairs of scales and arpeggios.

Improvisation

Module 5, either A, B, or C (candidate's choice), from the GSMD publication *Jazz Improvisation*. See p.210 for details and for further useful publications.

Pieces

Play TWO pieces, one to be chosen from List A and one from List B.

List A (Alto/Baritone)

Hagen, arr.
Long ....Harlem Nocturne (Blues for Saxophone)   (Wise/Music Sales 952028)

Brubeck, arr.
Long ....It's a Raggy Waltz (Classic Jazz for Saxophone)   (Wise/Music Sales AM937068)

Wilson ....Blues for Joseph (Creative Variations Vol.1)   (Camden Music CM183)

Desmond, arr.
Rae ....Take Five (Take Ten for E♭ Sax and Piano)   (Universal UE18836)

Goodman ....Flyin' Home (Jazz and Blues Greats for
                 Saxophone)   (Wise/Music Sales AM82298)

Bellson ....The Hawk Talks (Jazz and Blues Greats
                 for Saxophone)   (Wise/Music Sales AM82298)

Gershwin ....Bess, you is my woman now
                 (Play Gershwin B♭/E♭)   (Faber 0571517552)

Ellington, arr.
Rae ....Sophisticated Lady (Take Ten for E♭ Sax and Piano)   (Universal UE18836)

List B (Alto/Baritone)

Holcombe ....Prestidigitator *or* Night Song (Contemporary
                 Alto Sax Solos in Pop/Jazz Styles)   (Studio Music AS001)

Miles ....Bathwater Blues (Creative Variations Vol.1)   (Camden Music CM183)

Wilson ....12 Bar *or* Swing 8 *or* Jazz Waltz (Jazz Album)   (Camden Music CM097)

Lyons ....The Swinging Roundabout (New Alto Sax Solos Bk.2)   (Useful Music U8)

Gates ....Wonderland (Moodmusic)   (Camden Music CM061)

Rafferty, arr.
Harle ....Baker Street (John Harle's Sax Album)   (B&H M060065972)

Rae ....The Keel Row *or* Song Without Words
                 (Jazzy Saxophone 2)   (Universal UE19362)

List A (Soprano/Tenor)

Hagen, arr.
Long ....Harlem Nocturne (Blues for Saxophone)   (Wise/Music Sales AM952028)

Brubeck, arr.
Long ....It's a Raggy Waltz (Classic Jazz for Saxophone)   (Wise/Music Sales AM937068)

Wilson ....Blues for Joseph (Creative Variations Vol.1)   (Camden Music CM183)

Goodman ....Flyin' Home (Jazz and Blues Greats for Sax)   (Wise/Music Sales AM82298)

Bellson ....The Hawk Talks (Jazz and Blues Greats for Sax)   (Wise/Music Sales AM82298)

Gershwin..............Bess, you is my woman now (Play Gershwin B♭/E♭)   (Faber 0571517552)

List B (Soprano/Tenor)

Miles ....Bathwater Blues (Creative Variations Vol.1)   (Camden Music CM183)

Wilson ....12 Bar *or* Swing 8 *or* Jazz Waltz (Jazz Album)   (Camden Music CM097)

Lyons....................The Swinging Roundabout
(New Tenor Sax Solos Bk.2)   (Useful Music U10)

Norton.................Swing Out Sister *or* Riff Laden (Microjazz for
Tenor Sax)   (B&H M060085635)

Rae......................The Keel Row *or* Song Without Words (Jazzy Sax 2)   (Universal UE19362)

Wilson ....Tango in D   (Camden Music CM065)

List C: Study

Play ONE study, to be chosen from the list below.

Street ....Leaps and Bounds, No.2 (Street Beats)   (Saxtet Publications 120)

Gumbley ....Bebop Bounce, No.1 *or* Low Down, No.2 *or*
In the Groove, No.6 (15 Crazy Jazz Studies)   (Saxtet Publications 121)

Lyons....................No.24 (24 Melodic Studies for Sax)   (Useful Music U55)

Dorsey ....Ex.10, p.47 (Jimmy Dorsey Saxophone Method)   (IMP 50308)

Rae......................Groove It (20 Modern Studies for Solo Sax)   (Universal UE18820)

Niehaus ....Exercise No.15 *or* Exercise No.19 (Intermediate
Jazz Conception for Saxophone)   (Try/Elkin TRY003)

Sight-reading (see p.209)

Aural Tests *or* Initiative Tests (see p.207)

Musicianship Questions (see p.208)

Grade 6

Warm-ups

Warm-ups do not form part of the examination, but it is highly recommended that candidates prepare by using warm-up exercises immediately before entering the examination room. See page 6.

The Examination

Facility Exercises

- Play a long note *mf* for a prescribed number of beats (4 – 10 at ♩ = 60). The examiner will specify the note and the number of beats and will set the pulse.

- Play a long note *f* for a prescribed number of beats (4 – 6 at ♩ = 60). The examiner will specify the note and the number of beats and will set the pulse.

Scales and Arpeggios (Chord Shapes)

(See Notes on Scales and Arpeggios p.198)

To be played from memory. All scales and arpeggios should be prepared with the specifications listed in the grey box below. The examiner will request *two only* (e.g. one rhythm *and* one dynamic *or* one articulation *and* one character) when requesting each scale/arpeggio.

Range

Creative Exercise

Choose one of the scales or arpeggios from the list for this Grade and perform a creative version using elements chosen from the menu on page 205 and/or from the grey box for this Grade.

Candidates may notate their creative exercise and read from this or simply improvise a version.

Rhythms	♪s grouped in 3s or 4s as appropriate; i) straight; ii) fast swing
Dynamics	Within the range *pp – ff*, i) sustaining a level throughout; ii) cresc.; iii) decresc.
Tempi	♩ = 132+
Articulations	i) tongued; ii) legato Swing ♫♫♩
Character	Candidates to offer a selection of at least four of their own contrasting choices which reflect the jazz idiom, provided an explanation can be given.

In either case the same exercise should be performed twice so as to clarify the musical intentions. Candidates will be rewarded for adventure and invention.

Note Centres

Candidates should prepare the following note centres: ♮ ♭ (two octaves) *and* G (a twelfth).

When the examiner names a note centre the candidate will play:

- the major scale followed by the major seventh arpeggio
- the dorian scale followed by the minor seventh arpeggio
- the mixolydian scale followed by the dominant seventh arpeggio (starting and finishing on the note centre)
- the harmonic minor scale
- the melodic minor scale
- the minor arpeggio with the major seventh
- the blues scale
- the chromatic scale

Candidates may pause between pairs of scales and arpeggios.

Improvisation

Play once through then improvise two choruses of a modal tune, e.g., *Cantaloupe Island, Maiden Voyage, Impressions, Footprints, Little Sunflower, Milestones,* or a similar modal tune.

Or

Play once through then improvise two choruses of an original modally-based composition.

Candidates must provide a legible copy of the composition for the examiner's use.

Pieces

Play TWO pieces, one to be chosen from List A and one from List B.

List A (Alto/Baritone)

Wilson ....After Charlie....Joe (Creative Variations Vol.2)   (Camden Music CM184)

Meyer, arr.
Brown ....Crazy Rhythm (Jazz Sax 2 Alto)   (IMP 16461)

Gershwin, arr.
Brown ....Oh, Lady, Be Good! (Jazz Sax 2 Alto)   (IMP 16461)

Conrad, arr.
Brown ....Singin' the Blues (Jazz Sax 2 Alto)   (IMP 16461)

Jobim ....Desafinado [Getz Solo] (Saxmania Standards)   (Wise/Music Sales AM78262)

Parker, arr.
Williams ....Billie's Bounce [CD track 3] (In Session with Charlie Parker) (IMP 6613A)

List B (Alto/Baritone)

Harle ....Blues for Marguerite [improvisation optional]
(Encore) (Chester/Music Sales CH61090)

Dankworth ....Domnerus (Cascade Jazz Series) (Cascade CM29)

Wood ....Pressed and Dried (Saxtet Publications 002)

Gumbley ....The Girl from Sark (Saxtet Publications 009)

Holcombe ....Latin Quarter *or* Rise and Shine (Contemporary
Alto Sax Solos in Pop/Jazz Styles) (Studio Music AS001)

Lamont.................More Brothers (The Light Touch Bk.2) (Stainer and Bell H388)

Miles ....Candlelight (Creative Variations Vol.2) (Camden Music CM184)

Wilson ....Bebop (Jazz Album) (Camden Music CM097)

Joplin, arr.
Ferguson ....Maple Leaf Rag *or* Swipesy (Lemoine/UMP 25172)

Rendell ....Gold Dust Scramble *or* Blues Montage
(Saxophone Selection, Alto) (GSMD M570010219)

List A (Soprano/Tenor)

Wilson ....After Charlie....Joe (Creative Variations Vol.2) (Camden Music CM184)

Parker, arr.
Williams ....Billie's Bounce [CD track 3]
(In Session with Charlie Parker) (IMP 6612A)

Jobim ....Desafinado [Getz Solo] (Saxmania Standards) (Wise/Music Sales AM78262)

Harbison...............When? (20 Authentic Bebop Solos) (Aebersold/Jazzwise SU011T)

Bechet, arr.
Brown ....Bugle Blues (Jazz Sax 3 Tenor) (IMP 17063)

Simons, arr.
Brown ....All Of Me (Jazz Sax 3 Tenor) (IMP 17063)

Mandel, arr.
Brown ....The Shadow Of Your Smile (Jazz Sax 3 Tenor) (IMP 17063)

List B (Soprano/Tenor)

Wood ....Pressed and Dried (Saxtet Publications 002)

Wood ....Squiffy's Song (Saxtet Publications 004)

Miles ....Candlelight (Creative Variations Vol.2) (Camden Music CM184)

Wilson ....Bebop (Jazz Album) (Camden Music CM097)

Rendell ....Gold Dust Scramble *or* Blues Montage
(Saxophone Selection, Tenor) (GSMD M570010226)

List C: Study

Play ONE study, to be chosen from the list below.

Street ....Watch It, No.8 *or* Party Time, No.10 (Street Beats)   (Saxtet Publications 120)

Gumbley................Crazy Hepcats, No.3 *or* Reed Fever, No.5
            or Funky Monkey, No.14 (15 Crazy Jazz Studies)   (Saxtet Publications 121)

Rae ....Soho *or* Latin Jive (20 Modern Studies for Solo Sax)   (Universal UE18820)

Lewin ....Hawk Gets Bird, p.19 (Twenty-two Unaccompanied
            Pieces for Saxophone)   (ABRSM 185472 272 7)

Sight-reading (see p.209)

Aural Tests *or* Initiative Tests (see p.207)

Musicianship Questions (see p.208)

Grade 7

Warm-ups

Warm-ups do not form part of the examination, but it is highly recommended that candidates prepare by using warm-up exercises immediately before entering the examination room. See page 6.

The Examination

Facility Exercises

Play a long note *p/mf* for a prescribed number of beats (4 – 12 at ♩= 60). The examiner will specify the note and the dynamic, choose the number of beats and set the pulse.

Play a long note *f* for a prescribed number of beats (4 – 8 at ♩= 60). The examiner will specify the note and the number of beats and will set the pulse.

Scales and Arpeggios (Chord Shapes)

(See Notes on Scales and Arpeggios p.198)

To be played from memory. All scales and arpeggios should be prepared with the specifications listed in the grey box on the following page. The examiner will request *two only* (e.g. one rhythm *and* one dynamic *or* one articulation *and* one character) when requesting each scale/arpeggio.

Range

Creative Exercise

Choose one of the scales or arpeggios from the list for this Grade and perform a creative version using elements chosen from the menu on page 205 and/or from the grey box for this Grade.

Candidates may notate their creative exercise and read from this or simply improvise a version.

Rhythms	♪s grouped in 3s or 4s as appropriate; i) straight; ii) fast swing
Dynamics	Within the range *pp – ff*, i) sustaining a level throughout; ii) cresc.; iii) decresc.
Tempi	♩ = 132+
Articulations	i) tongued; ii) legato Swing ♫♫♪
Character	Candidates to offer a selection of at least four of their own contrasting choices which reflect the jazz idiom, provided an explanation can be given.

In either case the same exercise should be performed twice so as to clarify the musical intentions. Candidates will be rewarded for adventure and invention.

Note Centres

Candidates should prepare the following note centres: B (two octaves, with major scale two and a half octaves) *and* F (two octaves, with major scale extended down to lowest C).

When the examiner names a note centre the candidate will play:

* the major scale followed by the major seventh arpeggio
* the dorian scale followed by the minor seventh arpeggio
* the mixolydian scale followed by the dominant seventh arpeggio (starting and finishing on the note centre)
* the harmonic minor *or* melodic minor *or* jazz melodic minor *or* Spanish Phrygian minor scale (candidate's choice) followed by the minor arpeggio with the major seventh
* the blues scale
* the chromatic scale

Candidates may pause between pairs of scales and arpeggios.

The following should also be prepared:

* the whole tone scale, two octaves, starting on B♭
* the whole tone scale, two octaves, starting on B
* the augmented arpeggio, two octaves, starting on B♭
* the augmented arpeggio, two octaves, starting on B

Improvisation

Play once through then improvise two choruses of a blues-based tune, e.g., *Now's the Time, Billie's Bounce, Tenor Madness, Blue Monk, Watermelon Man, West Coast Blues,* or a similar blues tune.

Or

Play once through then improvise two choruses of an original blues-based composition.

Candidates must provide a legible copy of the composition for the examiner's use.

Pieces

Play TWO pieces, one to be chosen from List A and one from List B.

List A (Alto/Baritone)

Wilson .... Just a Ballad for Joseph (Creative Variations Vol.2)   (Camden Music CM184)

Parker, arr.
Williams .... Yardbird Suite [CD track 13] *or* Now's the Time
                   [CD track 17] (In Session with Charlie Parker)   (IMP 6612A)

Donaldson .... Wee Dot (Alto Sax Solos: The Blues)   (Corybant/Jazzwise SS037T)

Brubeck .... Blue Rondo à la Turk (Solos for Jazz Alto Sax)   (Fischer/B&H M060082252)

Rodgers, arr.
Brown .... The Blue Room (Jazz Sax 2, Alto)   (IMP 16461)

McHugh, arr.
Brown .... On the Sunny Side of the Street (Jazz Sax 2, Alto)   (IMP 16461)

Kern, arr.
Brown .... Why Do I Love You? (Jazz Sax 2, Alto)   (IMP 16461)

List B (Alto/Baritone)

Harle .... Matthew's Song
                 [improvisation optional] (Encore)   (Chester/Music Sales CH61090)

Sheppard/
Lodder .... The Fool [with improvisation] (Encore)   (Chester/Music Sales CH61090)

Miles .... Sideways On (Creative Variations Vol.2)   (Camden Music CM184)

Rendell .... Rock Major *or* Bebop Comet (Saxophone
                 Selection, Alto)   (GSMD M570010219)

Holcombe .... C minor, p.12 *or* E major, p.22, *or* G major, p.28
                 or E minor, p.30 (24 Jazz Etudes for Alto Sax)   (Music JE003)

Harbison...............Ridin' the Rails (20 Authentic Bebop Solos)   (Aebersold/Jazzwise SU011T)

Dobbins ....Echoes from a Distant Land for Alto Sax and
Piano [omit piano solo bars 90-106]   (Advance/Studio Music 7033A0)

Joplin, arr.
Ferguson ....Elite Syncopations   (Lemoine/UMP 25143)

List A (Soprano/Tenor)

Wilson ....Just a Ballad for Joseph (Creative Variations Vol.2)   (Camden Music CM184)

Parker, arr.
Williams ....Yardbird Suite [CD track 13] *or* Now's the Time [CD track 17]
(In Session with Charlie Parker)   (IMP 6613A)

Burke/Van Heusen,
arr. Stitt &
Keller....................It Could Happen To You
(Sonny Stitt Improvised Tenor Sax Solos)   (Columbia/IMP 50424)

Arlen, arr. Stitt
& Keller................Over the Rainbow (Sonny Stitt Improvised Tenor
Sax Solos)   (Columbia/IMP 50424)

Young, arr.
Brown ....Lester Leaps In (Jazz Sax 1)   (IMP 09974)

Mobley..................Crazeology (Rhythm Changes Tenor Sax)   (Corybant/Jazzwise SS024T)

List B (Soprano/Tenor)

Sheppard/
Lodder ....The Fool [with improvisation] (Encore)   (Chester/Music Sales CH61090)

Miles ....Sideways On (Creative Variations Vol.2)   (Camden Music CM184)

Harbison...............Ridin' the Rails (20 Authentic Bebop Solos)   (Aebersold/Jazzwise SU011T)

Rendell ....Rock Major *or* Bebop Comet (Saxophone
Selection, Tenor)   (GSMD M570010226)

Holcombe ....B♭ major, p.8 *or* F minor, p.14 *or* E major, p.22
(24 Jazz Etudes for Tenor Sax)   (Studio Music JE003)

Dobbins ....Sonata for Soprano or Tenor Sax, 1st Movt *or*
2nd Movt [with improvisation]   (Advance/Studio Music 07030)

Piazzolla, arr.
Sugawa.................Café 1930 (Histoire du Tango)   (Lemoine/UMP 26820)

List C: Study

Play ONE study, to be chosen from the list below.

Gumbley ....Merry-Go-Round, No.7 *or* Fourth Attempt, No.10
or Tough Guys!, No.11 (15 Crazy Jazz Studies)   (Saxtet Publications 121)

Rae......................Ignition, No.1 *or* Free Spirit, No.9
                 (12 Modern Etudes)   (Universal UE18795)

Wilson ....Monody for Solo Sax   (Camden Music CM099)

Niehaus ....Etude 20 *or* Etude 21 (Intermediate Jazz
                 Conception for Saxophone)   (Try/Elkin TRY003)

Sight-reading (see p.209)

Aural Tests *or* Initiative Tests (see p.207)

Musicianship Questions (see p.208)

Grade 8

Warm-ups

Warm-ups do not form part of the examination, but it is highly recommended that candidates prepare by using warm-up exercises immediately before entering the examination room. See page 6.

The Examination

Facility Exercises

- Play a long note *pp/p/mf* for a prescribed number of beats (4 – 16 at ♩ = 60). The examiner will specify the note and the dynamic, choose the number of beats and set the pulse.
- Play a long note *f* for a prescribed number of beats (4 – 10 at ♩ = 60). The examiner will specify the note and the number of beats and will set the pulse.

Scales and Arpeggios (Chord Shapes)

(See Notes on Scales and Arpeggios p.198)

To be played from memory. All scales and arpeggios should be prepared with the specifications listed in the grey box on the following page. The examiner will request *two only* (e.g. one rhythm *and* one dynamic *or* one articulation *and* one character) when requesting each scale/arpeggio.

Range

Creative Exercise

Choose one of the scales or arpeggios from the list for this Grade and perform a creative version using elements chosen from the menu on page 205 and/or from the grey box for this Grade.

Candidates may notate their creative exercise and read from this or simply improvise a version.

Rhythms	♪s grouped in 3s or 4s as appropriate; i) straight; ii) fast swing
Dynamics	Within the range $pp - ff$, i) sustaining a level throughout; ii) cresc.; iii) decresc.
Tempi	♩ = 132+
Articulations	i) tongued; ii) legato Swing ♫♫♪
Character	Candidates to offer a selection of at least four of their own contrasting choices which reflect the jazz idiom, provided an explanation can be given.

In either case the same exercise should be performed twice so as to clarify the musical intentions. Candidates will be rewarded for adventure and invention.

Note Centres

Candidates should prepare the following note centres:

B♭ (two octaves, with major scale two and a half octaves)
D (two octaves, with major scale extended up to highest F♯)
and F♯ /G♭ (two octaves, with major scale extended down to lowest C♯).

When the examiner names a note centre the candidate will play:

- the major scale followed by the major seventh arpeggio
- the dorian scale followed by the minor seventh arpeggio
- the mixolydian scale followed by the dominant seventh (starting and finishing on the note centre)
- the harmonic minor *or* Spanish Phrygian minor scale (candidate's choice)
- the melodic minor *or* jazz melodic minor scale (candidate's choice)
- the minor arpeggio with the major seventh
- the blues scale
- the chromatic scale (starting on lowest note of range and extended to cover the whole range for this Grade)

Candidates may pause between pairs of scales and arpeggios.

The following should also be prepared:

- the whole tone scale, two octaves, starting on B♭
- the whole tone scale, two octaves, starting on B

- the augmented arpeggio, two octaves, starting on B♭
- the augmented arpeggio, two octaves, starting on B

Improvisation

Play once through then improvise two choruses of a 32-bar song form, e.g., *Autumn Leaves, Whisper Not, Fly me to the Moon, Take the A Train, Stella by Starlight*, or a similar 32-bar song form.

Or

Play once through then improvise two choruses of a 'rhythm changes' tune, e.g. *I've got Rhythm, Oleo, Anthropology, Moose the Mooche, Lester Leaps in*, or a similar 'rhythm changes' tune.

Or

Play once through then improvise two choruses of an original 32-bar song form or 'rhythm changes' composition.

Candidates must provide a legible copy of the composition for the examiner's use.

Pieces

Play TWO pieces, one to be chosen from List A and one from List B.

List A (Alto/Baritone)

Wilson ....Funky Joe (Creative Variations Vol.2)		(Camden Music CM184)
Parker, arr. *Williams* ....Donna Lee [CD track 21] (In Session with Charlie Parker)		(IMP 6613A)
Parker/Gillespie, arr. Williams ....Anthropology [CD track 25] (In Session with Charlie Parker)		(IMP 6613A)
Monk, arr. *Brown* ....'Round Midnight (Jazz Sax 2 Alto)		(IMP 16461)
Arlen, arr. *Brown* ....A Sleepin' Bee (Jazz Sax 2 Alto)		(IMP 16461)
McLean ....Blues Inn (Alto Sax Solos: The Blues)		(Corybant/Jazzwise SS037T)

List B (Alto/Baritone)

Woods ....Sonata for Alto Sax and Piano, 1st Movt
[optional improvisation]   (Advance/Studio Music 07045)

McGarry ....Dreams of You   (Saxtet Publications 003)

Miles ....Struttin' in the Barbican (Creative Variations Vol.2) (Camden Music CM184)

Holcombe ....B♭ Minor, p.16 *or* E♭ Minor, p.17 *or* B Major, p.20
(24 Jazz Etudes for Alto Sax)   (Studio Music JE003)

Rendell ....Rock Study (Saxophone Selection, Alto)   (GSMD M570010219)

Harbison...............Say It! *or* The Pope's Way (20 Authentic
Bebop Solos)   (Aebersold/Jazzwise SU011T)

List A (Soprano/Tenor)

Wilson ....Funky Joe (Creative Variations Vol.2)   (Camden Music CM184)

Parker, arr.
Williams ....Donna Lee [CD track 21] (In Session with Charlie Parker)   (IMP 6612A)

Parker/Gillespie,
arr. Williams.........Anthropology [CD track 25] (In Session with
Charlie Parker)   (IMP 6612A)

Trad., arr.
Brown ....Indian Summer (Jazz Sax 3, Tenor)   (IMP 17063)

Young, arr.
Brown ....Stella by Starlight (Jazz Sax, Tenor)   (IMP 09974)

Green, arr.
Brown ....Body and Soul (Jazz Sax, Tenor)   (IMP 09974)

List B (Soprano/Tenor)

Miles ....Struttin' in the Barbican (Creative Variations Vol.2) (Camden Music CM184)

Holcombe ....E♭ Major, p.10, *or* B♭ Major, p.16 *or* B Major, p.20
(24 Jazz Etudes for Tenor Sax)   (Studio Music JE003)

Rendell ....Rock Study (Saxophone Selection, Tenor)   (GSMD M570010226)

Harbison...............Say It! *or* The Pope's Way
(20 Authentic Bebop Solos)   (Aebersold/Jazzwise SU011T)

McGarry ....Dreams of You   (Saxtet Publications 003)

Dobbins ....Sonata for Soprano *or* Tenor Sax, 3rd Movt
[with improvisation]   (Advance/Studio Music 07030)

Piazzolla, arr.
Sugawa.................Bordell 1900 *or* Nightclub 1960 *or*
Concert d'aujourd'hui (Histoire du Tango)   (Lemoine/UMP 26820)

List C: Study

Play ONE study, to be chosen from the list below.

Gumbley ...............D.D.D. Double Density Disorder, No.9
  (15 Crazy Jazz Studies) (Saxtet Publications 121)

Rae ....Tabasco, No.6 [no repeats] (12 Modern Etudes) (Universal UE18795)

Niehaus ....Etude 25 (Intermediate Jazz Conception
  for Saxophone) (Try/Elkin TRY003)

Rendell ....Ballad Improvisation
  (Saxophone Selection, Alto/Tenor) (GSMD M570010219/M570010226)

Rae ....Dick's Licks *or* Snookie Dookie
  (20 Modern Studies Solo Sax) (Universal UE18820)

Sight-reading (see p.209)

Aural Tests *or* Initiative Tests (see p.207)

Musicianship Questions (see p.208)

Notes on Scales and Arpeggios

A recommended resource for scale learning and practice is *The Scales Wizard* by Jeffery Wilson and Malcolm Miles, published by Camden Music (CM187).

Candidates should prepare all the scales and arpeggios listed in the syllabus for their grade, along with all the specifications listed in the grey box.

All scales and arpeggios are to be played from memory. The candidate may choose the first scale/arpeggio they play from the list of requirements for that grade. Thereafter the examiner will request a selection taken from the requirements for that grade.

Of the specifications shown in the grey box, the examiner will request *one only* for grades 1 – 5 and *two only* for grades 6 – 8 when requesting each scale/arpeggio/exercise. The candidate may choose the speed of the scale/arpeggio/exercise, provided that it falls within the given range of speeds listed for the grade.

Note centres

Note centres have been introduced from grade 1 in jazz syllabuses and from grade 2 in all other woodwind syllabuses. The candidate should prepare the relevant list of scales and arpeggios for the grade, based on the note centre. For example, for Jazz Flute Grade 2, the note centre is D, and the candidate should prepare:

- D major scale
- D major seventh arpeggio
- D dorian scale
- D minor seventh arpeggio
- D mixolydian scale
- D dominant seventh, i.e. D7, starting and finishing on D

Scale and arpeggio examples

The natural minor scale

The natural minor scale (aeolian mode) is a basic form of minor scale. It should be played according to the key signature, without using any accidentals, as in the following examples:

A natural minor

E natural minor

The whole-tone scale

There are two whole-tone scales; each one has six notes.

C whole-tone

D♭ whole-tone

The crabwise scale

Crabwise scales are an excellent method of developing fluency in scale playing. An example of the crabwise major scale, one octave, is below. Breathing places should be decided by the candidate.

The diminished (octatonic) scale

There are two forms of this scale pattern; one alternates intervals of tone, semitone; the other alternates intervals of semitone, tone. Both forms should be prepared for the examination.

F diminished scale (tone, semitone)

C diminished scale (semitone, tone)

The augmented arpeggio

C♯ augmented arpeggio

C augmented arpeggio

Scales and arpeggios with the range of a twelfth

Major scale (a twelfth)

Major arpeggio (a twelfth)

Chromatic scale (a twelfth)

A major seventh arpeggio (a twelfth)

F minor seventh arpeggio (a twelfth)

Extended major scale

Major scale (two octaves) extended down to the dominant

Other scale and arpeggio examples

G pentatonic major

C pentatonic minor

C dominant seventh (C7)

C jazz melodic minor

C Spanish phrygian minor

C minor arpeggio with major seventh

F major seventh arpeggio

D dorian scale

E minor seventh arpeggio (swing)

C blues scale (swing)

E♭ mixolydian scale

Scale/arpeggio exercise

Flute, Clarinet, Saxophone, Grades 6 – 8

Scale rhythms

The following scale rhythms are referred to in the 'grey boxes'.

Ex. 1

Ex. 2

Ex. 3

Ex. 4

Jazz Creative Exercises

This exercise will be marked as part of the Scales and Arpeggios section.

The menu below is to be used for the Creative Exercise. The grid is cumulative, i.e. at each grade the options from all previous grades can also be used. Candidates may also use elements from the 'grey box' (the scale and arpeggio specifications) for the relevant Grade.

Grade	Rhythm	Articulations
1		Slurs
2		(as previous grades)
3	Combinations of Ties and anacrusis	Staccato Tenuto
4	Triplets	Accent
5	Combinations of and	Stylistic vibrato Mezzo staccato sf
6	More complex ties	Effects e.g. 'Growl' or 'Smear' 'The hat' – marcato
7	(as previous grades)	(as previous grades)
8	(as previous grades)	(as previous grades)

An example for each Grade is given below. These examples may be used, but candidates should bear in mind that marks for this exercise will be awarded for adventure and invention.

Grade 1 example
G mixolydian (N.B. Do not be afraid to repeat the top note of the scale/mode.)

Grade 2 example
D7/Dominant seventh on D, Rock 'feel'

Grade 3 example
A dorian

Grade 4 example
C pentatonic minor, Latin 'feel'

Grade 5 example
E dorian, funk 'groove'

Grade 6 example

G blues scale, fast swing

Grade 7 example

B Spanish phrygian, bebop - fast

Grade 8 example

C whole tone, straight 8s

Aural and Initiative Tests

The following support materials are available:

M-57001-048-6	Aural Training book 1, Introductory – Grade 4 (book & CD)
M-57001-049-3	Aural Training book 2, Grades 5 - 8 (book & CD)
M-57001-001-1	Aural Tests, Grades 1 - 5 (book only)
M-57001-999-1	Specimen Initiative Tests, Grade 1 – Diploma

Details of the individual tests are available from Guildhall Examinations and can be downloaded from the website **www.gsmd.ac.uk.**

Musicianship Questions

The Musicianship Questions, which are a component of most practical examinations, reflect the holistic, person-centred philosophy and outlook of the Guildhall School. The questions relate directly to the performance that the candidate has just given and will aim to encourage an attitude that understanding the music itself provides the most appropriate path towards realising the music in performance. They should also develop an awareness of the value of positive detailed critical reflection as a tool for self-development.

The Nature of the Questions

Examiners will ask three groups of interrelated questions (one to three questions per group), to ascertain fundamental aspects of the candidate's learning. These questions will focus on **Musical Awareness** as communicated through **Performance**. One group of questions will relate to a piece in its entirety (e.g. What does the title suggest about the mood of this piece? What did you do to help create that mood?); the other groups will relate to specific moments and/or their interrelationship (e.g. What aspects of the music at these two points led you to choose to play them so differently? What technical choices are you aware of making to highlight these contrasts?).

In responding to these questions, candidates will be able to show their understanding of:

*   all aspects of the written score
*   the style, background and context of the music
*   how best to prepare and perform pieces
*   the interrelationship between musical ideas and musical lines
*   the impact of the music
*   the essentials of good practice with regard to instrumental technique and its application in music
*   the nature and care of the instrument

1. Musical Awareness
What to communicate and why

Structure

Relationships established through time: phrases, patterns, melodies, cadences, dynamics, timbre relationships, repetition and return, variation, extension, new material, modulations.

Character and Style

Nature of the piece and its distinguishing qualities: mood, musical gestures, feel, energy, space, movement, texture, harmony, context.

2. Performance
How to communicate

Interpretation
Relating technique to the music; reasons governing performance decisions; type and choice of sound, fingering; reasons for certain phrasing, tempi, dynamics, expressive colouring, etc.

Physiology and Technique
How to prepare for performance: posture, breathing, coordination, flexibility, balance, articulation, dexterity; balance of tension/relaxation; vibrato, fingering.

3. Communication
Within this basic framework (i.e. what/why/how), examiners will ask questions that are appropriate to the standard and demands of the grade, exploring the apparent musical personality (as demonstrated in performance) of the candidate.

Sight-reading

For Grades 1-5, the candidate plays the complete test, as written, twice. The examiner will assess both playings, but only marks for the better of the two performances will contribute towards the final result. For Grades 6-8, the candidate will play the complete test once only.

Candidates will have a minimum of 30 seconds to prepare for the sight-reading component of the examination in all grades.

Specimen sight-reading tests are published by Guildhall Examinations as follows:

M-57001-013-4	Graded Flute Sight-reading
M-57001-057-8	Graded Clarinet Sight-reading (including Jazz)
M-57001-058-5	Graded Saxophone Sight-reading (including Jazz)

Each book contains a chart of sight-reading requirements for each grade.

Specimen sight-reading tests for Jazz Flute and a chart of requirements are available free from the website **www.gsmd.ac.uk.**

Useful Publications

Jeffery Wilson and Malcolm Miles: *The Scales Wizard*   (Camden Music CM187)

Jeffery Wilson: *Progressive Guide to Melodic*
Jazz Improvisation   (GSMD M-57001-054-7)

accompanying CD   (GSMD M-57001-052-1)

Jamey Aebersold Play-a-long series (Jamey Aebersold).

General Notes

Facility exercises and Creative exercises
Facility exercises have been introduced to all Grades, and Creative exercises to all Grades of the Jazz syllabuses. Both will be marked as part of the Scales and Arpeggios section.

Performing on more than one instrument
Candidates may choose to perform on more than one woodwind instrument as follows:

Flute examinations: one piece/study may be played on the Piccolo from Grade 6 as indicated in the repertoire lists; one piece/study may be played on the Alto Flute at Grade 8

Clarinet examinations: one piece/study may be played on the Bass Clarinet from Grade 6; one piece/study may be played on the Eb Clarinet at Grade 8

Saxophone/Jazz Saxophone examinations: candidates may choose to play two different types of saxophone (soprano, alto, tenor, baritone) from Grade 4

Candidates who choose to present more than one instrument may alter the order of their programme to accommodate the move from one instrument to the other.

Lyons/Kinder Clarinets
The Lyons or Kinder Clarinets may be used for Clarinet/Jazz Clarinet examinations up to and including Grade 4. For Lyons clarinets and Kinder clarinets in C, the solo parts of the studies/pieces set for the examination should be played as written and the accompaniments should be transposed as necessary.

Order of performance in the examination
It is recommended that candidates play the facility exercises, scales and arpeggios before their pieces in the examination. However, this is not compulsory.

Choice of repertoire

Candidates should pay attention to the length of pieces when making their choices, balancing for example a longer piece from List A with a shorter one from List B. Examiners may have to stop a performance if the total length of pieces offered is likely to make the examination run over time.

List C (Studies)

All List C choices must be performed unaccompanied.

Repertoire lists – Boosey Woodwind Method

The syllabus uses the Boosey Woodwind Method (Boosey & Hawkes) as repertoire books for Flute, Jazz Flute, Clarinet, Jazz Clarinet, Saxophone and Jazz Saxophone for Grades 1 - 3. Pieces from the Boosey Woodwind Method are shown in a box at the beginning of the relevant repertoire list. IMPORTANT: Any preparation exercises, practice hints or alternative arrangements given or suggested in the books are not to be included in the exam. Each book contains a CD of accompaniments. Candidates are strongly advised to use a CD player *with balance control* in their exam, and to set the balance to the left (this will provide the accompaniment only, without the melody). See Boosey Woodwind books for further information about the balance control. Accompaniment books, containing keyboard accompaniments which may be used in the exam as an alternative to the CD, will be available from 2003.

Details as follows:

Flute accompaniment book	B&H M060113161
Clarinet accompaniment book	B&H M060113000
Saxophone accompaniment book	B&H M060114311

Prescribed note range

For each Grade, a note range is indicated. All scales, arpeggios and technical exercises will fall within this note range, as will the vast majority of the repertoire. However, occasionally repertoire has been included which is considered suitable for the Grade, but which falls slightly outside the prescribed note range.

Tuning

Instruments should be tuned outside the examination room by teachers or candidates. During the examination, instruments may be re-tuned briefly as necessary using the piano. For examinations up to and including grade 4, either the accompanist, if present, or the examiner may help with tuning. For examinations from grade 5 upwards, candidates are expected to tune their own instruments.

Additional notes for jazz examinations

General

The jazz syllabuses for flute, clarinet and saxophone are designed to reflect the richness and diversity of the genre and to introduce the candidate to elements of style and jazz phrasing through repertoire and improvisation. A stylistic approach with idiomatic phrasing will be rewarded. Examiners will listen for rhythmic and melodic interest and invention, with a relationship to the pulse and wide use of dynamics and colour. In higher grades, they will expect greater awareness of underlying chord progressions, and of form and structure (for example, motivic development and building of solos). As in the classical syllabuses, a sense of ensemble and interplay is important.

Accompaniments

Accompaniments can either be played live or pre-recorded on a good quality sound system. Where accompaniment is played on the piano, the solo line should not be doubled. Some of the repertoire has an accompaniment published only as chord symbols. In these cases, an accompaniment should be played by interpreting the chord symbols given. Improvised intros, codettas, fills and breaks are welcomed where appropriate.

Improvisation

Candidates should play extended improvisation sections only where stated in the syllabus. Improvisation may be terminated by the examiner once sufficient evidence of attainment has been established.

Performance Assessment and Expectations

One of the most popular aspects of the Guildhall School's graded examinations is our commitment to using discipline **specialist examiners** wherever possible. That means that players who understand the processes involved in teaching and learning instruments will examine this syllabus.

Our commitment to **specialist examiners** has enabled us to develop a unique way of assessing musical performance that we have called Clear. Clear enables us to share formative information directly related to teaching objectives.

How we mark musical performance

Playing a musical instrument or singing involves a unique synthesis of physical and expressive skills. Development of imagination, musical awareness, technical skills, aural awareness, reading ability and self-expression are among the many facets of musical learning.

Using Clear, we aim to support the teacher's planning process and to provide a formative assessment framework that reflects the skills central to learning an instrument successfully and with enjoyment. These skills are gathered together in our Assessment Categories.

What are Assessment Categories?

Guildhall School examiners listen for the performer's mastery of musical and technical skills in each of five Assessment Categories:

- Musical Awareness
- Quality of Sound
- Accuracy
- Communication
- Control of Instrument

You will see the Assessment Categories on the Assessment Record.

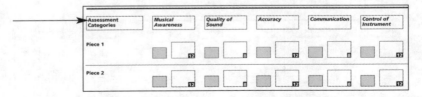

You can find more detail about each Assessment Category in the Marking Schemes on pages 217 to 221.

How is each Assessment Category marked?

During the performance of each piece the examiner will listen for recognisable qualities in each Assessment Category to determine the degree of mastery evident. The examiner judges which of the descriptions in the Marking Scheme best fits the candidate's perfomance.

You will find the Marking Schemes on pages 217 to 221.

How does an examiner record a judgement?

Having judged an Assessment Category, the examiner will record this as a code. The available codes are N, L, S, C and CC, one of which will be inserted in the relevant grey box on the Assessment Record.

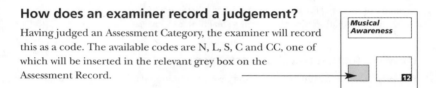

This code is then converted into a mark using the appropriate table. Here is an example when the maximum available mark is 12.

Judgement	Code	Marks
Clear and consistent evidence of attainment	CC	10–12
Consistent evidence of attainment	C	8–9
Some evidence of attainment	S	5–7
Limited evidence of attainment	L	1–4
No evidence of attainment	N	0

When all the Assessment Categories have been marked, the examiner will total the marks to arrive at the mark for the examination component.

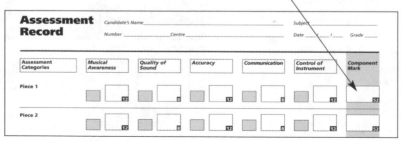

The final mark

The final mark falls into one of five bands. These bands represent thresholds in the cumulative degree of mastery evidenced throughout the entire examination.

90% – High Honours

A high honours pass is awarded to an exceptional musician who shows clear and consistent attainment across all Assessment Categories.

80% – Honours

An honours pass is awarded to a musician who shows clear and consistent attainment in most, but not all Assessment Categories.

65% – Merit

A merit pass is awarded to a musician who shows consistent attainment in most Assessment Categories.

50% – Pass

A pass is awarded to a musician who shows consistent attainment for some Assessment Criteria, with evidence of some attainment in most of the Assessment Categories.

Less than 50% – Fail

The candidate has not satisfied the minimum requirements for an award at this stage.

Assessment Pattern

Assessment is carried out during a single examination of performance and understanding. Each single examination is comprised of a number of components, all of which are assessed by an external examiner on the same occasion. These components include:

- The performance of up to three pieces from a specified repertoire
- A practical test of technique and control
- A sight-reading test
- Aural or equivalent tests of understanding

Each component is given a score derived from marks given for specific criteria. These scores are combined to form the total score for the candidate.

There are no components that are assessed separately from the examination of performance and understanding (e.g. written examination paper).

How can we learn from the results?

The final mark, while of prime interest to many pupils and parents, should not distract from the valuable and detailed picture contained in the Assessment Record. A Clear Assessment Record offers many opportunities for analysis of an individual's results and herein lies the key to gaining formative assessment information from the examination.

The Assessment Record provides insights into the candidate's achievements. You can consider the detailed balance of strengths and weaknesses within an individual examination component, for example, by considering the marks awarded in each Assessment Category for a piece. You can also consider the various component marks.

However, perhaps the most valuable insights can come from studying the Assessment Category Totals that can be found in the shaded bar above the final mark box. These give you a view of the overall degree of mastery in each Assessment Category (Musical Awareness, Quality of Sound, Accuracy, Communication and Control of Instrument) and are the most valuable in identifying future learning needs.

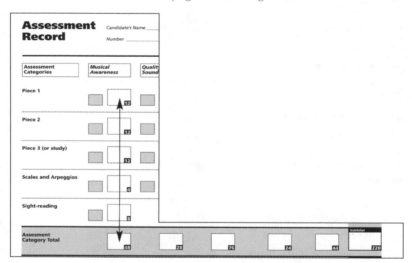

Marking Schemes

Assessment Category: Musical Awareness

Criteria

Expression
The candidate's innate musicality and sense of shape, mood and character.

Structural Awareness, Style and Period
Interpretation of the composer's musical intentions and the understanding of stylistic and structural elements such as part writing, melody, accompaniment, cadences, modulation and larger-scale elements of form.

Summary of Knowledge, Skills and Understanding

Coverage:

- that the chosen sound world is appropriate to the music's style;
- an understanding of how style, phrasing and expression contribute to performance;
- a naturalness of expression, phrasing and a sense of line;
- an ability to shape phrases;
- a sense of musical coherence;
- an understanding of overall structure;
- a sensitivity to the relationship between parts within a texture;
- the ability to realise and explore the composer's intentions;
- an ability to capture mood and character.

Degree of Mastery Recognisable in Performance for Musical Awareness	Judgement	Code
Clear and consistent sense of overall form and shape together with an artistic and individual response to style and period. Ability to use structural features to convey the meaning of the music and a sense of mood and character.	Clear and consistent evidence of attainment	CC
Consistent evidence of sensitivity to structural features such as form, style and shape of the music with an overall sense of interpretation.	Consistent evidence of attainment	C
Recognisable stylistic awareness and some variety in mood and character. Some evidence of an ability to react, although not necessarily always appropriately, to structural elements.	Some evidence of attainment	S
Limited or variable evidence of stylistic awareness and musical understanding.	Limited evidence of attainment	L
The performance demonstrated no evidence of attainment for any aspect of the category.	No evidence of attainment	N

Assessment Category: Quality of Sound

Criterion

Consistency, Clarity of sound and focus

Evenness over the instrument, attack, dynamic range and projection, ability to sustain colour, vibrato, intonation.

Summary of Knowledge, Skills and Understanding

Coverage:

- a sensitivity to quality of sound;
- a sensitivity to intonation and its relationship to sound quality;
- an ability to project their sound;
- an evenness of tone over the range available;
- an ability to sustain tone at appropriate dynamics;
- an appropriate use of vibrato;
- the expressive use of tone and colour.

Degree of Mastery Recognisable in Performance for Quality of Sound	Judgement	Code
An engaging sound, focused and sustained, with a convincing ability to project and use colour and variety of attack to convey meaning.	Clear and consistent evidence of attainment	CC
A good sound quality with evidence of an ability to vary sound to project musical intention. Confidence in attempting a range of techniques to convey musical intention.	Consistent evidence of attainment	C
An acceptable basic sound with some capacity for effective use of tonal variety. Evidence of attempts to explore sound quality to convey musical intention.	Some evidence of attainment	S
A poor basic sound with limited potential for expression.	Limited evidence of attainment	L
The performance demonstrated no evidence of attainment for any aspect of the category.	No evidence of attainment	N

Assessment Category: Accuracy

Criteria

Observation of Performance Directions
Reading of notated detail such as notes, tempo, rhythm and dynamics.

Fluency and Expression
Continuity, line, tone, articulation, rhythmic character, phrasing.

Summary of Knowledge, Skills and Understanding

Coverage:

- an understanding of and ability to reproduce notation and written directions accurately in performance;

- ability to perform music fluently, sustaining line, tone and phrasing;

- an ability to choose and sustain an appropriate tempo;

- an ability to interpret and sustain rhythmic character.

Degree of Mastery Recognisable in Performance for Accuracy	Judgement	Code
Accurate and fluent with an awareness of the nuance of notated detail.	Clear and consistent evidence of attainment	CC
Accurate and fluent.	Consistent evidence of attainment	C
Generally accurate and fluent with only occasional slips.	Some evidence of attainment	S
Limited or variable evidence of accuracy and fluency.	Limited evidence of attainment	L
The performance demonstrated no evidence of attainment for any aspect of the category.	No evidence of attainment	N

Assessment Category: Communication

Criterion

Intent and Sense of Performance
Presentation, commitment, conviction, confidence, flair, individuality, sensibility.

Summary of Knowledge, Skills and Understanding
Coverage:
- an ability to play with style and communication;
- a sense of occasion and performance;
- commitment, confidence and poise;
- flair and individuality in performance;
- an awareness of presentation;
- a sense of intent and musical sensibility.

Degree of Mastery Recognisable in Performance for Communication	Judgement	Code
A confident and effective capacity to engage an audience with a convincing sense of an individual and committed response and musical sensibility and personality.	Clear and consistent evidence of attainment	CC
A recognisable capacity to engage an audience with an overall sense of individuality and confidence.	Consistent evidence of attainment	C
Some recognisable capacity for audience engagement with variable evidence of an ability to create a sense of performance. Some evidence of commitment and individual interpretation with a basic general level of confidence in performance.	Some evidence of attainment	S
Limited evidence of potential for conveying musical intent and a variable commitment to sense of performance.	Limited evidence of attainment	L
The performance demonstrated no evidence of attainment for any aspect of the category.	No evidence of attainment	N

Assessment Category: Control of Instrument

Criteria

Technical Control

Physiological control, co-ordination, posture, relaxation, balance.

Production of Sound

Physical aspects of sound production, range, intonation.

Summary of Knowledge, Skills and Understanding

Coverage:

- an awareness of balance, posture and relaxation;
- an understanding of the importance of mobility and stability and how they contribute to the quality and variety of sound production;
- an understanding of tone production and its relationship to posture and physical co-ordination;
- an understanding of the relationship between technical skill and musical feeling;
- an appropriate control of breathing, posture, physical co-ordination, finger movement; physical control and co-ordination;
- appropriate stamina.

Degree of Mastery Recognisable in Performance for Control of Instrument	Judgement	Code
Sustained and convincing command of the instrument with a full understanding of the relationship between physical co-ordination and musical interpretation.	Clear and consistent evidence of attainment	CC
Consistent and convincing command of the instrument.	Consistent evidence of attainment	C
Technically proficient with only occasional technical limitations.	Some evidence of attainment	S
Limited or variable evidence of command of the instrument with notable limitations in some aspects.	Limited evidence of attainment	L
The performance demonstrated no evidence of attainment for any aspect of the category.	No evidence of attainment	N

Mark Weightings

This is the importance that the Guildhall School gives to the various components within most graded examinations:

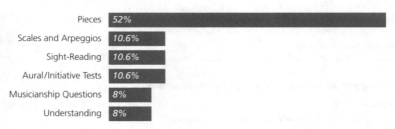

Pieces	52%
Scales and Arpeggios	10.6%
Sight-Reading	10.6%
Aural/Initiative Tests	10.6%
Musicianship Questions	8%
Understanding	8%

The weighting may change where there are fewer or more components in an examination, such as Preliminary.

In Jazz examinations, there is the additional component of Improvisation. Mark weightings for Jazz are as follows:

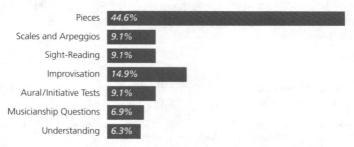

Pieces	44.6%
Scales and Arpeggios	9.1%
Sight-Reading	9.1%
Improvisation	14.9%
Aural/Initiative Tests	9.1%
Musicianship Questions	6.9%
Understanding	6.3%

All pieces have a maximum mark of 52. The weighting given to each of the assessment categories is shown below:

Musical Awareness	23%
Quality of Sound	15.5%
Accuracy	23%
Communication	15.5%
Control of Instrument	23%

Understanding

Examiners have marks available to reward overall aural and instrumental awareness, enjoyment, musical discipline and commitment, sense of ensemble and sense of performance as appropriate. Playing from memory can be rewarded here along with other facets not otherwise marked e.g. pianists who include harmony in initiative tests.

Entering for Guildhall Examinations

Examination Regulations

It is the applicant's responsibility to ensure that they and their candidates are aware of all the pertinent regulations and conditions of entry. The Entry Leaflet, containing Examination Regulations, is available from Guildhall Examinations or from the website **www.gsmd.ac.uk**.

This leaflet contains regulations concerning the following:

* Examination entry
* Prerequisites
* Exemptions
* Fees
* Examination appointment
* Absence and illness
* Venues and equipment
* Accompaniment
* Awarding of marks
* Results and certification
* Special needs

Entry information and instructions

For examinations in the UK, a leaflet containing entry information and instructions is available, including a list of local examination centres with dates of examination sessions. Private visits can also be arranged. Separate entry information is published for Northern Ireland, Eire and Channel Islands. Entry forms can be obtained from Guildhall Exams or downloaded from the Guildhall School's website. For examinations overseas, please contact the local Agent or Representative.

Further information

If you need any further advice or information, please contact the Guildhall School Examinations Service, 3 Lauderdale Place, Barbican, London EC2Y 8EN.

Tel: 020 7382 7167
Fax: 020 7382 7212
Email: **exams@gsmd.ac.uk**
Website: **www.gsmd.ac.uk**

How to obtain music for Guildhall Examinations

Your local music shop

In the UK, all music required for Guildhall School examinations should be available from your local music shop.

Trade orders

Music shops can obtain music for Guildhall School examinations through the Guildhall School's trade distributor, Boosey & Hawkes. E-mail **trade.uk@boosey.com** or telephone +44 (0) 20 7291 7163.

The Barbican Music Shop, London

The Barbican Music Shop can supply all the music required for Guildhall examinations. You can order by telephone or e-mail and your music will be posted to you. You may pay by cheque or by using a major credit card.

Tel: +44 (0) 20 7588 9242
Fax: +44 (0) 20 7628 1080
Email: **barbican@chimesmusic.com**
Website: **www.chimesmusic.com**

A World-Class Performance

The Corporation of London is no stranger to world-class performances.
As the local authority for the City of London, its prime role is to support and promote the City as the world's leading international financial centre. Within the Square Mile are over 560 foreign banks from over 80 countries: it is quite simply where the world does business best.

Keeping the world spotlight on the City's financial status also reflects its cultural excellence. Providing in the region of £30 million annually in arts funding, the Corporation is the third largest sponsor of the arts in the UK. It owns, funds and manages the Barbican Centre which attracts over two million visitors each year, and directly funds its two prestigious residents, the Royal Shakespeare Company and the London Symphony Orchestra. It also provides half the annual costs of the enormously popular Museum of London and supports a year round programme of major arts festivals and events in the City and neighbouring areas.

International standards of excellence run through the host of other responsibilities the Corporation holds and which extend far beyond the boundaries of the Square Mile. It is the port health authority for the whole of the Thames estuary, runs four premier food markets at Smithfield, Billingsgate, Spitalfields and Leadenhall, manages a portfolio of property throughout London and maintains and safeguards over 10,000 acres of open space in and around it, including Hampstead Heath, Epping Forest, Burnham Beeches and a string of parks and commons in Kent and Surrey. It also runs the four bridges that cross the Thames into the City, including Tower Bridge, a major tourist attraction and an international symbol for London as a whole.

Add to this the unique and influential role played by the head of the Corporation, the Lord Mayor of the City of London, in promoting the City's financial services at home and overseas and the Corporation has a cast and company fit for the world stage. Indeed the Corporation has taken many roles over the centuries – whether playing the lead or acting in a supporting role it is dedicated to delivering a world-class performance.

The Guildhall School of Music & Drama was founded in 1880 by the Corporation of London and in 1977 it moved into the Barbican Centre

CAMDEN MUSIC
real music for growing musicians

CREATIVE VARIATIONS

by Jeffery Wilson and Malcolm Miles

Creative Variations was developed specifically to cater for the new Guildhall Exams woodwind syllabus. Covering all grades for Jazz Flute, Jazz Clarinet and Jazz Saxophone, these superb books contain a wide variety of engaging pieces designed as a graded approach to improvisation.

Each of the six books comes with a free CD of demo recordings and play-along tracks. No bland and sterile MIDI accompaniments here - all tracks are played by professional jazz musicians. Hear examples on the Camden Music website (www.camdenmusic.com) which will be launched in June 2002.

Vol. 1 - Grades 1-5 / Vol. 2 - Grades 6-8
Versions for Flute, Clarinet (Bb & C) and Saxophone (Bb & Eb)

JAZZ ROUTES
for Flute
by Malcolm Miles

Eight progressive pieces for flute covering all grades in the Guildhall Jazz Flute syllabus. Miles's engaging music is fully notated with optional improvisation, making this a truly versatile collection.
A free CD is provided, offering full performances and playalong tracks.

COLOUR STUDIES
for Clarinet
by Jeffery Wilson

These unaccompanied studies are featured on grades 1-7 of the Guildhall Clarinet syllabus.
Drawing inspiration from different colours and their character, this attractive set of pieces prove that studies don't have to be dry technical exercises!

LEADERS IN QUALITY MUSIC PUBLISHING

www.camdenmusic.com

Single Reed Specialists

All titles for clarinet and saxophone listed in this syllabus are kept in stock and are also available by mail order.

31-35 CHILTERN STREET LONDON W1U 7PN
TELEPHONE: 020 7935 2407 FACSIMILE: 020 7224 2564
E-MAIL: sales@howarth.uk.com
INTERNET: www.howarth.uk.com

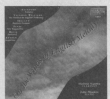